DAUGHTER
OF
FIRE

DAUGHTER
OF
FIRE

A Novel

SOFIA ROBLEDA

Published by Amazon Crossing, Seattle

www.apub.com

Amazon, the Amazon logo, and Amazon Crossing are trademarks of Amazon.com, Inc., or its affiliates.

ISBN-13: 9781662517976 (paperback)
ISBN-13: 9781662517983 (digital)

Cover design by Kimberly Glyder
Cover images: © Yurlick, © Mark Yarchoan / Shutterstock; © ZU_09, © freestylephoto, © aldra, © logaryphmic, © Martina_L / Getty

Printed in the United States of America

For my son, Hugo, who will hopefully grow up to be the exact opposite of nearly every male character in this novel.

Where are my companions now? They have fallen in battle, or been devoured by the cannibal, or been thrown to fatten the wild beasts in their cages. Their remains should have been gathered under monuments emblazoned with their achievements, commemorated in letters of gold; for they died in the service of God and of his Majesty. They came to give light to those who sat in darkness . . . and also to acquire that wealth which most men covet.

—Bernal Díaz del Castillo, Spanish conquistador, 1568

FOR GOD, GLORY, AND GOLD

Alvarado led the conquest straight to the K'iche'.

In 1524, following a successful two-year onslaught against the Mexican Empire, the ruthless Spanish commander advanced south into present-day Guatemala, along with the Tlaxcalans and other Indigenous allies. The land was populated by several competing Maya kingdoms, each with its own system of stratified rule, language, military, and advanced civilization.

The K'iche' were the dominant Maya group, and their capital city, Q'umarkaj, was situated in the rocky Guatemalan highlands.

Like all the other Indigenous people the Spanish encountered, the K'iche' put on a brave and prolonged fight. However, against a population ravaged by smallpox and other deadly diseases brought over by the newcomers, and with the advantage of steel swords, firearms, and horses, the Spanish were soon victorious.

After this apocalyptic clash of worlds, a society of violent extremes began to forge a new identity. A new mixed race and class structure emerged, with the Catholic Spanish on top, dictating whom and what to believe in. The newly relegated lower class of Indigenous people, however, continued to resist and strive to preserve their rights and culture, including their great works of literature, of which the *Popol Vuh* stands above the rest.

CHAPTER 1

Santa Cruz del Quiché, Guatemala
Summer 1540

When I was a child, Mother would tell me bedtime stories only when Father was away. They were secret stories, forbidden stories. Mother always said I had to be careful not to tell anyone about them, not Cook, not Beatriz, and especially not Father. She said if anyone heard about them, we'd end up like the twitching *Indígena*, the one who'd died with a rope tied around his neck.

I couldn't see why I had to keep the stories from Father. I thought he would've rather liked them, and I would've liked to have been the one to share them with him. They were much like the stories he loved to tell us whenever he came home. After giving my mother a kiss and his other daughter—my half sister, Beatriz—a warm embrace, he'd sit me on his lap and begin. He'd tell us stories of powerful gods. Of creators, shape-shifters. Stories of love forbidden, of wounded heroes, and tricks of war.

Father's story gods had names like Hephaestus and Hera.

Mother's were Auilix and Xbalanque.

One such night, after Beatriz had dressed me for bed, combed and braided my hair, and sang me to sleep in her honeyed voice, and probably many hours after she'd herself gone to bed, Mother entered my room and woke me up again.

She showed me a dance from one of her stories, a dance called the Armadillo, and after I'd shown her that I could do it just like her, I asked the question burning in my heart. "Mother, why can't I show Father how well I dance?"

She stared at me with a sad expression, then walked to the four-poster bed. A long, rough, rectangular piece of bark paper lay folded on the mattress. Our ancestors had named it the *Popol Vuh*, the *Book of Council*, though it had many other names. Mother called it "our hidden treasure," and it was filled with colorful symbols and pictures I loved to stare at.

One day she'd teach me to read all the symbols. One day I'd know all the stories inside it by heart, just like she did.

I pointed at the book. "Why can't I tell him the story of One Death and the mighty twins?"

She gestured at me to come close. We were in my chamber. I was only five, but I remember that everything except the burning fireplace was made of wood and iron—the large chair, the dressing table, the trunk at the foot of my bed, the floorboards, and the candlesticks—all timber and metal. Nothing was remarkable, though I knew we were not poor. Only the green woolen coverlet and the walls were a different shade. If the curtains had been open, the layer of white lime plastered on the walls would've made them shine, even in moonlight.

Mother made me sit on the mattress with my back to her. With tender fingers, she undid my two braids and pulled me into an embrace. I compared my arms to hers. They were much shorter but the same color, tawny brown and bronzed from our day spent out in the sun. I watched the flames as they twitched and fluttered. We needed to add another log or soon they'd die.

"Our world is full of stories," she whispered in our secret language. It was a real language. Other people used it all the time, other K'iche' Maya like my mother. But I wasn't supposed to know it; we spoke it only when we were alone.

"People are always arguing about which stories are true and which are not. It's a pointless argument, for all contain a speck of truth about our world and ourselves. The only thing that matters is this: some stories are protected, safeguarded, and others are left to fade with time."

I didn't know why she was telling me all this, or how it answered my question, but I breathed her lingering fragrance, the echo of incense caught in her hair, and allowed myself to enjoy the sound of her voice. It was low and clear and strong, like a current in a dark underground river.

"Some people, like your father and sister"—her voice was measured—"would disagree. Others are even worse than them. They see only one truth, one story, and they take it so seriously they're willing to kill those who think differently."

"But they're only stories," I said, and ran a finger over the cherry-red thread framing the edge of her white cotton blouse. "Zeus doesn't strike people with lightning, and Plumed Serpent didn't create the world out of mist; God did."

She sighed and walked to the window. I felt the absence of her warmth on my back and regretted that my words had pushed her away.

Mother pulled the curtains, opened the wooden blinds, and said, "Come. Look outside." I ran to her, relieved, even though an odd note had caught her voice. I forgot that quickly, for I was tall enough that I didn't need her to pull the chair to stand on anymore, and this filled me with a spark of pride. The view from my room was of a wild field of grass, shining blue in the night and waving with the breeze.

"The two mounds you see on the field were made by men. They are pits, deep burial pits. One for those murdered during the war with Alvarado, and another for those killed by the plagues he brought. Thousands of dead K'iche' were flung in there."

My heart felt as though a vicelike grip had taken hold of it. As if a skeleton hand, like one of thousands concealed by the swaying lawn, was shaking it against my ribs. I threw my arms around my mother's waist and buried my face against her belly. She held me tightly, but what she said next did nothing to soothe my terror.

"My mother and father are in there, my older brothers and their children. Our entire family. I was four years old when Alvarado rode in with his mighty horse, his sword, and his golden cross. He was one of those single-minded men who believe in one story, and even though we were one of the great K'iche' families, we were not spared. Every family suffered, no matter how high or lowborn. I survived only because I was led to safety by Cook."

"Cook?" I looked at her with wonder.

Mother nodded. "She gathered as many children as she could and took us to a secret cave in the ravine. When she wouldn't tell the Spanish where we were, they . . ." She averted her eyes and stared back out the window. "They hurt her very badly. That is why you mustn't tell her about the *Popol Vuh*. You mustn't burden someone who already carries a heavy load."

I said nothing. I knew I ought to have felt sorry for Cook, and I did, but mostly I felt a selfish pang of frustration. Here was something I was great at, and I wanted Father to see it. I wanted him to see how I shone, and I wanted him to be proud of me. In the end, I couldn't help myself. I mumbled, "So, I can never tell him I'm learning the *Popol Vuh*, ever?"

Mother turned, and I could no longer see myself in her dark, angular face. "No. Never." Her voice was rough. Her eyes, usually black and beautiful, flashed with flame so real it sent a barb of fear through my core. She saw this and her lips set. She knelt down and grabbed both of my arms.

"It's our family's sworn duty to protect this book. It's a dangerous thing, but it keeps our ancestors alive; it is a way to honor them—"

"I know, but Father—"

She growled, "Your father wouldn't understand. No Spaniard does."

"But—"

"No buts!" She covered her mouth and glanced at the door. "Stay," she whispered, then tiptoed toward it, placed her ear against the grain, and waited. She opened it a fraction and peeked into the shadowy hall before shutting it again.

She walked back to the bed and lifted the *Popol Vuh* into both of her hands with petal-like fingers, as though it were made of quetzal feathers and written in molten gold.

"Listen to me." She knelt to my level and took a heavy breath. The warm scent of cacao and sapote lingered as she exhaled and said, "A long time ago our family was entrusted with keeping this book safe. The god of our house, Lord Hacauitz, commanded it so. He said his Sons of Fire would never fail him."

I nearly rolled my eyes. I knew this story already. But then she added, "The book should've never come to me. There are no more Sons of Fire. Hacauitz has but two daughters left. You and me, and one day, perhaps soon, perhaps not for many years, I will be gone."

I stuck out my bottom lip and gave her a petulant frown. "No, Mama."

"Nature is cruel, and people are worse." Her gaze pierced into mine, her face softened, and her voice wavered. "I *do* hope to have many, many years with you, little bird. But if something were to happen to me, I need you to swear that you'll guard it . . . with your life."

My frown deepened. I didn't know the name for what I felt in that moment. It was a new sensation to me, the weight of her words upon my slender back, the lengthening of my young spirit as it plunged itself into the future and saw the dark, tangled, desolate road ahead.

She placed the book between my hands and spoke my secret name. She was deadly serious then, for she rarely used it, even when we were alone. Usually, she called me by my Christian name, Catalina.

"Ab'aj Pol," she whispered. Her tone was urgent. "Promise me."

Her eyes suddenly shone with a film of tears. The awful, strange new feeling disappeared and was replaced by the need to make my mother happy again. I knew just what to do. I smiled my bravest of smiles and kissed the book to show her I meant what I said next.

"Yes, Mama. I swear."

CHAPTER 2

Santa Cruz del Quiché, Guatemala
Autumn 1551

Eleven years later, it was my sixteenth birthday party, and like any good and proper lady, I should've been sitting on one of the benches arranged around the hall, waiting to be asked to dance.

Instead, I hid in part shadow by the door to the kitchen and tried not to fiddle with the frill collar tickling my neck. I smoothed down my green silk gown and avoided eye contact with all. This was not unusual.

As the only legitimate mixed-blood child in town, the only Mestiza, I was used to being set apart. No one quite knew what to make of me. When I was a child, Father had always said I was one of a kind, and I'd fancied myself a mythical creature, a sort of griffin, hovering above Spaniards and K'iche' alike with my eagle wings and jaguar's tail.

But life was different now. My childhood was gone. It had come to a swift, brutal end almost seven years ago, although this party today marked my official entry into adult society.

I knew any moment I'd be asked to dance, yet I couldn't bear the thought of it, even though I dearly loved dancing and the cheerful tune was much to my liking.

The musicians were most impressive. Father had brought a whole band—guitar, tambourine, bells, cornet, and castanet players—all the way from Santiago, the capital. They played in the corner of the long inner patio by a pillar that supported one of the four white archways. The crowd danced under the stars and by the light of the many flickering torches, which infused the fresh pine air with the pungent smell of mutton oil.

My guests made two lines in the center of the red tiled floor. Limbs, skirts, and capes swished and circled in perfect harmony. Every step and pointed toe were memorized by heart, and each face appeared delighted, eager to shine. Everyone who was anyone in the little town of Santa Cruz was there. I knew I might not have an opportunity to enjoy myself like this again for years. I told myself over and over to sit.

But I could not, for I was fighting a battle no one could see, one I was losing. Two of the most important people in my life were missing from my party, and it was impossible not to think of them. It was impossible not to hear Beatriz's chiming voice greeting each guest, or picture Mother, avoiding notice, yet still standing proudly by my side. Neither of them had been mentioned in over seven years. Beatriz was still alive, though I knew not where she lived. But my mother was worse than dead.

It was as though she'd never existed at all.

Everyone pretended as though I'd sprung fully formed from my father's head, like Athena. Even I sometimes found it easier to pretend, because thinking of her made me ache for her, or worse, picture the last time I saw her, when those hooded men—

I gasped as the memory hit me, fresh and raw and gutting, and I drew closer to the shadows so no one could see my face.

"Don't cry, don't cry," I muttered, "it's not real. Breathe." I pinched my forearm so hard I knew I would be bruised the next day, but I had to remind myself of where I was. I forced myself to look at the dancers again. I went through their moves in my head: step left, twist, step right, bow, again. When I felt stronger, I whispered a silent prayer too. Slowly, the familiar Latin words grounded and soothed me.

My breath had just returned to normal when the doorman, who stood by the arched entrance, banged his staff on the floor and yelled out, "Lord Juan de Rojas of House Kaweq, Cacique de Q'umarkaj."

I nearly choked. Even the music stopped as Lord Juan stepped into the room, proud and scowling. Son of the Jaguar. He would've been *ajpop*, king, my mother's king, if the Spanish had never come. But the red cape draped over his shoulders and cotton vest, while most impressive, was frayed and patched. I shifted and tried to hide the frown on my face.

Poor man.

I sighed, for nothing could be done. I couldn't help him, or any of my mother's people, who were my people, too, though I couldn't freely admit it. I wished I could do something, anything at all really, to change the way things were, to give them back some of what they'd lost. But I had no money, no say, and no power.

I was only a girl, and a half-Spanish one at that. With my thick black hair, brown skin, and defined nose, I might've looked K'iche', but I dressed like a Spaniard, spoke Castilian with a courtly accent, and rode on the back of a fine Andalusian horse with more flair than a Moorish princess. There was no doubt in my head that I'd never be fully trusted, even if I could do more than just give alms and pray all day long, which is all I ever felt I did.

Even in that moment, I prayed. *God, help them, help the cacique. Keep him well and grant him good health. Send him a good woman to care for him and give him children.*

For an outrageous, yet rather thrilling moment, I pictured myself as his good woman. My gaze fell on the bright-red loincloth that jutted out from under his short white skirt, and then I blinked and shook my head. What was the matter with me? It wasn't like I'd never seen K'iche' regalia before, so why was I staring like a common wench?

I huffed and decided I'd best begin my silent penitence in advance. *Ave Maria, gratia plena.* The first one of at least ten I'd probably need to say, and there would be more if I didn't keep my eyes off the cloth, or his beautiful, powerful, bare legs.

It was hopeless. I studied each curve and vein until I reached his sandals. There they were, finally, on the floor, close to hell, where I'd surely be going. From the way some of the other women were looking, it was clear I wouldn't be going alone.

Perhaps they were just surprised, though. No one had expected Lord Juan to come to my party. He'd received an invitation, of course. Father couldn't overlook him. He was much too important to the *Indigenas,* and they weren't on bad terms, all things considered. But he'd never responded, so we'd assumed he wouldn't come.

Why he wanted to come was beyond me. This land was his birthright. This house, the president's country home, had been given to my father, who was the head of government in all of Guatemala and Nicaragua—but it ought to have been Lord Juan's. We should've all been bowing down. Instead, all reverence and honor went to my father, who, I'm afraid to say, was no blood noble, unlike my mother. Shameful, it was.

Still, Lord Juan knew things could've been worse. Before my father had come, the young cacique had been little more than a slave, along with most of the Maya in Q'umarkaj. Illegal slaves, of course, for our Holy Emperor had decreed that all his native subjects be free, their labor paid, and any mistreatment be punishable. The emperor's unpopular New Laws had been in effect for more than ten years, but Father was the only leader in all the Indies who'd bothered to implement them. That is, with the exception of Viceroy Vela, who'd been murdered for his efforts in Peru.

Father's zealous reforms had earned him widespread hatred. At least two Spaniards had tried to kill him. But there he was, alive and older than most, walking up to Lord Juan. They shook hands and Father gave him a genial pat on the shoulder. The cacique's whisper carried throughout the hall.

"I thank you for the honor of your invitation, Don Alonso."

"The honor is ours, Cacique. I'm sure I speak for my daughter when I say we're both delighted you've graced us with your presence."

The Spaniards muttered. A compliment from my father was as rare as a pink quetzal, and he'd just paid it to a K'iche'. Father smiled at the sound, as if he'd drawn four of a kind in primero. Lord Juan ignored them and scanned the room. I didn't know what devilry possessed me, why I wanted *him*, out of everyone, to see me, but I stepped into the light.

He found me with ease, for I'd inherited Father's mountainous height. There was a tiny flicker of something in his gaze when he looked at my face, something ardent, and I burned in response. I bowed my head and hid my features. Even though my brown skin rarely betrayed me, this heady rush of triumph felt too powerful to conceal.

I took a breath to compose myself and lifted my chin. He was halfway through nodding in what seemed an elegant, congratulatory gesture, when he froze.

I gulped and tensed in response.

"I beseech your permission to dance with your daughter," Lord Juan said. He did not take his eyes off me, nor did he wait to hear my father's response.

I should've been exhilarated by those words, and a part of me was, but my pulse also spiked in terror. Not because every face, including my father's surprised one, had suddenly turned toward me. No, it was because for some unfathomable reason, Lord Juan was suddenly vexed . . . with me! In a blink he'd led me to the open floor, and I felt certain I'd not imagined it. The man was livid. I knew because I'd studied him most of my life, even though until tonight, he'd never looked at me twice.

"Is anything amiss, my lord?" I whispered, but he didn't respond.

We bowed to each other, and I glanced up at his eyes. They were normally a shade of caramel, but now they were black and fixed down on my neck. His fresh warm breath hit my face in rapid gusts, and his calloused hand shook as he held mine.

11

The other dancers lined up in a row beside us and the music started.

Thank goodness it was a sober, graceful pavane. After a few beats, I felt its soothing effect on him, and when he spoke, his voice was low, a soft growl.

"You're wearing a most unusual shade of jade, Ab'aj Pol."

My jaw came loose at his use of my Maya name. Stone Orchid. My secret name. The name Mother whispered to me but twice, and never again used for fear of Father's wrath. How did he know? She must've told him, but why? When? I had no response. My head spun.

"The necklace, was it a gift from your father?"

I looked down. I wore a long, heavy necklace of fat jade beads. A birthday gift from my father indeed. I had no idea where he'd gotten it from, but I nodded with the beat to disguise the fact that I was answering him. He smiled, but for some reason, the change in his countenance did nothing to ease my discomfort.

"There is a story about a necklace just like it. Would you like to hear it, Ab'aj Pol?"

"I beg you, my lord, use my Christian name, Catalina."

His smile died. I looked up into his eyes again. They were deep, clear, cold pools, and I was swimming in them, drowning in them. When the music brought us closer, he whispered in K'iche', "Would you like to hear the story?"

I shook my head. No one except Mother had ever told me a story in K'iche'. No one else had spoken more than a few words to me in that language in years. Many had tried, for my features gave away my lineage as clearly as the sun gave away the day. I usually responded with a grimace of apology, pretended not to know what they were saying, and endured the disappointed shakes of their heads. I told myself it was safest. In truth, I also did it to keep my crippled heart from dwelling on her too much, from breaking apart again.

"I see . . . well, it is a mighty treasure. It seems you hold two such treasures in your possession. One you are not worthy of. The other does not belong to you."

I was unsure what to make of his tone, but a spark of anger lit inside me at his words. We spun away from each other, round the room, and faced each other again.

"This necklace belonged to Waqib' Kaj, Lady Six Sky, an ancient queen. One of my great- great-grandmothers." We pivoted and our hands brushed again. His touch seared beyond my skin, and I nearly missed what he said next. "It is said that she was held in high favor by the goddess Xkik', the Lady Blood."

I reeled and he tightened his grip on me to keep me standing. To call upon Lady Blood! To say her name! He must've been stone mad! He stepped away from me and danced toward the other ladies. He did so without smiling and returned to me, led me in a circle again, and whispered, "It is said that only the heirs of Lady Six Sky may wear this necklace, for all others shall be cursed by Lady Blood with a slow and painful death."

The necklace suddenly weighed down on me. A tight feeling squeezed my neck, and between the music and the staccato and hush of a language I wasn't meant to know, I feared I would faint. Terror gripped me at the thought of our enemies, hidden in plain sight, for they'd say we spoke of evil things, and they'd brand me a pagan witch and sentence me to death.

He smiled, as though he knew the effect his words had on me. "Perhaps I could help you, though . . . if you were willing to help me back."

My eyebrows knotted. His words riled me and broke whatever spell his fingertips had laced through me before. My voice was hoarse, but I responded, "How could I help you? I have no gold. And even if I did, what makes you think I'd entertain these fanciful notions?"

The music rose, and the piece neared its end. He took both my hands and we swayed.

"I do not wish for gold. But I shall have the necklace, for it is mine by rights. And I have come to ask for something else. The treasure of your mother's lineage," he went on. "The Dawn of Life. The Light from Beyond the Sea." He paused to enjoy whatever look of horror was crossing my face, then struck true. "The *Book of Council*, the *Popol Vuh*."

I stumbled back, speechless. The music came to an end. The room burst into applause, and as we bowed to each other, he looked me in the eye and whispered, "We shall speak on the matter again very soon. Until such time, you will see how fanciful my notions can be."

His pupils turned pitch black. Even the whites of his eyes faded. The blood drained from my face. I stepped away, dizzy, back across the hall into the outer courtyard. There was enough moonlight to illuminate the fountain at the center, surrounded by Father's orange trees, which were loaded with fruit. Several couples sat around the fountain's edge, but I was so quiet no one noticed me in the shadows. I took out my fan from my purse and tried not to gasp for air while I fought the urge to tear the necklace off. Its weight seemed to increase by the moment, and I was sure I'd soon topple into the ground.

I did what I could. I prayed, *Father in Heaven, I renounce this blasphemy. There is but one God and no others. There is but one Holy Trinity, one Savior, one Christ!*

But . . . just in case, Lord Jesus, if Lady Blood should be out there, oh please, please save me from her wrath.

For I knew with absolute certainty.

I'd been cursed.

◆ ◆ ◆

I couldn't recall the walk back to my bedchamber. I couldn't remember when I changed and climbed into bed. My curtains were open, and moonlight streamed through the shutters, bright enough to illuminate the swirling flecks of dust. I followed the slanting beams, and jolted when the damned necklace came into focus, glittering lilac in the silver light. Someone had placed it on a cushion on top of my vanity.

I stared at it, and it seemed to stare back. An owl hooted, right outside my window.

The dust slowly spun into a shape, arms, and a head. A woman! I bolted upright. Her gray, terrible face was clouded in shade, but I knew it was Lady Blood. She was a creature of Xibalba, the underworld, a creature of the night.

Her fingertips trailed along the surface of the necklace. The owl hooted again.

"Daughter of Fire, you're no daughter of mine," she whispered.

My body felt warm, too warm, and my throat itched to scream, but I was frozen stiff. I felt sure someone would hear my thundering heart and come running.

No one did.

She floated to the foot of my bed, in part shadow, part moon.

I trembled and whimpered, "Forgive me, forgive me!" My tongue spoke the K'iche' words instinctively, over and over.

She hovered above me.

"I'll—I'll give it back, I swear! I'll give the necklace back to him."

Her gray eyes sank into my soul. An icy cold feeling, like a hand, gripped my stomach.

"Please, no! Stop! Mama, Mama, save me!" I cried out, dreading the sting of death. It would arrive at any moment. It was inevitable. I wouldn't survive the night.

The moment the cock crowed, I sat straight up, touched my cheeks, arms, and belly, and looked around my room, though I purposefully averted my gaze from the necklace. Dawn light filtered through the wooden blinds. Too feeble, I needed more of it. I stumbled out of bed, nauseated, and struck the window open, then gulped in the misty, cool air, all the while praising God, for I'd been spared. I'd survived!

There was a light rain. Before long, the damp and cold began to seep into my forearms. I turned and grabbed my mother's cotton sarape, then wrapped it across my shoulders. It was red with zigzag stitching, a pattern typical of her people. I opened the door and tiptoed barefoot over the cold tile floor into the kitchen.

Cook turned, and I fell into her arms.

She shushed me, and I knew she would've loved to say more words to comfort me, but it was impossible. She had no tongue to speak with. She sat me down on my favorite stool and started crushing roasted cacao beans into a paste. She scooped the paste into a clay mug, added boiling water and cornmeal, then handed it to me along with a jar of honey. She always refused to add any to mellow the bitter taste, but she had learned to forgive my weakness. I breathed in the steam and took a sip. Frothy and heartwarming. Cook served it only in dire circumstances.

I wiggled a little closer to the edge of the table. My back was to the fireplace, and I didn't want the soot and smoke to ruin my shawl. I stared at the loaves in the basket in front of me, but found I wasn't hungry. In fact, I was developing a pounding headache.

"Perhaps I drank too much wine," I muttered. I'd been permitted two full glasses the night before, whereas normally I might've had a sip or two at most.

Cook huffed and began to grind maize with her stone tools at the edge of the table. Every so often the mano and metate collided with a grating sound that made my teeth clench. Whenever this happened, she winked at me and gurgled a laugh. I pouted at her in return.

For all the aches in my body, though, there was a part of me that was relieved to have a body at all. I'd come so close to dying, and this was only a reprieve. She'd be back. I needed to make amends, fast. Now, I could not possibly give Lord Juan the *Popol Vuh*, but perhaps I could find a way to return the necklace to him and hope it would be enough.

How I'd manage to do that was another question. Father never let me be seen in public without him. He read all my letters—not that I sent many. Whenever he went away, he locked up the ink and took the key so I couldn't write at all. He used to say it was because he didn't wish to come back and find he didn't have enough to do his work, but I knew better. I wasn't even allowed to attend church when he was gone.

We didn't live in the new town, Santa Cruz. Our villa was about a mile west, across the plateau on a hill, closer to the ravine and ruins of the ancient K'iche' capital, Q'umarkaj. When I stood on the veranda, I could see glimpses of them both—the white cross atop the bell tower to the east, and to the west, the canyon with the colorful, crumbling walls of the temple of Auilix, goddess of the moon. To her left, I could also see the tip of the pyramid of Hacauitz, god of the fire mountain, god of my mother's house.

I wondered if he would still protect me, let's say, if I slipped away to see Lord Juan on a cloudy, dark night, while Father was away. Perhaps there had been some misunderstanding; perhaps we could start over. My heart fluttered and I felt the imprint of his hand on mine again, the rush of pleasure from capturing his gaze in that first, brief instant.

"*¡Hija!*" I was jolted back into reality by Father's booming voice and spilled lukewarm chocolate all over my hands. What was the matter with me?

Cook shook her head and handed me a cloth. Father burst through the door.

"Why are you here?"

My brows crumpled; I was confused by the question. I was always there.

"You're no longer a child, and you're certainly not a servant. The kitchen's no place for you. Do not let me find you here again, understood?"

"Yes, Father," I whispered.

"Now—give me a hug."

I rushed to him and he held me close. I inhaled his scent: horsehair, charcoal, and ink.

"That was a good party last night. The turkey broth was magnificent, Cook."

Cook nodded. Her real name was too difficult for Father to pronounce, so he'd always called her Cook. It was his favorite English word. Probably the only one he knew.

"And how about the music, eh?" Father continued. "You'd be hard pressed to find a guitar player like that Luis, even in the emperor's own court! I'll have to thank the lord treasurer for the tip. Anyway, did you enjoy yourself, daughter?"

"Yes, sir. Thank you."

He let me go, but before I could take two steps back, he grabbed my chin and forced me to look up at him. I blinked in shock, not at the rough gesture, familiar like blue skies in May, but at his round, wrinkled face and silver beard, at his speckled white skin, so different from mine that if it weren't for my height, I would've doubted I was his.

"The cacique showed great interest in you. Tell me, what was he whispering about, during your little dance?"

I hesitated and tried to pass it off as confusion. "I'm not entirely sure, for he spoke to me in K'iche', and I felt too ashamed to say I could barely understand." I blushed a little, both at the memory and at the blatant lie, which he didn't seem to quite believe.

"Is that so? Well, what *did* you understand?" He squeezed tightly enough to hurt.

I frowned. The guilt I'd felt from being dishonest evaporated. "I would like to answer, but I can hardly feel my tongue with that grip upon my face."

He flinched and let go immediately, murmuring something about arthritis making it difficult to control his joints.

I rubbed my jaw and let him feel his discomfort a moment longer before responding, "Well, I can't be certain what he said, Father, but I think he complimented my dress."

"Is that all?" He stared as if he'd burn a hole through me, but I made my face as open as possible and nodded. A frown tugged at his lips. "You should've said you didn't understand him. You should've said it loud for all to hear. Half the room thought you were talking back."

I looked down. "I felt sorry for him, sir. I didn't want him to feel foolish."

"Softhearted girl. Well, I suppose he was foolish enough to come—and dressed like a savage too. Does himself no favors, or me for that matter. I've told him, 'You're nearing twenty now, you must start acting like a man.' Cook—fetch me water, will you?"

The old woman moved like the wings of a hummingbird, the colorful flowers of her huipil blurring before my eyes. Even though Father always spoke to her as gently as his nature allowed, her speed stank of fear. Not for the first time in my life, I felt a twist of hot shame, a surge of anger at what she must've lived through, to feel the need to rush so. I knew better than to say anything, though, to either of them. She might crumble. He would burst.

"At least the other one had enough sense to stay away," I said, thinking it might amuse him and maybe even throw him off asking me any more questions.

"Ha! There would've been blood if that ruffian had come." He took a gulp of water.

We spoke of the other king of the highland Maya, whose Christian name was Don Juan Cortés, also known as Juan "El Grande." He and the cacique, Lord Juan de Rojas, would've ruled together, like their fathers and grandfathers before them.

They would've been brother kings, twin kings, like Hunahpu and Xbalanque, who defeated the lords of Xibalba before transforming into the sun and moon.

I started at the voice, as vivid and clear as the glass of water Cook had placed in my hand. I swayed, light-headed. My vision darkened, and my hands grew numb.

"What in heaven?" Father rushed to me and sat me down on the stool.

"Pardon me, Father. I believe the wine from last night has done me ill."

Father frowned. "Little wonder you went to bed so early last night."

"Oh, sir. I must've shamed you." I covered my face and took deep gulps of air to settle myself.

"Let this be a lesson to you, do you hear me? There is nothing more repugnant than a woman with a taste for drink."

"She should be avoided and detested like an ill-omened apparition," I whispered, quoting from Vives's *The Education of a Christian Woman*, which he'd asked me to memorize a few years back. In reality, I thought about Lady Blood again.

"Indeed! Now, finish that water and return to your chamber to sleep it off." He held out his arm. I didn't want to go back to bed, but I recognized an order when I heard one, so I did as he said and let him guide me down the hall, which was decorated in his spartan taste. There were no carpets covering the red tiled floor, no tapestries on the white plaster walls, no portraits, paintings, or relics of any sort.

Only one large wooden crucifix hung opposite my door.

"In you go." He stroked my cheek gently this time, his way of making amends.

I hesitated, then blurted out, "Father, the jade necklace—where did it come from?"

His eyes narrowed. "Why do you want to know?"

I thought quickly. "It seems quite old, and valuable."

He shrugged. "Bishop Marroquín had it in his collection. He gave it to me as a token of welcome when I first arrived. Said it was a symbol of leadership. I thought you'd like it."

"Oh, I do—I really do." I beamed, and a spark of pleasure lit his eyes too.

"Go rest now," he said.

I curtsied before closing the door. My room was almost as simple as the rest of the house. The only furnishings were a four-poster bed with thick green curtains, a wooden vanity with a small silver looking glass, and a chair with carved animal paws at the base, a furry fox's maybe, or a jaguar's.

Something gave me pause. I'd left the wooden shutters open. I studied the room, and a sick realization started to sink in.

The velvet cushion was still there, but the necklace was gone.

I looked for it everywhere. My hands shook both with fury at the violation and fear of the repercussions. It wasn't just Father who'd be upset. My mind turned again and again to the Lady's hovering gray eyes, enveloping me in a storm of dread. I tore my room apart first, then spent the rest of the day surreptitiously opening drawers and cupboards everywhere else, but it was truly gone. I cried myself to sleep and woke up in the middle of the night. It was windy and raining, and I'd somehow twisted the sheets into a tight knot around my legs. It felt like a net was pulling me down to the foot of the bed.

I kicked off the sheets and tried to ignore the throbbing in my belly and the eerie sensation like my spirit was being drawn to the right. To the side where, lying under a layer of carpet, floorboard, and loose stone, was a flat wooden chest containing the ancient manuscript I swore as a child to protect with my life. I almost laughed—who in their right mind made a child swear to something like that?

It was absurd.

A chill ran through my bones, as if my K'iche' ancestors were rallying against me, chiding me for my insolence. Then I heard her voice again.

Ab'aj Pol, you must love the Popol Vuh *and keep it safe. This book is our history, our treasure. Without it, our people are lost, for it is the Sight of our ancestors, who saw everything. Yes, they knew everything, whether there would be death, whether there would be famine, they knew it for certain. They wrote their knowledge here, their Sight, which passed beyond trees, beyond rocks, through lakes, through seas, through mountains and plains, the first families, molded from corn flour by Grandmother of Day and Light. Kaweq, Nija'ib', Ajaw-K'iche', they were gifted, they were thankful.*

I sat up on the bed, shaking, and looked around. "Mother?"

A bead of sweat fell down my temple as I waited for her reply, but she said nothing else. My jaw loosened in partial relief, for no matter how I missed her, I was not thrilled by the prospect of a ghostly call. I did not wish to be haunted by anyone, not even her.

The sound of heavy rain splattered against the walls. Why visit now, anyway, after all this time? Was it because I'd cried out to her last night?

And why remind me of the vow? I didn't need her to. It was impossible to forget.

I rubbed my face. Could this all be part of the curse? Not to die from Lady Blood's wrath, but to hear Mother whispering stories to me, like she used to when she was alive and Father was away? Or perhaps Mother was here to punish me. After all, I hadn't been as diligent in my study of the *Popol Vuh*; I hadn't burned incense for her in years. Once, I'd even prayed to God to make me forget her, although I'd felt so nauseated with guilt afterward that I hadn't been able to sleep for days.

Or perhaps it went even further back. Perhaps she was angry at me because I'd disobeyed her last order. The memory engulfed me and latched my throat shut.

"Close your eyes!" she'd yelled. Her hands were bound behind her. A fierce wind whipped her dark, glossy hair over her furious, defiant face. Everything else was a blur, except her face and the male fingers, a stranger's, which dug into my collarbones and held me in place. Unlike me, she didn't scream, shout, groan, or tear her windpipe crying.

No other sound came from her mouth again.

"Stop!" I stood up and went to the mirror, looked at myself, and slammed my palms down on the wooden surface of the vanity. The searing, prickling pain brought me back to my senses. I thought of seeking out Father, the only family I had left. Sometimes he comforted me, on days when I had difficulty reining in my mind, but it always troubled him deeply.

"You'll unlearn whatever she might've taught you," he'd said. They'd come for Mother when he'd been far away, unable to help us, to save her. He'd returned from Santiago with a head full of chalk-white hair, and sunken eyes that would not smile again for a year.

"If it's not in the Bible, it's not in your head, you hear me? I'll not have you ending up like her." He never spoke of her again.

With quaking fingers, I wiped my wet cheeks and crossed myself.

If this was the curse, I had to break it somehow, but the necklace was gone.

CHAPTER 3

Santa Cruz del Quiché, Guatemala
Autumn 1551

Father and I sat next to each other on the veranda and tried to make the most of the remaining light. It was a beautiful evening; a breeze carried the scent of fresh rain and pine needles from the nearby forest. We did this often, when he was home. He no longer told me stories, but he worked beside me while I read whatever he might've brought.

Books were a luxury even to us. He usually brought me pamphlets and scrolls about legal and religious matters, which were rather dense, but he said it mattered not if my role was confined to having children and managing the household, I had to be clever about the realities of this world. He said the emperor had *his* daughters educated, and so *I* had to be educated, and in any case, there was nothing worse than a stupid wife. So, even though I preferred poetry and new takes on the Greek classics, I never complained. To read something was better than nothing. It was an escape from the quiet, dull life I was forced to lead.

My thoughts were interrupted by Noble River, Cook's son, who also worked for Father. He brought us a jug of spiced, watered-down wine with orange slices, and I thanked him as he left. Father grumbled as he read a long letter from one of his fellow judges in Santiago. Too tired to read, I attempted instead to embroider what I hoped would resemble an amaranth and heliconia pattern onto one of my old black cotton skirts.

It was difficult because every few moments either my belly throbbed in pain or my head nodded down to my shoulders. I'd thrice pricked my fingers with the needle, which was good as it kept me awake. I truly hoped if I could make it through the day, I'd be able to sleep through the night. Maybe then I'd be guarded against Mother, against the words and stories she told. Even though I loved them, even though I missed hearing them, I also feared them.

They reminded me too much of her and that awful day. It was hard enough to cope with the memories when they flooded me. But even when I managed to push them aside and catch my breath again, they still nipped at me. They poked and whispered a lingering threat.

It could happen to you, too, if you're not careful.

Then there was my father. He'd expressly forbidden me from entering that world ever again. If he found out that I had the *Popol Vuh* in my possession, that I sometimes caved in and studied it . . . well, I didn't know what he would do. I just knew he wasn't above casting off his daughters. That's what he'd done to Beatriz.

My lungs clenched at the thought of losing him.

Yes, he could be cruel and unbearable at times, but he was my father.

He was my father, and I loved him.

"I must put Marroquín in his place when I return to Santiago tomorrow," he said. He folded a letter and opened another one. "From our relatives in Granada." His moustache twitched with the kind of pleasure that only our perfect Spanish relations brought him.

His relatives here, or more specifically, his daughter Beatriz, were another story.

I still prayed for her at night. After all, she was the only sister I'd ever known. She'd taught me my letters and numbers. She'd taught me French and Latin and played with me when Cook was too busy and Mother had one of her sleeping spells. But we never spoke of her now, and I was forbidden from writing to her. She was the real reason Father kept his ink locked away, because she'd done an unforgivable thing. She'd eloped with a common silversmith, the day after Mother died.

"Everyone sends their regards and hopes your party's a success. They cannot wait until we go back one day."

He sighed and kept reading. Poor man, I knew he wished to return to Spain, but the emperor refused to end his contract. He'd said Father was doing too good a job, and he had no one to replace him with.

I stitched on and hoped he'd share whatever news of Europe they'd sent, the latest fashions or the royal scandals, but I never found out, because the stable boy suddenly shouted and ran out from the back of the villa.

He stepped onto the brick and took off his hat in salute. "Señor!"

"What is it?" Father asked.

"Two men are coming." He pointed with his right pinkie. The rest of his fingers were missing from his hand. "They came out of the forest. I thought they'd head to town, but they're making their way, on foot. One's walking funny, limping-like. The other's holding him up."

Father groaned. "Fetch my horse; bring the mule."

The boy ran back.

"Who could it be?" I asked.

"Don't ask stupid questions. Take this letter inside and stay there."

I pulled up my skirts and ran past the arched door, through the sitting room, and into my bedchamber. I flung open the window and squinted. Father was already halfway down the field on his horse. He shouted something, probably cursing the mule to hurry.

He reached the men. I couldn't see much because the light was fading fast, but one of them looked in bad shape. The other man, who was lean and tall, helped the injured man onto the mule, jumped behind him, and held him to prevent him from falling. Father turned and trotted back.

I gasped when I finally made them out. Lord Juan, the cacique, had his arms wrapped around my cousin and dearest friend, Cristóbal, whose swollen face was battered purple and whose shirt was torn to bleeding rags.

"Cook!" I screamed and rushed through the inner patio to the kitchen. "Cook!"

The old woman was nowhere to be found, but the fire was burning strong. I grabbed the biggest pot and plunged it into the barrel of water. The coals hissed and spat when I whacked the dripping pot on the stove top. I stacked more wood and roused the flames with my fan. "Hurry!" I groaned.

I heard a crash and a flurry of sound, a grating chair, a moan, the harsh barks of voices arguing, and a shout—an order—then running footsteps echoing louder.

The stable boy crashed through the door as I poured vinegar into the water.

"Señorita, if you please—we need bandages."

"Here—grab my fan and keep going. Bring the pot when it's boiling."

I rushed to the pantry where Cook kept a basket full of fresh muslin, grabbed it, and ran back out. Father was leaning over Cristóbal, who lay sprawled on the large dining table. Lord Juan stood at the head of the table. He helped Cristóbal take his shirt off, rolled it, and tucked it under his head. Father and Lord Juan frowned at each other.

I ignored them and wiped the blood from Cristóbal's brow. He flinched and tried to open his bruised eyelids. "Cata . . ."

"Shh," I said.

The stable boy waddled in with the pot.

"Put it on the floor," I mumbled. "Take this, quickly." I handed him a clean swab. "Don't burn yourself." The stable boy tossed the wet cloth back to me and I wiped again. Cristóbal sucked in a breath and clenched his jaw.

"Sir, I have to talk to you about Captain Lobo," Lord Juan said.

Really? I thought. *Politics? Now?* I climbed onto the table next to where Father stood and dabbed at Cristóbal's chest. It was covered in cuts, but they weren't too deep. I let out a sigh of relief.

"He's still using illegal slaves," Lord Juan continued. "He pays them not, feeds them less, and works them to the bone in that encomienda, that land granted to him."

Father threw his arms in the air. "I've gone there three times. Without support from the neighbors, it's an impossible task."

"With all due respect—"

"Oh, do tell! What would you have me do, young cacique? Hand the slaves to you?"

Lord Juan remained silent.

"Tempting offer, eh? Once upon a time you would've jumped at it. Fodder for the altar, and their legs and arms for dinner too?"

I gaped. The cacique glared at Father, his nostrils flared.

"Perhaps, but since our customs have changed, praise God, I would have you set them free, like your lordship's done to countless others, because it is the emperor's law."

"Yes, and because it is right! I only jest about these old dinnertime customs of yours. In truth, I abhor seeing the awful looks on their faces. I abhor slavery with every hair on my body. Each time I inspect one of Lobo's mines, I hardly sleep for a week. Child, show the cacique your hand." The boy did as he was told.

"Mining accident right there. I took him to get treated myself, and now I can't get rid of him." He ruffled the stable boy's hair and pushed him away. "Anyway, I'll decide what to do with Lobo in my own bloody time. Now, what in heaven's name happened to my godson?"

Cristóbal moaned, and his eyes reeled as if he were drunk.

"I believe he was robbed," said Lord Juan.

"Bastards," mumbled Cristóbal. "They—they took my boots and sweet Berruga, ay!"

Father banged a fist on the table. "Damn them! That was a fine horse. Did you see the direction they went?"

Cristóbal rolled his head and looked up at Lord Juan. "Did—did you, Cacique?"

"They ran when they heard me coming. North-northwest, I believe."

"I'm sorry, Godfather. There were four of them, otherwise I could've fought them off."

"Why were you alone, you pigeon-headed fool?"

"I felt bad that I couldn't make it to Catalina's party." He shut his eyes. "I'd been delayed by all these storms and didn't want anyone slowing me down."

"Witless son of a donkey! Where do you think we live, Utopia? Boy, take the cloth. Catalina, go see that the cacique is recompensed for his efforts. Now, donkey-man, what did these robbers look like? I shall send out letters to the mayors north of here, see if we can catch them."

I glanced at Lord Juan and he nodded. I slid off the table and grabbed a fresh cloth to wipe my hands with as I walked into the library. The cacique walked behind me, and his presence, so close again, sent shivers down my neck and back.

The moment we were inside and out of earshot, he said, "I do not want a reward. You know what I've come for."

I sighed and turned, clenching my hands. There was no use delaying.

"Cacique, the necklace was stolen too."

His response was so brief that if I hadn't been looking for it, I would've missed it. There was a flash of dismay, a dilation in his eyes, a drop of color, before he collected himself.

"Forgive me," I whispered, and nearly reached out to touch his arm.

"You lie," he spoke in K'iche', his voice a rasp. "You wish to keep it."

My jaw dropped. I answered in Castilian. "I wish no such thing."

"You do!"

"I do not!"

"You may look like your mother, but you're nothing like her. You Mestizos always take after your Spanish fathers, and they're all the same, greedy old invaders—"

"Hold your tongue," I hissed in K'iche'. My cheeks were aflame, and my eyes were daggers, as sharp as his. "You forget yourself."

Lord Juan stepped away and crossed his arms behind his back, but he offered no apology, no sign of regret. *Shameless scoundrel,* I thought. *How dare he?*

"I may be a liar, but I'm no thief," I said. "Somebody stole it from my room, probably the same men who attacked Cristóbal. Come, see, I'll ask Father to add the necklace to his letter to the mayors."

I turned, but he put a hand on my shoulder. "Wait," he said, and stepped so close our faces were inches from each other. My body was rattled, like a flag in a thunderstorm, my chest heaved, and for a brief moment, he, too, swayed in a daze.

Then he blinked and said, "Where is the *Popol Vuh*? I *must* have it."

"But why?" I shook my head.

"That, I cannot say."

"Well, I could not give it to you anyway, or anyone else. Not for any reason."

His jaw set. He took a slow breath, as though he were readying himself to speak to an insolent child. "You do not understand. This is not a request; it's a command from the king of your mother's house."

In my heart, he was not my king, but as head of House Kaweq, he ultimately ruled over all of us, over House Ajaw-K'iche'—and even though both my mother and I, as women, had no right to preside over its noble duties, we were the only ones who'd survived.

And now, I was the only one left.

"I'm sorry, Cacique. I—I can't. I promised. I swore to my mother I'd keep it safe."

"It shall be safe."

"No, I can't. I won't, and we mustn't speak of it," I whispered.

The heat between us rose dangerously, like coals blasted by a pair of bellows. He replied through gritted teeth, "Oh, we must, and you will. Or I'll revoke your right to keep it at all, and I shall set the full might of Lady Blood against you."

I gulped. My heart sped to a frenzy.

His brow twitched, as if he knew my feelings, as if he'd won. He smiled the way a boy smiled down at the smaller child he'd knocked to the ground for no other reason than because he could. It was all the power he had in the world, and he used it without mercy.

The seeds of fear were scorched by a furnace of rage. I raised my chin and met his glare with my own. "I don't care. I'll not give it to you."

It was his turn to feel fury, and he didn't hide it well. He clenched his fists. His eyes turned pitch black, and too late I remembered, this man could've been a god.

"Oh—you will," he breathed, right in my face, so close our noses dabbed together. I sucked in a breath. I was so shocked I didn't realize when he turned and left. I blinked when I heard a bang and looked behind. My stomach swooped like I'd fallen off my horse. The stable boy was standing by the door, a big frown on his face. Bad. That was bad.

"Señor is wanting you."

Oh Lord, the boy was going to tell him what he saw, and God only knew what would go through my father's mind.

"Th—thank you, child—ah!" I clutched at my stomach, my womb.

"Señorita?"

"Ay!" I shut my eyes. I felt like a knife was ripping me open. Warmth leaked out of me, down my legs, my stockings, a river. I walked away and there it was, a trail of blood. Red against red. I gasped.

The Lady had come to claim me.

The next day, Father left for Santiago without saying goodbye. Perhaps he wanted to avoid the sight of me in that shameful condition. Perhaps the stable boy had talked, and he was too angry to speak with me. Whatever the reason, I was in a state of utter misery. I could hardly move, and the pangs were endless. I wished Father were home, with his strong arms and fiery temper. I thought maybe with him there, I'd be less afraid, less alone.

For I was afraid.

Three days had passed. I'd had my monthly bloods for a year, so I knew this situation wasn't normal. It was the curse, and I'd bleed to death unless I yielded.

But no, I could not. I'd sworn to my mother, whose voice I'd not heard once since that night. Still, I knew, the *Popol Vuh* was my burden, my treasure. I would rather have died than see Lord Juan take it. I pictured his stupid grin and my resolve strengthened.

But another night passed, and then another, and nothing changed.

I trembled and cried, "Christ in heaven, save me!"

Cook and Noble River were frantic. They fed me raw meat and forced glass after glass of water down my throat. By my counts, they shoved an entire lamb into my body, but the flow was unstoppable, the Lady's knife entrenched. My poor Cook scarcely brought me a basket of clean rags when she had to take them back to be washed. It was worse in the night, a torrent. I refused to lie on my bed. When I could, I slept on my leather chair, head on the mattress, and the blood dripped from the seat into my chamber pot. Cristóbal, who'd healed by then, stood by the door for hours and tried to distract me.

"Remember when we were children, and we would sneak off to the old ruins to play lords and ladies?"

"You wanted to be the ladies and I the lords," I said with a trace of a smile.

"We'd find secret tunnels and make up stories about the symbols and murals."

"You'd teach me the ones you knew, and I'd teach you the ones Mother taught me."

"And now your father insists I join the Dominicans."

"You really want to be a monk?" I strained to say.

"It'll please your father."

"So you don't."

He shrugged. "He's given me so much, cared for me well. Lord knows it's not been easy since my parents died. I thank your lady mother every day in my prayers, for asking him to be my godfather. So, if he wants me to be a monk, it's the least I can do."

After that, on the eighth day, Cristóbal and Noble River rushed to town to call on the doctor, but came back saying the doctor believed I was simply bringing balance to my new adult body by expelling my childhood sins. He would've bled me, but what was the point? He sent back a rabbit's foot for luck and recommended I inhale tobacco smoke to ease the colic. I threw the rabbit's foot back at Cristóbal's face with such little force it barely left my hand. The smoke left me feeling so nauseated I spent the rest of the day gasping out the window.

That night it felt like the phantom knife inside me was thrown into a forge and plunged back. It twisted and turned, and after an hour of groaning and crying, I finally gave up. Cook sat next to me, held my hand, and wept for me. I knew she longed to say the kind of sweet, soothing words I'd not heard since Mother died, and not for the first time in my life, I wished to God they'd never cut out her tongue.

"I yield," I cried in K'iche'. The stabbing pain eased to a throb. "I yield," I croaked.

Cook's face was pale. Noble River held a wet cloth to my forehead. They must've thought One Death had finally come for me. I shook my head. "Please, fetch Cristóbal."

He rushed into my room and held my hand. He looked like he hadn't slept for days. "Cousin, what can I do?"

"Send a message to the cacique. Tell him he can have it."

There was a flash of confusion on his brow, but I felt too exhausted to explain. He nodded and I fell asleep. When I woke up, however, many hours later, the river had run dry.

CHAPTER 4

Santa Cruz del Quiché, Guatemala
Autumn 1551

Two days later, we sent the stable boy to town with a long list of errands. Only Cristóbal and I were in the house with Cook and Noble River, who stayed in the servants' quarters whenever Father went away, for my protection. Regardless, Noble River was loyal to Cook, which meant he was loyal to me.

Father was always telling me I could never be too careful with servants, that too many people hated him and might seek revenge on him through me. He always said everyone had a price, and I knew Mother had learned that lesson the hard way.

It was a maid who'd betrayed her.

But I couldn't help it. Cook had kept my mother safe during the conquest, so I trusted her with my life. I trusted her with the secret of the *Popol Vuh* as well, because she'd walked in on me taking it out one night, about four years ago. She didn't need her tongue to turn me in, and yet, she never had.

I was still too weak to walk more than a few steps, so I decided to greet Lord Juan in the sitting room right outside my chamber. Cook and I sat, embroidering handkerchiefs by the window. A large sewing basket lay between our padded chairs, and her bare feet were up on a footstool, leather sandals arranged neatly by its side. She hummed tunelessly the way she did when she felt most relaxed. She would be by my side the entire time, for my reputation, and maybe even my protection.

Cristóbal walked in with a book, nodded, and sat across from me. He looked every bit like a Spanish gentleman, except for his skin. We were dressed in our Sunday best, with ruff collars around our necks; doublet, cape, and spotless white breeches for him; and full Spanish farthingale, slashed sleeves, and velvet slippers for me. It was too much trouble for a man who'd almost killed me. I resented it. But Father had always been very clear about treating his few friends with every honor, and I wasn't about to let him down, in that regard at least. I tried not to think about every single other way I risked his ruin.

If word had gotten out that the cacique had paid me a visit, at best it would've been a scandal, and Father would've been disgraced. At worst, his enemies might've inquired about the nature of the visit. If they'd somehow found out it was about a manuscript that contained the Maya story of creation, among several undoubtedly forbidden subjects, well, I imagined I would've been branded a heretic like my mother. I didn't wish to put Father through that again, and, if I was being honest, I didn't much fancy the notion of being tortured and then burned alive, or having my head sliced off, or whichever punishment was most in vogue at the time.

"Thank God you're here," I said. We knew everything about each other, always had and always would. The year before, when I'd been sick with fever, I'd told him where the *Popol Vuh* was buried, in case I died.

If he'd wanted to betray me, he would've done it already.

"The cacique shall keep it safe." He shook his head and murmured, "It's unfair, though, him taking away the ancient rights of your house."

Cristóbal was of the Nija'ib' lineage, the second most important house to the K'iche'. He had a title and rights of his own. "Are you certain you don't want me to intervene?"

There was a tremor in my stomach, a warning. "I am."

The sound of footsteps approaching set my heart aflutter. Cook's son knocked on the door and said in K'iche', "Lord Juan is here."

"Thank you, Noble River," I said. "You may show him in."

Lord Juan walked in, his movements fluid and purposeful. He was irritatingly handsome, with his full lips, high cheekbones, and piercing, catlike eyes. And he was so tall, taller than most men, with broad shoulders, which were lean but defined. I could see the muscles through his plain linen clothes, which were the same as last week's.

He nodded at Cristóbal and pressed his hand to his heart when he looked at Cook. It was a sign of deep respect. She was one of the oldest K'iche's in Santa Cruz and had been only slightly older than me when the Spanish arrived. At the kind gesture, my anger toward Lord Juan mellowed, until I caught the gleam of triumph in his eyes.

I sat up straight and folded my hands on my lap to keep them from shaking. "You'll excuse me for not rising to greet you, Cacique, but I took ill after we last met, and I'm trying to preserve my strength."

"My lady, I'm sorry to hear that. Is there anything I can do?" He bowed to hide it from the others, but when he looked me straight in the eye, the corner of his lips twitched. I felt certain then that he knew what he'd done, the dog. I kept my face still, smiled even, though in that instant I loathed him with every hair and fiber of my body. I would not give him the pleasure of guessing how sick he'd made me, or how much he affected me, even now.

"I thank you, my lord," I said. "Was but a trifle and I'm very much on the mend."

"That's a relief."

Noble River nodded and turned. Cristóbal closed the door behind him, and all pretense on my part faded away.

"Right, you're here to steal away my inheritance. Cristóbal, if you'd be so kind as to assist our *great* lord."

"Catalina." His tone pleaded with me to behave.

"Cristóbal said your father asked the mayors to keep an eye out for . . . your . . . necklace," said Lord Juan. "I thank you, and I give you my word, once I'm finished with it, I shall return the manuscript to you, and we can put all this unpleasantness behind us."

I scoffed. "What do you need it for anyway? Why now, after all these years?"

Lord Juan glanced at Cristóbal. I remembered suddenly that they knew each other well. They'd both gone to the missionary schools as children to learn to read, write, and speak Castilian. They'd both been forced to be acolytes together in their youth.

I threw a look at Cristóbal, wondering if my cousin had anything to do with this, but I failed to catch his eye. He seemed innocent enough, so I dismissed the thought.

Lord Juan responded, "I cannot say, only that it is important."

I wished to argue back, but my stomach gave an unpleasant jolt, and I was cowed. "Do take a seat." I picked up my half-finished handkerchief and stabbed the needle, in and out, in and out, and tried to ignore the way Lord Juan patted Cristóbal on the shoulder as he walked past him into my chamber, or the way he leaned sideways on Cristóbal's chair like it was a throne. I bit down on my tongue to keep from cursing him, though I wouldn't have known how.

After a moment, there was a rustling, and a dull clatter like wood hitting wood. Cristóbal must've been digging past the floorboard. There were two separate thuds, and a gasp. Lord Juan and I looked up at each other and at the door.

"No!" Cristóbal's voice reached us, thick with horror.

We stood at the same time and I rushed inside, the cacique behind me.

Cristóbal was kneeling with half an arm inside the open floorboard. He pulled out a large rock and I sucked in my breath. His sleeve was drenched and muddy.

"Oh my Lord." I covered my mouth.

He reached back in, pulled out the dripping wooden chest, and placed it beside him. My knees failed me. Cook pushed past the cacique and tried to help me, but I was too weak.

"What's this?" said Lord Juan.

"Give it to me," I croaked.

Cristóbal gently pushed the chest over to where I sat. It was a long, thin wooden box, about the length of my forearm, although twice as wide. A small puddle started forming around it, soaking into my knees.

"I—I took it out in the middle of the night, when Father was traveling, and studied it just last month," I whispered. "It was fine!"

But I could see that it was no longer fine. The wood was soft and spongy, and reeked of dampness. The copper clasp dangled off its top hinges, rendering the lock useless.

"It must've been the storms," said Cristóbal, who slipped next to me and wrapped an arm around my shoulders. "Maybe it's not as bad as it looks. Open it and make sure?"

It took me a moment to hear him. When I finally moved, it was like someone else's hands were reaching out. But no, they were my hands. They pulled off the clasp with ease and lifted the lid. I stared at the ancient paper, folded like a fan, no longer plump and healthy, but slopped flat like a dead fish.

"It was fine last month," I whispered in disbelief as the truth sank in. All those beautiful stories I loved, our magical history, our people's legacy. Gone. It was as if Mother were dying all over again. The terror and grief gripped me, tore me down. I was on the verge of screaming when Lord Juan slapped the door with his palm, and I jumped.

"Argh! First the necklace, and now this?"

I covered my face to hide the shame rising in me like a lance.

Cristóbal's arm tensed around me. "Cacique, please, this is not her fault."

He was wrong. I'd failed. I'd failed my mother, my house, my blood, my people. This was my one job, my promise. My mother had died to keep this book alive, and I'd let it rot.

"Do you even realize what this means?" Lord Juan asked. His voice trembled.

I glared at him through my tears.

"How will we interpret the auguries now, if we need to? How will we divine the sky? We shall be blind! Our children shall run forth in darkness, all thanks to you."

"Oh yes, all thanks to me! I made the earth flood, did I?"

"Ha! You have no such powers, Mestiza." He threw the word at me as if it were the dirtiest thing in the world, to be mixed-blood, neither here nor there, an insult to both races.

My stomach dropped. Before that moment, I'd felt many things about being Mestiza. I'd felt lost, torn, confused about who I was and where I belonged, for I was always on the fringes. In rare moments, however, I'd also felt proud, lucky to be privy to the beauty of two completely different worlds. Hopeful that I could make them both better. But in that moment, I felt tiny, insignificant, crushed. Like a worm whose fragile body had been dug up and ripped in two by a clumsy child's hand.

"Enough," said Cristóbal. He stood up, and even though he was a head shorter than Lord Juan, even though the blood had drained from his face, he seemed to radiate light, like a stag in a forest clearing.

"Bickering won't help. Let the paper dry first; only then can we ascertain the damage."

"Stop trying to make her feel better," Lord Juan said. "Look how the ink runs all over the paper. Look at that glyph; I can't even make out the symbol."

I looked at the one he pointed to and whispered, *"K'a katz'ininoq."*

Cristóbal looked down at me. "What did you say?"

I wiped my eyes and took a shuddering breath. I wouldn't allow the cacique to see how I trembled. *"K'a katz'ininoq,"* I repeated.

Cook sat next to me and hugged me close to her, like Mother once had. The memories flashed in my mind, of when we had studied the pages and recited the words together like a prayer. Sometimes Mother had danced around me. She'd glided like satin and water, her steps lighter than lace. She'd soared like a heron, and nothing had been more beautiful in this world. Her voice chimed in my ears again, and her fingertips braided ribbons through my hair.

I leaned closer to Cook, closed my eyes, and said,

> *K'a katz'ininoq*
> *All is still silent and placid.*
> *All is silent and calm.*
> *Hushed and empty*
> *is the womb of the sky.*
>
> *There is not yet one person,*
> *one animal,*
> *not one bird, fish, crab,*
> *tree, rock, hollow,*
> *canyon, meadow,*
> *forest.*
>
> *All alone the sky exists,*
> *the face of the earth is not yet clear.*
> *Alone lies the expanse of sea,*
> *under the womb of the sky,*
> *and nothing else is gathered.*
>
> *All is at rest, nothing stirs,*
> *all is languid under the sky,*
> *only the tranquil sea lies alone.*
> *All lies placid and silent,*
> *in the darkness, in the night.*

My voice faded to a scratch, but I felt more grounded, slightly more at ease. I opened my eyes and stared at the box again. No one spoke for a long moment. There was only the soft rustling of Cook as she rubbed my arm. Then, Cristóbal hunched down and grabbed my hand. I looked up and, to my surprise, he was smiling.

"You know the book by heart?"

I blinked, taken aback. My first instinct was to be modest. "Well, I mean, I—maybe?"

"Catalina," he said, raising his brow.

"I suppose I know it well enough, but most of us do, don't we? All of the K'iche' know the deeds of Hunahpu and Xbalanque, and the three attempts to forge mankind, do they not?"

Cristóbal shook his head. "All of us would've known the basic storylines, years ago. But they have not been performed for decades and our people have been, well, focused on surviving—" Lord Juan let out a snort, and I flinched, mortified, but Cristóbal ignored us. "Many are too frightened to teach them to their young. Some of us remember some parts, but I doubt we would be able to recite them word for word. Am I right, Cacique?"

Lord Juan crossed his arms. His gaze trailed my room, lingered on my large, comfortable bed, my expensive looking glass. I wasn't sure if I imagined the look of jealousy and scorn, before he said, "It was the sacred task of House Ajaw-K'iche', of the Sons of Fire specifically, to fully memorize and be able to recite the *Popol Vuh* from start to finish, but I doubt *she* has achieved this feat."

My eyelids narrowed. "It's been a long time," I said plainly. "I am out of practice, true, but I was eight the first time I did it." I remembered the glow in my mother's eyes, the pride in her grin that night. It was one of my greatest comforts, to know I'd given her that small pleasure, the reassurance that her efforts were not in vain.

But Lord Juan scoffed. "Really? What of the first true dawn, the wandering of the tribes, the history of my people, do you know *those* parts? Because I do."

I rolled my eyes at his use of the words "my people" rather than "our people." I stood up, and helped pull Cook back up to her feet.

"I know it all." I bit back the urge to tell him that the story of the first dawn was my most beloved. It felt too raw an admission, so I smoothed down my skirt instead and said, "Although I must admit, I always found the end dreadfully boring, reciting generation after generation of dead kings. I can see why you'd find it interesting."

"Well!" Cristóbal interjected. He threw an apologetic look at Lord Juan, who was clearly shocked by my impertinence. "I can tell you disagree on most things, yet both of you cannot deny this: it is our duty to preserve this book."

We stared at Cristóbal for a moment, until Lord Juan said, "I agree, but the fact remains that there is nothing *left* to preserve."

The implication was clear; it was all thanks to me.

Well, I'd be damned if I was going to let him hang this over my head for the rest of my life. I refused to be remembered as Catalina the Destroyer. And just as I thought that, I realized I didn't have to be.

Look upon it, my bird, whenever it's safe for you. Know it as you know the Lord's Prayer. Sing it to yourself when you're alone. Never forget. She'd made sure I knew that book in and out. She'd kept her vow, and by God, so would I.

"I disagree, my lord," I said, placing a rather venomous emphasis on the last word. "The book lives inside me, and I swore to protect it, like my ancestors did. So *I'll* make amends. I'll rewrite the *Popol Vuh.*"

There was a long, astounded pause. The cacique's eyes narrowed in confusion and mistrust. Cristóbal blinked at me. Then Cook stepped in front of me and cupped my face in her hands. I looked down, for the top of her head barely reached my shoulder. Her face was grim and hard like flint. A warning, I felt, of what lay in the path ahead, of what I myself had to become.

Cristóbal cleared his throat. "Your valor is admirable, but I'm afraid you cannot possibly do this on your own."

Cook tapped my cheek, as though giving me leave to fight. I put my hands on my hips and said, "Why not?"

"Well, for one, you don't know all the symbols, so how will you write it?"

I raised a brow. "I'll simply write in Latin script, as it sounds."

Cristóbal looked impressed, then worried again. He glanced at the cacique, and at Cook, as if pleading for assistance. "It's too dangerous. What if you're discovered? The Church will show you no mercy."

"Exactly! I'd not ask it of you. I could not ask it of anyone else." I stole a glance at the cacique, for it was the truth. No matter how much I disliked him, I would've been loath to see him burn. We all looked down at the box.

Lord Juan crossed his arms and said, "No."

"Excuse me?"

His body went rigid. For a split moment, he had a far-off look and his eyes turned pitch black. Then he shook his head. "I mean, you'll not be the only one to write it. Not only do I not trust you, a Mestiza, a woman, to do the task properly, but it'd not be right. This book *must* be written by all three masters of the great K'iche' houses, not just the least."

"Oh, it *must*? And how does your superior male brain propose we do that, huh?" I said. "We'd have to meet in some abandoned, hidden place at some godforsaken hour. Don't you think it was difficult enough to arrange *this* pleasant gathering?"

But before Lord Juan could answer, we heard the sound of footsteps running.

"Hurry!" Cristóbal said.

Lord Juan grabbed the box with the wet manuscript, and we rushed back into the sitting room, closed my door, and sat. Noble River knocked and entered.

"The stable boy is on his way back, galloping hard."

Lord Juan stood and bowed. "I believe that's my cue to leave. Thank you for your hospitality, my lady."

"It's been a pleasure," I responded with a voice like ash poured from an urn.

"May I escort you, Cacique?" said Cristóbal, and they turned and left.

I grabbed my handkerchief and tried to stitch, but Cook gave me that hard stare again.

"I know, I know. Don't worry, we'll be fine," I said, but I couldn't meet her eyes.

Because in my heart, I knew we wouldn't be.

CHAPTER 5

Santa Cruz del Quiché, Guatemala
Autumn 1551

It took several weeks for me to fully recover from Lord Juan's curse and for us to arrange and prepare everything for our next meeting. On the allotted night, I lay on my bed, fully dressed in a simple cotton kirtle. I was waiting for Cristóbal to knock on my door. Father had come and gone again, and I finally felt like myself once more. Well, the petrified version of myself, as I was about to do the most daring, most foolish thing ever. I was going to sneak out of my house to meet with not just one, but two full-blooded Maya men.

I told myself for the hundredth time that we'd taken every precaution. Cook had slipped some essence of white lotus into the stable boy's soup during supper. He would've slept through a hurricane. We were indeed meeting in some abandoned, hidden place at a godforsaken hour. The ruins, where no one dared to go at night except, of course, the type of people who tended to slit your purse *and* your throat for good measure. But, I reminded myself, the old citadel was large and it was unlikely we would run into them. Cristóbal was an excellent swordsman too. We would be safe enough, and we had to try. Father wouldn't be home for another five days. It was the right time.

The quiet knock came, and I jumped up, pulled a cloak around my shoulders, and raised the hood so my face was hidden. I felt so light-headed when I opened the door that I looked down to check whether my feet still touched the ground. Cristóbal, also hooded, reached out for my hand. I was about to take it when I saw the crucifix behind him and froze.

"What is it?" he whispered.

I'd been so worried about my body coming to harm, I'd forgotten about my soul. Our souls—Cristóbal's, Juan's, Cook's.

"What is it, Catalina?"

"Are we doing an evil thing?"

He raised an inquiring brow.

"What if, what if God sent those rains to destroy the *Popol Vuh*, just like he sent the floods to Noah?"

Cristóbal sighed and looked at the crucifix too.

"It's true," he hesitated. "The priests would say the *Popol Vuh* is evil. That it spurs idolatry. They'd damn us to hell for keeping alive words that gainsay the Holy Bible. They'd say we'd led others astray and ruined their souls."

I blinked. "Well, then, should we be doing this?"

He smiled. "I cannot tell you what to do. It's a matter of conscience. I've searched my soul and found my answer, and you must find yours, for you'll be judged one way or another, in this world or the next."

I closed my eyes and leaned on the doorframe, aware of time slipping by.

"There's no time for this!" I grabbed his hand and pulled. Cristóbal laughed and we walked away, past the crucifix, past the courtyard, into the hall, through the kitchen, out into the orchard, and toward the trees that lined the way from my house down the hill. We avoided the narrow pass that led up to the ravine and the ancient stone citadel with its palaces and temples with tips like polished mountains. That's where most robbers waited to ambush their prey. Instead, we went past it, toward a second, secret pass, one only the highest nobility ever knew of, or used.

The chilled wind blew harder the closer we climbed up the hidden steps on the side of the ravine, shaking both trees and nerves alike, but by the time we'd climbed over the canyon top, I was drenched in sweat and panting from both fear and exertion.

Cristóbal led the way through the abandoned city, although the shifting light made the carvings on the walls come alive. Kings emerged from screeching eagle beaks and the gaping maws of beasts, warriors with pierced tongues pointed their razor-sharp maces, musicians banged on their turtle-shell drums. We skirted around the boulders and vines, the weeds and ferns that crept around and on top of the buildings. With a pang of sorrow, I noted the forest was reclaiming the land, and had advanced greatly since I had last been there, when I'd visited as a child, with Mother.

We walked toward the main square, where the colorful temples of Tohil, Auilix, and Hacauitz faced each other. To fend off the rising panic, I crossed myself and prayed.

We circled around until we were hidden in the shadows of the tallest temple, Tohil, where we waited. I kept praying and praying. Lord Juan was meant to meet us there, but time stretched on. An effigy with black eyes and scorpion tails for hair looked down on me, and my skin crawled. Finally, after the longest quarter of an hour of my life, the cacique walked out, at a most leisurely pace I might add, into and across the courtyard. Even though he was hooded, he glided as if he were leading a procession, as if there were hundreds of people gathered around, watching him, adoring him, their king.

I glanced behind me, at Cristóbal, and shook my head in disbelief. He placed a hand on my shoulder to placate me. I had promised him I would try to be civil, so I held my tongue when Lord Juan met us and said, "Follow me."

It wasn't long before we reached the burnt remains of the palace of House Kaweq, Lord Juan's ancient family seat. The steps were still there, and the large, flat platform where the palace complex once stood, but apart from a smaller tower and one or two colonnades, most of the structure had turned to rubble. The larger stones were gone. They had been used to build the church in Santa Cruz. I stole a glance at Lord

Juan, but whatever emotions he felt at the sight of his destroyed home, he hid well.

The cacique did not climb the steps, but instead took us to one side, where a budding avocado tree grew sideways out of the joint between the structure and the ground. He reached into the sack he carried under his cloak and took out two wooden sticks. He squatted down by the rustling tree and swept a square, flat rock with his hand, sending dirt flying in all directions. He took out what appeared to be a short rope with hooks on both ends, inserted them into the two holes on the boulder he'd revealed, stood back, and pulled. With a grating sound, the rock lifted up like a hatch, and revealed a few narrow steps that led down into a pitch-black hole.

"Grab the poles and fix them on the corners," he said to Cristóbal, who did as he was told. Once the hatch looked well supported by the sticks, Lord Juan let go of the rope and put it back in his sack.

"Only those of stout heart dare enter the Kaweq lair." He looked at me, eyes glinting.

"I guess I'll have to show you what that looks like," I bit back, piqued by his tone, by the implication that I was weak or terrified, which, of course, I was. But before they could stop me, I gathered my skirts, sat on the edge, and squeezed into the dark tunnel. I descended each step on my bottom, until I reached some kind of landing.

My fiery indignation was quickly extinguished, however, by the cold, dank air, and the realization that I couldn't even see the end of my nose.

I backed into the musty wall next to the steps, jerked my hand away from its sleek, frog-skin feel, and fought the urge to scream my lungs out. I was suddenly nine years old again. Mother was gone, and I was petrified of dirt.

Yes, dirt. Soil. I detested it, and anything like it—earth, mud, sand, even small rocks. I couldn't leave the house. I couldn't step outside the safety of our tiled floors. I didn't want to be touched by it, those tiny particles. I feared a gust of wind might thrust them up toward my face, and I imagined breathing it all in, all that dirt rushing up my nostrils and the back of my throat, accumulating behind my eyelids until the world was smothered in darkness. I couldn't bear it. My chest would seize, and I would scream until I lost my voice.

Father helped me, in his way. He made Noble River dig out the hydrangeas and then held me down on the fresh soil until I was still as a tomb. I was stock-still in the cave, but not calm. Thankfully, I could hear the others shuffling down, and it wasn't long before Cristóbal's echoing voice called out my name.

"I'm here," I croaked. There was a clack as his boots hit and stumbled on the stone. He stood next to me and I gripped his hand. He squeezed back, even though his palm was as clammy as the wall behind us.

"Hold on, I'll light a torch," said Lord Juan, who sounded like he was seated on the last step. There was a number of sharp clicks followed by the pungent smell of sulfur and smoke. A golden light flickered and glowed from near my feet, slowly illuminating the cave.

Its sheer splendor snapped me out of my terror. It was no bigger than my kitchen, but decorated with a beautiful, elaborate frieze, replete with brightly painted busts and sculptures of birds and jaguars, and gods crowned with feathered headdresses, playing ball. In the center there was a small circle of carved stones, some of which supported different colored vases, a large bowl of water, and my mother's fan-like manuscript, laid out, looking worn but dry. In the middle of the stone circle was a neatly laid pile of dried wood. The ground was strewn with large pine needles, forming a fragrant carpet.

"You did all this, my lord?" Cristóbal asked.

"No, I asked El Grande, who is like a brother to me. He prepared everything," Lord Juan said as he walked toward the center, lowered his hood, and lit the kindling, which let off so much black smoke it brought tears to my eyes. He reached into one of the vases and threw a pinch of something into the fire that filled the room with a strong aroma.

Copal.

Immediately, I thought of my mother, who'd always smelled like that, like resin, the blood of trees. The smell comforted and strengthened me, and I steeled myself to do whatever I had to do to keep the vow I'd made to her.

The cacique washed his hands and arms, closed his eyes, and whispered, "Heart of Sky, Heart of Earth, the Kaweq speak to you, pray to you, keep your days. On this night of the *oxlajuj kej*, a night that carries the destinies of humankind, we ask for your blessing."

Cristóbal and I walked together until we stood in front of the fire. He took a pinch of copal too, threw it in the fire, and said, "Maker, Modeler of humankind, Giver of breath and heart, the Nija'ib' praise you, you who know everything. We ask for your blessing."

Cristóbal handed me the vase and I took it. I glanced involuntarily at Lord Juan, who looked at me just like I thought he would, with unfiltered, unmistakable disdain.

You don't belong here, Mestiza. I was certain those were his thoughts. I would never be K'iche' enough for him. I was tainted. But there was some kind of shield around me then and, for once, I didn't care. My blood claim might've been less than his, but my love for our heritage was just as strong.

My eyes moistened as I realized how much I'd tried to push that love away. I'd tried to swallow it down and contain it, hoping it would contain the grief that came along with it. Now I knew it couldn't be done. I was no Athena. I couldn't deny half my being, and if I wanted to honor my mother and truly keep her memory and her promise, I would have to feel her loss, no matter how deeply it hurt.

With that weight on my chest, I reached into the jar and threw in the incense, closed my eyes, and whispered the way she had, "Mother-Father, Bearer, Begetter of life, begotten in light, the Ajaw-K'iche' call upon you and seek your blessing."

After several quiet breaths, Cristóbal cleared his throat. "Good. We mustn't waste time. Catalina, we've agreed the cacique will scribe, for we know the creation story best."

I nodded and he continued. "It's important we do this the right way, the old way."

My cheeks burned. "With dancing, you mean?"

He nodded and took off his cloak and boots. I was in the middle of doing the same when he said, "And *balché' ki'*."

We stared at each other for a moment, until I nodded again. He turned and so did I—to tighten the lacing on my bodice. Cristóbal said, "You made the drink, sir? The *balché' ki'*?"

The cacique nodded. "As you instructed, I soaked and ground the bark, crushed it, and added all the different mushrooms and flowers. Thorn apple, greenheart, wild tobacco, and honey. It's in the wineskin there; the instruments are here, and all the ink and amate." There was enough amate paper to write the book three times over. "And I brought something of my own for you to wear, Nija'ib'."

Out of one of the larger vases, he removed a delicate panache of striking red and blue feathers; I guessed macaw by their size. Cristóbal walked with his head bowed, and Lord Juan tied the panache around his head.

"I am honored," said Cristóbal.

"It's only right. We'd best get started," replied the cacique. He took off his cloak, and laid it on the ground neatly before sitting on it and setting up a kind of desk on one of the smoother stones.

Cristóbal grabbed the first jar he pointed at and took a long draft, then handed it to me and said, "Drink the rest."

The *balché' ki'* was surprisingly sweet and fragrant, with a bitter after-taste, and it wasn't long before its soothing effects tingled up my chest and cheeks. Cristóbal gave me a rattle and started a slow, steady beat on his handheld drum, giving me a brilliant smile.

I realized the *balché' ki'* was hitting him too, and I beamed and rattled away.

"Ah, I do love you, cousin." He laughed for a long time, although he kept the beat going. For a long while after the last echo of his voice was gone, the drum kept on beating.

Then, in between beats, Cristóbal nodded and said, "This is the beginning of the Ancient Word, here in a place called K'iche'." I caught Lord Juan scribbling away. "Here we shall inscribe the Ancient Word; we shall demonstrate our shadow past, and how life and light were brought to being."

Cristóbal and I circled each other, and all the while his steady beat reverberated inside the cave, inside my heart. My soul lifted.

"We write about this now, even now, amid the preaching of God, in Christendom," he said, voice trembling. "We bring it out because the original *Book of Council* is no more. But this is the account, here it is. Tell it, Stone Orchid."

I hummed for a little while and waited for the words to come. The tip of my tongue quivered. I shook my rattle and recited, "All is silent and calm. Hushed and empty, is the womb of the sky." I kept speaking, and something curious happened to my voice.

I could *see* the sound, my breath, a blue vapor. It echoed, expanded. It cloaked the room in a peaceful fog, a vast emptiness, where a single drop of water falling into the crystal pool below would've resounded for millennia.

I was alone in this eternal dusk, and I was not me.

My body was long, powerful, covered in thousands of dazzling scales each the size of my old human body, and my arms were no longer arms, but wings. They spanned continents, dazzled in emerald feathers. I stretched them and soared, delighted in my grace.

I flew through the cool, quiet mist for eons, encountering no one, until finally, another point of light caught my golden gaze.

Hurricane and Thunderbolt gathered around each other and hovered above the calm sea. Their shattering voices ripped through clouds, through the fabric of space.

"Join us, brother," they said, "and we shall bring forth the world."

I lingered beside them, and our consciousnesses melded together in a perfect beam.

"Earth!" we called in unison, and the earth rose with the groan of a thousand crushed stones; the sea foamed and split in half. Mountains and trees sprouted as we thought of them, and grass and flowers grew in every hue and shape we could conjure. Our wisdom was endless, and so was our creation.

I danced below the trees and slithered my body next to rough bark and fragrant petals, overjoyed. "They should have guardians," I hissed, "these beautiful trees."

"Indeed! And those guardians should praise and worship us," replied the other gods, and as soon as we thought of them, deer and birds sprouted from our heads. They bucked and fluttered in all directions and began to build nests. The jaguar, monkey, and lizard emerged too. How beautiful they were, how marvelous.

"But listen to them—they can only growl, and screech, and hiss," said Thunderbolt. His diamond body sparkled and fizzed with unspeakable force.

I listened and hoped to hear my name praised and sung, as it ought to have been, but these animals could not do it. A sudden rage filled my belly, as endless and powerful as the savage heat that simmered underneath the mountains I'd created.

"This won't do!" I pounced on the useless creatures and devoured their meat.

"Stop, Q'ukumatz," said Hurricane, and his dark cloud of a body swirled all around me, enveloping me in screeching wind and freezing rain. "Let us seek advice from Grandmother of Day and Light. She will know how to make the best worshippers."

We flew to Grandmother of Day and Light, who stood with her back crouched as she warmed her wrinkled hands over a smoking mountain. "What you need is men," she said.

"How do we make such men to worship us, oh wise one?" I asked.

"Hmm . . . why don't you try making them out of mud and clay?" she replied, and smiled with her starlike eyes.

We mixed the soil and water and sculpted our men from mud. But their windpipes were too soggy, too loose to make sounds and name us. They could not raise their wobbly arms to praise us. We dismantled them, and flew back to Grandmother of Day and Light for more advice.

She said, "Hmm . . . why don't you try making men out of wood?"

We split our forests in two, and made men with one half. It did not work. We watched in horror as armies of our wooden men destroyed the other half of the forest and beat our animals with stones. They never once called our names in worship, never once remembered us in their vacant minds.

"They are heartless, senseless! Let's destroy them!" I said to the other gods.

A moment later we flooded the earth and drowned the wooden beings in wave and foam. We called upon the demons of Xibalba, and they rose from the underworld in a fury, gouging out eyeballs, snapping off heads, devouring ligneous flesh.

We flew back to Grandmother of Day and Light one last time. "Please, wise one," said Thunderbolt. "How do we make men to worship our names?"

"Hmm . . . ," she said, and rubbed her warm hands, clapping them once. Stalks of maize suddenly sprouted from the ground and rose over our heads. "Help me collect the harvest."

We gathered thousands of cobs by her feet and picked out the life-giving kernels—green, white, and golden. She conjured a grinding stone, made the dough, and said, "This shall be their body." Then, from the river beside her, she scooped and poured pure water. "This shall be their blood." She mixed the paste with the water and molded three perfect men, with flawless brown skin and eyes alight with goodness.

Immediately, they bent their knees and began to pray to us.

"Now all they need to be truly happy," Grandmother of Day and Light said to me, "is to see the first true dawn." She touched my shoulder, the joint of my left wing, and I slowly retreated into my human body. It wasn't painful, but there was a hollow ring inside me as the underground cave came back into focus and my beautiful wings became heavy arms, and the unearthly power was removed from my being, leaving me weak.

I realized I was down on one knee.

I was about to stand again when I noticed Lord Juan for the first time in what felt like days. We were a few feet away from each other, but his gaze burned into me. There was something like wonder, or a mixture of desire and fear. I was suddenly conscious that my hair was loose, I was covered in sweat, and I'd drawn my skirts so high that my thighs were exposed. I had worn no stockings, as they'd all been ruined by my recent cursed cycle, so my skin was bare. I rushed to pull down my dress and looked away.

Cristóbal lay on the floor across from me, and he was also drenched. All the fastenings in his shirt had come undone. I moved to sit next to him.

"I can't go on," he wheezed, and sat up and placed his head on my shoulder.

"Neither can I," I responded after a moment. For a long while there was only the sound of our breaths and the quill as it scratched the paper.

"We have nearly completed the first part," said Lord Juan without looking up. "There's an hour or so before daybreak, so have a rest while I check the old paper for any mistakes and finish writing. I think it's safest if I keep the manuscripts in here, until we are done. What do you think,

Nija'ib'?" But Cristóbal was already asleep. He let out such a violent snore that both Lord Juan and I started, then broke out into laughter.

I'd never seen him laugh before.

The change was drastic, breathtaking. I couldn't help but stare. Our eyes locked, and then he looked away, as though embarrassed. I pretended to close my eyes, but really I studied him while he wrote. And I could've sworn a part of him was attuned and roused to my gaze, but of course he, too, feigned otherwise.

The next night we did it all again.

That time, I was the scribe. I watched Lord Juan and Cristóbal as they drank *balché' ki'* and danced to the story of Seven Macaw, a bejeweled, though rather pompous, bird god who claimed to be the first true dawn and was punished for his vanity.

Lord Juan, of course, was chosen to be Seven Macaw. He stomped and leapt and kicked like a proud warrior, while Cristóbal assumed the role of the mischievous twin heroes, Hunahpu and Xbalanque, who tricked him into his death.

I must admit, I had a hard time concentrating, for both men danced as if touched by flame and lightning, and though they took no note of me, lost in the otherworld as they were, I'd never felt more alive. I stopped writing altogether when Cristóbal began his victory dance and Lord Juan splayed out on the floor next to me. His head was so close to my thigh that his hair fell onto my dress. I simply could not focus.

He was meant to be playing dead, but his eyes were wide open, back on earth. He looked up at my face and said, "Our turn to dance tomorrow."

"So it is," I replied, wrote a few more lines, and acted calm.

"I wish to bear no more ill will to one another," he whispered.

I glimpsed at him, but he was watching Cristóbal and I couldn't tell if he was sincere.

"And why's that?" I asked. I couldn't keep the edge from my voice. He took a breath. "Perhaps—perhaps I was hasty, in drawing my opinion of you."

How magnanimous, I wanted to say. We stared at each other, and my eyes narrowed. "So, is that an apology?"

"It's a peace offering," he snapped, with a touch of his old arrogance. So, instead of seeing the merit in his words and practicing Christian mercy, I bit.

"Your *ill will* nearly killed me. Whatever I feel for you now is your own doing, so best learn to live with it."

His features clouded over, and I was filled with regret. But I didn't say anything as he rolled away. I simply dug my nails into my palms and tried not to think what a fool I was.

Cristóbal and I barely said a word to each other on the way home. He was still drunk and half-dead from exhaustion, and I was too cross with myself. Mother had always said, *A lady never shows her anger.* Until recently, I'd never had trouble following that rule, even though I'd felt angry enough. But with Lord Juan, I couldn't seem to rein it in.

I was so sick of thinking about him, I actually let out a growl.

"What's wrong?" Cristóbal murmured.

"Nothing," I began, but I couldn't help myself. "I just hate him! I hate the cacique!"

Cristóbal laughed and sped up to walk next to me, suddenly wide awake.

"He's the most obnoxious wretch I've ever met in my life," I said.

"Obnoxiously handsome." Cristóbal winked. "You do seem to get under each other's skins an awful lot."

"He's impossibly irritating! Worse than a mosquito in the dark!"

He bumped my arm. "Like an avocado you leave *just one more day.*"

I giggled. "And when you cut it open it's stringy and gray, and disgusting."

He laughed again, then glanced at me from the corner of his eye. "They say it's a fine line, you know, between love and hate."

My jaw dropped and I spluttered, "Ab-absolutely not—he *cursed* me, Cristóbal!"

"What?"

I told him everything I hadn't already, about our conversation during the dance, Lady Blood's visit, and how I'd stopped bleeding the moment I'd yielded the *Popol Vuh* over to him.

Cristóbal shook his head. "I have always known him to have a cruel streak, for life has been terribly cruel to him, but this is . . . shameful, appalling behavior."

I nodded in response, mollified by his support. "Well, I cannot wait until we finish writing this book so I can be rid of him."

"Only three more parts to go." He put an arm around my shoulder, and I leaned into his neck. We walked like this the rest of the way, and for a brief moment I felt the kind of peace that had eluded me since Father had sent Cristóbal off to live with the Dominicans.

The villa came into view, and I let out a little cry of relief. All I wanted was to crawl into bed and sleep until noon. There was only one problem.

The instant we opened the door, we were greeted by my father, who'd obviously arrived earlier than expected. He was sitting down, holding a musket by his side.

He raised his arm, and pointed it straight at my heart.

Whenever she put me to bed, my sister, Beatriz, told me tales of Africa. She told me stories about all sorts of animals, but the ones from Africa were her favorites. She described the gigantic elephants with ivory tusks large enough to skewer eight men sideways, the giraffes with necks as long as the trunks of palm trees, and the lions with sun-like eyes and fangs the size of my face. She made me stand and say, "There is only one way to survive an encounter with a lion. I must stand my ground.

Tall and firm." She made me pretend to stare back into those feline orbs and say, "I'm the one going to dinner, not you."

That was the way I faced Father. Even though I didn't think he was capable of killing his own daughter, he was a judge by profession and a dragon by reputation, and this was, without a doubt, our trial.

Cristóbal was a little behind me. I couldn't see him, but I knew he'd sobered up.

"Where've you been?" Father asked me.

The best way to lie is to tell the truth. Mother again.

"The ruins," I responded.

"I forbade you to go there."

"I went to pray, for Mother," I said. "Cristóbal came to protect me."

He blinked once. Good.

"To whom did you pray?"

"We prayed to God, of course." I was amazed by the question, and by my father's formidable intuition, but I didn't blink. His mouth set in a small line, and for a moment I panicked, thinking he knew.

"You pray to God in a sanctified church, not in some pagan ruins! You realize that's how they got her, your mother? Aha! That's right. You want to end up like her?"

He never spoke of her. Ever. His mention of her shook me to my core.

"Come here," he said. I walked forward. My courage wavered, and I held my hands together, one on top of the other, like a nun.

He grabbed my arm and pulled me down so we were nose to nose.

"Did you debase yourself with that boy?" There was such a flash of pain in his eyes that I couldn't help my voice breaking.

"No! Father, I swear," I said.

He stared and stared, and even sniffed me out. All I could think of was how lucky we were that he hadn't arrived yesterday, when I'd reeked of sweat and drink.

"Copal," he said.

I nodded. "I burned incense for her."

"Triple fool. Go to your room," he whispered.

I bowed and walked away. Before I turned the corner, I glanced at Cristóbal. He also stood tall and firm.

I sat on my stained chair, taut like a harp string. I wasn't fooled—this wasn't over. I heard the murmur of voices for about half an hour but no shouting. I didn't think that was a good sign when it came to Father. No shots were fired, however, so I assumed Cristóbal had passed the test. There was a slam of a door, and silence. Despite my trepidation, after an hour or so I was so exhausted I fell asleep.

The next thing I knew I was woken up by Father.

Standing behind him was the midwife.

"Sir, there are many other ways, foolproof ways, to ascertain if the señorita is pure. With your permission, a simple inspection of her chamber pot should tell us. If her urine is clear and odorless, it is a sign that she lives without sin. Or, I have with me a sieve, which, in her blessed and virginal hands, should retain all water."

"I'm paying you for the examination, so get on with it. And I do not wish to hear a word from you, dear daughter."

Eye contact would only provoke him, so I kept my eyes on the floor as I curtsied and sat on the mattress. I waited for the woman to tell me what to do. Father drew the curtains around my bed, though his presence filled the room like a cloud blocking out the sun.

"I'll need you to lie on your back, my lady, so I can take a look," she said in the kind of voice that told me she was sorry.

I nodded, and not a sound escaped me, even when she hitched up my skirts and I was stung by a humiliation so formidable that tears spilled from my eyes, unbidden. After a pause, she pulled my skirts back down and patted me once on the knee.

"Virgo intacta," she grumbled to my father, and walked out.

I sat back up and tried to arrange my features into something resembling dignity before Father pulled back the curtains. I watched his face reflected in the mirror as he pulled his beard and vacillated. For a moment I thought he would admit he'd gone too far, but then he raised his hand and yelled, "You left me no choice, both of you!"

I bit my lip and nodded, but inside, I only wished he'd go away.

"He's gone. I've sent him off. You will never see him again, do you understand?"

More tears poured out, but I nodded again.

"You're also coming to live with me permanently, in Santiago. Cook will help you pack, but you'll come alone. No Cook, no nothing! She's spoiled you far too long. If she weren't an old, crippled woman I'd throw her in the dungeons—"

"You wouldn't!"

"She should've stopped you last night. And don't you dare deny it. She knows everything you do!"

I glared at him like I'd never done before in my life and growled, "That woman raised me like her own child, and if you hurt her, I swear I'll never forgive you."

To my surprise, his eyes widened, and he took a step back toward the door. He turned and said in a more subdued tone, "We leave tomorrow. Be sure to say goodbye."

CHAPTER 6

Santiago de los Caballeros, Guatemala
Winter 1551–1552

Father's rage burned hot for almost two whole months, longer than I'd ever experienced it. His punishment was severe—I was forbidden from leaving the palace where I was now living. It wasn't until Christmas Day that he eased his grip.

As a treat, he took me to hear Christmas Day Mass. After the service ended, we walked arm in arm, behind Bishop Marroquín, who headed the procession out of the cathedral and down the main plaza. He held a resplendent golden cross high in the air.

The morning sun was warm, when the breeze lulled. The bells tolled and there were celebrations and music everywhere. Stalls had popped up along the center of the cobbled square, with woven baskets stacked with fresh dahlias, ceramic bowls full of cacao beans, trays replete with cakes of indigo and cochineal powder for dyeing cloth, and displays of Italian wine and olive oil. Encomenderos, Spanish men who'd been endowed with land, labor, and tribute grants, rode around on horseback, wearing plumed hats and smoking tobacco. Ladies in wide gowns and puffed sleeves pranced around in twos and threes and talked behind painted wooden fans, trailed by their multicolored servants. *Indígenas*, Creoles, Black men and girls—some free, some not—carried baskets of food on their heads or squirming children in their arms.

I searched the crowd, hoping to catch a glimpse of Lord Juan or Cristóbal, though I knew Father wouldn't have sent Cristóbal to Santiago.

I wished I knew where he was. We'd been such fools, to not discuss what we'd do if a situation like this arose. It had been ages without news from either of them, not to mention Cook, although she couldn't write.

I, of course, had been unable to go anywhere without Father, and Santa Cruz was a three-day journey by carriage, so I couldn't seek them out. Even when Father was busy, his eyes were on me. The palace was full of his people. Servants of the Crown, servants of his own, and dozens of clerks who ran around all day, bringing letters and taking letters. It was infuriating to behold so much paper and ink and be unable to use it. He'd ordered a maid, Maribel, to keep me company during the day. We spent our time in the library, sewing all day in suffocating silence, waiting for Father to call me to dinner.

I thought today would be different. Father always hosted the Christmas feast for the court in Santiago. I wasn't sure if Lord Juan had been invited, but I prayed he would appear. My heart fluttered at the thought, but I told myself it was only because I was desperate to find out if the *Popol Vuh* was safe. I longed to continue writing it. It was a constant thought, an unceasing worry during the day that carried through to my dreams at night. Even at that moment, I recited the familiar words in my head, the next part we needed to write:

On went One Hunahpu and Seven Hunahpu, guided by messenger owls. They descended the path to Xibalba, down trembling canyons and turbulent rivers . . .

We didn't have to walk far before we reached the north-facing palace, adjacent to the cathedral. It looked much like our villa in Santa Cruz, except it was two stories tall with elaborate arched windows, two courtyards, and a large garden, framed in the background by three magnificent volcanoes.

We crossed the iron gates and I gasped at the sight. Normally, Father loved a banquet, just for the opportunity to publicly humiliate his enemies en masse. If left to his devices, he would've thrown a somber affair, a pitiful feast, to remind everyone present what he thought they deserved. But they'd gotten ahead of him that year. They'd written to the emperor to complain of last year's meager portions, and said it was an insult to His Majesty's honor.

Father had been ordered to provide. There was no argument to be had, and so the garden was sumptuously decorated. Since the weather was so pleasant, the tables were out in the open air, ornamented with the palace's gold-embroidered cloth and silver dining set. The fountain in the middle of the main courtyard was draped in fruits and flowers. A harpist, brought in from Chiapas, plucked an airy tune as we made our way in, trailed by our many guests, who exclaimed as they took in the delights of the garden. Impeccably dressed servants in their blue livery rushed forward with wine served in Venetian glassware.

Father had done his duty, but by the look on his face, he'd rather have swallowed poison than bring so much joy to people he so disliked. People who constantly opposed him, who threatened him and the New Laws, every single day. His mood blackened as his two worst rivals, Bishop Marroquín and Captain Lobo, the lord treasurer, approached him together with broad, satisfied smiles. They gave me a small nod, which I hesitantly returned.

"Don Alonso, what a pleasant change from last year's gathering," said Captain Lobo, a grizzly, middle-aged conquistador who was as wolfish as his name. He had a scar across his left cheek and light hazel eyes that could've been mistaken for yellow. "Could this be a sign that times are changing for the better, perhaps?"

The feast was one of Lobo's triumphs over Father, who forced a smile. "The emperor may want you to sup in splendor for the night. But his New Laws remain the same."

"Come now, another two families left us in the last month. Good, honorable families, gone back to Spain," said Bishop Marroquín, who was tall and slim, with a small white goatee and balding head. "I implored them to stay, but I had nothing to say against their protestations."

"Which were?"

"That since your so-called reforms, they've had no *Indígenas* to help with construction, no *Indígenas* to plow their fields, or work their mines," said Captain Lobo.

Father laughed. "Meaning they were too cheap to pay for labor they were stealing for free."

"Prices are going up. Just the other day I paid a hundred reales for a shirt that would've cost no more than twenty only three years ago. One must cut off an arm nowadays to pay for good firewood. *Indígenas* ask for such excessive wages you simply cannot hire them."

"Come now, Javier. Both of us know if you spent less on lard and honey, three reales a week to each of your poor workers would be of no consequence."

"You can't expect the neighbors to live like this," said Lobo, turning purple.

The bishop placed a placating hand on Lobo's shoulder. "My lord," he said to my father, "I agree we need to improve the treatment of our natives. But your passion, however admirable, has made conditions unendurable to settlers. More will leave. The *Indígenas* will rebel and return to worshipping their false idols. All the hard work of our missionaries will be for nothing."

"Your Excellency! It'd be a pity if you worried yourself to death. Needless, too, as for every four vagrants that leave, there are another four hundred ready to take their place. So, have a glass of wine. To His Majesty's health and long life!" Everyone shouted in response, and Father steered me away from the dour-looking men.

"Unendurable conditions," Father muttered. "The emperor has *explicitly* stated that *Indígenas* are our countrymen now, and they need to be treated fairly. It's a legal fact, if not a moral one. But see—greed is blinding, Catalina. They don't see the suffering." He shook his head. "They give beasts of burden more consideration than their fellow human beings."

"Don Alonso!" We turned and Father groaned. Judge Ramirez walked up to us, arm in arm with his young wife, who'd arrived from Spain only in the last month.

"You're back," Father said.

"I am! My journey was comfortable, thank you for asking."

"Have you made any progress with all these robberies happening about the place?"

"I'm afraid not, and I've no news on the necklace you reported missing. I believe it was your daughter's? Is this she?" he asked Father, who proceeded to introduce me.

"I am sure you give thanks every day, señorita, that you look nothing like this man." Judge Ramirez beamed up at me, bowed, and kissed my brown hand without hesitation. He was a full head shorter than me, but I could see why he was a favorite among the ladies of the court, why rumors were rampant about his many mistresses, with his easy manner, dark Spanish brows, tanned skin, and sparkling green eyes.

I was taken aback, unsure of how to take this conflicting greeting, but he did not wait for my response. "I've been telling your father it's not healthy to keep young people locked up, but you need to be a muleteer to steer him. May I introduce my wife to you, Isabel."

We exchanged the usual pleasantries. Isabel was cold at first and studied me closely, especially when her husband spoke, and though I found myself laughing at one of his remarks, she appeared to decide something in my favor, for when Father and Judge Ramirez were called away by some of the other men, she stayed by my side.

We sipped on our wine for a few silent moments. I wondered what I could possibly say to this strange woman, but she spared me. She cleared her throat and asked, "Are winters always so mild in this country?"

Ah, yes, one could always speak of the weather. I nodded. "We don't see much change in seasons, I'm afraid."

She looked deflated. "I see."

"It's something Father misses very much about Spain, among other things."

"You have family there, I believe?"

"An aunt, and several cousins, though I've never met them."

"I'm sorry," she sighed. "I guess it's the way of the future, for families to be split across oceans, all for the sake of gold and adventure. Have you seen the ocean, my lady?"

I shook my head.

"Weeks upon weeks, I gazed in all directions and could see no end. I've never been more terrified. That is one thing that gives me comfort about this place, those still, solid mountains."

We both looked up at the volcanoes at the same time. I thought it would be imprudent to tell her of the terrible eruption from a decade earlier, which destroyed half the city. Agua's fractured tip was draped by clouds, but Fuego and Acatenango smoked gently, as they did often enough that we sometimes forgot to stay vigilant.

"I hear the Maya have many legends about those mountains," she whispered.

"I wouldn't know," I said straight-faced. Some people were curious, and some people were out to test your faith. I wasn't interested in finding out where she stood. I knew the consequences of one of those sides too well.

"Of course not," she said, and studied my face again.

I cleared my throat, and she shook her head and said, "It's peculiar, but you remind me of my sister. You have a similar expression . . . I always say she can look through an apple and know whether it's rotten without taking a single bite."

I laughed, though I was unsure about her. She gave me an odd feeling, the type I realized I hadn't felt since I'd last seen Beatriz. Suddenly, I missed my elder sister. Perhaps it would be nice to have someone like her in my life again, or if not, at least some sort of ally. Someone I could ask to borrow ink and paper from to write a letter, for example. It was imperative that I reach Cristóbal or Lord Juan and get back to writing the *Popol Vuh*, so I took my chance.

"You remind me of my sister too," I said. "Perhaps we should take that as a sign that we ought to be friends. I should like to see you again."

Isabel beamed. "Oh, I would very much like that! In fact, I've been hoping to meet someone to help me with a little project I've undertaken."

She explained that she was helping an older gentleman. "He can no longer see well enough to write his memoirs. I've offered to help, but it would be unseemly to pay him a visit on my own. Would you like to accompany me?"

"Oh, that's very kind, but I believe you'll have to speak to my father first."

So she did.

◆ ◆ ◆

I shall never know exactly what Isabel said or did, but she not only convinced my father to let me go—for an entire day he raved about how the New World hadn't seen a woman of her caliber since Our Lady of Guadalupe had blessed Mexico with her virginal feet.

"It'll be good for you to mix with the likes of her, an intelligent, devout Catholic," he said, "and let's pray she also elevates the rest of the poultry we're forced to trade feathers with."

Two days later, Isabel came to pick me up, and we walked down the main street to the right of the palace, past several entrances to villas painted in different shades of marigold, tangerine, and rust, framed by heliconias cascading out of their rooftops.

Several times she stopped and spoke with passersby, both Spaniards and *Indigenas* alike, not that the latter always understood her. She bought trinkets, hugged the stiff-backed Indigenous children, gave words of advice and encouragement, or recited poultices and recipes. Always, without fail, she offered prayers.

Isabel made a point to introduce me too, which made me shuffle in discomfort.

When she finally noticed, she said, "It's important to be seen, Catalina. *You* especially have a unique role to play in the shaping of our new society. We may not be here by choice, but we *are* here, and it is our duty to be models of virtue and propriety. Especially after so many terrible years full of suffering. Men cannot help their brutality, but I am ashamed that none of our fellow females has taken up the mantle assigned to our sex." She sighed. "Never mind, I am determined to rectify things."

Isabel threw me a quick smile, as though the matter was settled.

I wondered if this was what she'd said to my father. How she'd recruited me to be her ally, her puppet, in this second, moral conquest. I swallowed hard, thinking it had been a mistake to befriend her, but it was too late. We stopped outside a towering wooden door with a brass knocker shaped like a lion's head. This brought me out of my reverie.

"Wait, the older gentleman you're helping is Don Bernal? Does my father know?"

Everyone knew Don Bernal Díaz del Castillo, an original conquistador and the present-day governor of Guatemala. The man had been one of Hernán Cortés's soldiers. He'd met Moctezuma, and Cuauhtémoc the brave, the last Mexican emperor.

His eyes had seen Tenochtitlán in her full glory.

His hands had ripped her down to his knees.

Isabel nodded and banged on the door. "He's a fascinating man, although your father seemed to disagree. I gather they've had their differences, but I convinced him it would be a priceless lesson for you to hear his recollections in person."

My heart raced as we waited for the door to open. I felt both apprehensive and excited, for I was about to listen to a man who was *there*, sword in hand, when the whole world changed, when my two worlds collided.

Twice I'd asked Mother to tell me about the conquest, but she'd refused. She'd brushed my hair and said it was not a story for children. I'm sure that was only part of the reason. Looking back, it must've been too painful to recall, based on the few things she did say, based on how her entire family was killed.

Perhaps it would be too painful for me too, especially coming from *him*. Or perhaps hearing this story would help me understand this strange, breached life I lived. I shook my head and reminded myself this was all secondary. I had to focus on my one true purpose. Paper and ink. I could not leave the house without writing this letter, today.

I realized with a jolt of hilarity, which nearly made me squeak with laughter, that I could simply ask politely for some. After all, it was only Father who made such a fuss about me writing. No one else should find it odd.

Don Bernal's pretty maid, a lovely, wisp-like creature with golden skin and amber eyes, let us through to the garden and into the house, which wasn't lavish, as one would've imagined a conquistador-turned-governor's home to be. In fact, it was smaller than Father's country villa, although with a few more creature comforts and modest yet elegant touches one would've associated with a person of quality: portraits of saints holding lambs, silver candlesticks, hanging tapestries of lush scenery, and even a small carpet. But there was no Aztec gold, no gilded doorframes or painted murals. I preferred it that way.

She guided us up the stairs and into the drawing room.

"I shall go and fetch my lord," she said with barely a hint of a K'iche' accent. I vaguely wondered if she was Mestiza like me. "Do take a seat."

It was a fine room, airy and bright, with four plush armchairs around a small ornate table. The plastered walls were painted in a tasteful pattern of white and yellow honeysuckle intertwined with pink pomegranates. The large window opened to a magnificent view of the volcanoes in the distance. To the right of the window there was a great writing desk piled with papers, a few candlesticks, a drawer for outbound letters, and not two, but three feathered quills.

My spirits soared.

We did not have to wait long for Don Bernal, who walked in on the arm of his maid. He was bald at the top of his head, but his remaining hair and full beard were a rich brown with barely a fleck of silver. He was dressed in an overlarge frill collar and an armored vest, which I thought was strange. It was not unusual for conquistadores to wear their old armor to formal affairs, as if to remind everyone of the debt they were owed. But to wear it in his own home? Maybe he was one of those old soldiers who were never at ease, who felt the shower of arrows whizzing toward his back, even in his sleep.

He smiled and looked in our direction, although his eyes were unfocused. "Welcome, welcome, dear creatures!" His voice was soft and had an odd, gravel-like quality. He shook our hands. "You have no idea what this means to me. Come."

He took us to his writing desk and then showed us his diaries and the notes he'd kept the past thirty years, all the faded maps and letters and dozens of lists of supplies and names of people, horses, and places. He also showed us the part of the memoir he'd written on his own.

"My dear wife, God rest her soul, pestered me to finish it, but I was much too embarrassed, and now that I want to, I can't. My maid, Carmen, helps me write my letters, but this, I feel, is too important. I need someone I can fully trust."

"We are honored by your trust," said Isabel.

"I'm not like those famous chroniclers," he said. "I'm no scholar. I've no eloquence or great rhetoric. I'm sure you'll be bored to pieces, especially you, Lady Cerrato. Is there anything you might require to pass the time? A book, perhaps? Carmen could show you my birds, or you could draw?"

The polite thing would've been to say that I could not possibly be bored while listening to him, but this was a stroke of luck I could not ignore. In a demure tone I said, "Oh, Don Bernal, I do need to write a quick letter, if you don't mind. Would you be so kind as to oblige me with some ink and paper?"

To my relief, he was delighted. "Of course, of course! Let me fetch you some bits."

He then proceeded to give me three sheets of paper, real Austrian paper, smooth and soft and white like fluffy summer clouds. A generous gift to anyone, but as I was categorically forbidden them, they were priceless. Best of all, he handed me a small bottle of ink and one of his quills.

I shall never forget the thrill, the sense of freedom, from holding those innocuous items. I was so excited that I didn't even hear Isabel and Don Bernal's ensuing conversation. It was as though everything around me, sights, sounds, and time itself, all went still. Only the quill in my hand quivered as I wrote the following:

> *December 27, 1551*
> *Dear cousin,*
> *How I'd love to wish you a merry Christmas in person.*
> *It would bring me much comfort. Father and I are well,*
> *though he complains of stomach pains now and again.*
> *Pray for him, I beg of you.*
> *Now, you shall not guess where I'm writing from.*
> *I've made an acquaintance with Don Bernal Díaz del*
> *Castillo, who wishes to write his memoirs of the conquest*
> *of Mexico. I know you would have much to say on the*
> *subject.*
> *Oh, how I wish I was allowed to write a book! Some*
> *would argue a woman cannot possibly have a book's*
> *worth of things to write about, but I happen to disagree,*
> *of course. It shall be nice to be able to visit Don Bernal*
> *every few days, for otherwise I'm stuck in the palace, and*
> *it's so very dull. In fact, when you respond, it's probably*
> *easiest if you write to me here. Do tell me more of your*

travels, and don't waste so much ink next time on news of your Cooks and other servants.
God bless you and keep you well.

I read it fifteen times over. I couldn't see how anyone would've found anything suspicious, should it have fallen into the wrong hands. Father would've been terribly unhappy and would've understood the meaning behind my last sentence: that I wished to know where Cristóbal was, and for news of Cook, but even that was forgivable. I'd begged him to tell me anything about her, to let me write to her, but he'd flatly refused. He couldn't blame me for growing desperate.

Don Bernal stopped speaking and I glanced over. He yawned. Isabel shook her wrist loose. Suddenly, I realized I couldn't send the letter directly to Cristóbal, because I had no idea where he was. I also didn't think Don Bernal could be trusted to not ask a servant to read my letter. I would have to sneak it into Don Bernal's pile of letters and send it to Lord Juan in Santa Cruz. I folded the letter and, imitating Don Bernal's small, garbled hand, wrote the cacique's name and address on the outside. I thought about adding a note to him, something amicable perhaps, but my pride sparked against it.

I wondered what his reaction to my letter would be. Would he smile the way he'd done that night, in the cave? Would he be disappointed that I'd not written anything to him? Would he care at all? Probably not. Not about me, anyway. He'd want to make a plan to rewrite the *Popol Vuh*. For some reason it seemed to be just as important to him as it was to me. Maybe he felt it was his kingly duty. One thing he could do for his people.

One fewer thing for them to lose.

I jumped as Don Bernal's five-year-old son, Diego, burst through the door and ran screaming through the room, then crashed into one of the many chairs. Carmen ran behind him, huffing and puffing and begging pardon. She caught the child by the waist and attempted to lift him away, but he jerked his body out of her arms and tore around the room, turning over furniture, screaming something about his toy soldiers.

Pieces of paper flew in all directions, candlesticks rolled over the carpet, a glass of water Isabel had been drinking from smashed and spilled on the ground. She joined Carmen in her frantic attempts to calm the boy down, but everything they tried seemed to only make matters worse. Don Bernal stood, arms outstretched, begging for his child to stop. As for me, I was eyeing the candlesticks and the letters, my stomach coiling with tension.

I knew this was my chance.

A moment later, all four of them ran out of the room, where the screaming continued right outside the door and then appeared to move down the stairs. I leapt out of my chair, grabbed and burned the wax with the nearest candle, and stamped it with Don Bernal's seal.

The shouting abated. My upper lip broke into sweat as I waited for the wax to cool down. *Quickly now!* I blew and gathered things around me, trying to make it seem as though I was mopping and tidying up the mess.

As soon as the wax hardened, I shoved the letter in among the others in the tray and walked back to my chair. I took some slow, deep breaths, and wiped the sweat off with my sleeve, then waited for several moments, long enough that I began to feel like I'd been forgotten. I thought perhaps I ought to come out of the room and see if they needed my help, but as soon as I did, I was pulled up short by Don Bernal's voice in the staircase landing below.

"Isabel dear, please beg Catalina for her discretion in this awful ordeal. It's terribly embarrassing that she has witnessed my son in such a state. I'd hate for her father to know." He sighed. "I'm desperate to find him a tutor."

"He needs one, indeed. But pray, do not worry, I shall make a case for you."

"Thank you. I hope you will be taking her for a stroll around the market, poor girl. Always stuck inside the palace."

"Yes, it's not healthy. I've already had a word with her father," murmured Isabel.

"Oh, good. Do bring her back again. She is most agreeable. To tell the truth, I didn't know what to expect from the daughter of a heretic and a beast."

My cheeks burst into flame. I strained my neck to hear what Isabel would say.

"One must not condemn a child for the sins of their father." She sounded surprisingly sincere. Even though in my case, she was clearly in the wrong, I blinked, conflicted at her willingness to stand up for me. She barely knew me, so why would she say that? Maybe she was one of those rare people who thought only the best of others.

Credulous morons, Father called them.

I waited for Don Bernal's response. He wasn't moved. "Quite right, quite right," he said. "But one must never forget, a tiger cub will always have stripes."

CHAPTER 7

Santiago de los Caballeros, Guatemala
Spring 1552

I received no response to my letter. I thought constantly of all the reasons why this could be. Perhaps it had gone astray. Perhaps the cacique felt it was too dangerous to reply. Perhaps everyone was dead, and he wanted to spare me the grief.

Or, perhaps, he enjoyed the thought of me waiting in agony.

Oh—how I hated thinking about him! Worse, I hated that I couldn't stop.

I held my breath each time we visited Don Bernal's, and hoped he'd say something had arrived for me, but he never did. I sat for hours in bitter disappointment, feeling a twisted sense of rage. It galled me, how easy it was for him, a Spanish man, to do, say, and write anything he wanted. He had no need to hide, to sneak in the dark, or be afraid.

He sat, proud as a peacock, in the comfort of his own lovely home, in broad daylight, writing the story of our world as though it had never existed until he set foot on it, until his eyes saw and gave it meaning. No matter if it had meaning before, the deepest, most beautiful meaning in the world. It was his way, his views, his opinions that mattered.

And here I was, helping him! How I hated myself for it! The worst thing was, I would constantly get lost, listening to him. Hours would pass where I'd sit, enthralled, then wake as if from a terrible dream, wishing Mother had told me her side so I could tell lies from truth, wishing he'd never come and Mother were still here, alive. Even if it meant I wouldn't have been born. In those moments, where I ached for her in a way that made me want to double over and scream, I knew without a doubt that I would've traded my life for hers.

All I had left of her was the *Popol Vuh*. I needed to write it, for her, to show him, to make sure it was not just *his* memories that lived on. But I couldn't bring myself to write more letters. After hearing his comment about my mother, it was clear the man was wary of me, and I had to remind myself that I ought to be even more wary of him. After all, beneath that old, gallant veneer there lay a battle-hardened soldier, a warrior who'd not hesitated to draw his sword to end countless lives in his quest for fortune and glory.

I thought again and again about asking Isabel for ink and paper. When she wasn't trying to parade me, or giving unsolicited advice, she was pleasant enough company. Well, compared to Father and the ever-silent Maribel. At the very least, I enjoyed our walks through the market together. Still, there was something about her. She was much too private, too guarded. I understood her, in a way. I wasn't one to openly trust either. But the thing that really put me off asking was how friendly she was with Father. He always made time to speak to her, and so I could not risk her mentioning my request to him.

I felt adrift, lost, alone. A powerless little girl again.

Until I met Nicolao.

He called one morning to offer his tutoring services to Don Bernal's son. Don Bernal planned to interview him that evening, and had asked me to keep him company until Isabel got tired of writing. They were upstairs in the drawing room, and Nicolao and I sat awkwardly beside each other, downstairs, on a wooden bench in the small interior patio.

"Do you mind if I sew?" I wanted to decorate one of my old Spanish shawls in bright K'iche' colors, and had brought a straw basket with all my needles and yarn.

"Of course not." He cleared his throat.

I nodded with a smile and he leaned back against the blue tiled wall, more relaxed.

"So, Señor Lopes, you are Portuguese?"

"Indeed, but I was living in Florence, you see, for I'm a great lover of the classics, and have been filling my head with the words of Homer and Cicero since I can remember."

"Florence must've been heaven for you," I said, and he smiled.

He was quite plain, with a pallid complexion and a thin, childish moustache that ought to have been shaved, but his manner was warm and open, and he reminded me so much of Cristóbal that I soon felt much at ease.

"You understand me perfectly! There's nowhere in the world better to live and breathe among others who share my passion."

Don Bernal's maid, Carmen, walked out into the courtyard with some bird food and set the parrots aflutter. She sprinkled the seed on her tiptoes, and accidentally showed her delicate ankles. I sneaked a glance at Nicolao, who studied her closely.

"I hear Florence is a most beautiful city," I said, drawing his attention back.

"Oh yes, the lowliest brick is beautiful there. At least, it was when I left. But alas! It's not an easy life for a humanist tutor in a city of humanist tutors. I thought perhaps I might have better luck in the New World. I hesitated for months, but when France allied herself with Suleiman, I feared I would be forced back into war unless I left."

"But don't the Portuguese hate the Turks?"

He laughed and eyed me with interest. "Well, yes, but everyone hates the Turks, even the French, who are forced to bed them. No, do not think me a coward, señorita. It is a matter of conscience. *Homo, sacra res homini.*"

"Man is sacred to man," I translated.

He sat up, hazel eyes glowing. "You are a most accomplished lady," he said at the same time as I added, "My father would disagree."

"Indeed? I'd be proud if my daughter had a grasp of the politics of our world, and indulged a poor scholar when he tried to impress her with his Latin nonsense."

"Oh no, what I mean is, Father would say to you, *homo homini lupus.*"

"Man is wolf to man. I see." He squinted in inquiry, but a smile of delight danced on his lips. "And what is your opinion, if you don't mind me asking?"

I blinked. No man had ever asked for my opinion in my entire life. I was suddenly at a loss. I wanted to say something deep, something lyrical. I racked my brain for a quote, a proverb, anything substantial, preferably in another language, but in my panic, I was left stuttering, "I—I," until Isabel emerged from the hall.

"Señor Lopes, Don Bernal is ready to see you."

We both rose. "I'll have to wait to hear your answer, my lady. Pray it won't be long before that happy moment."

I forced a smile, still mute and annoyed at myself. He lifted his hat to Isabel when he walked past. Her eyebrows shot up at me. "Well!"

"Shall we go?" I shoved my work back into the straw basket and walked out onto the dusty road. Isabel emerged. Her gaze burned into me, and I feared she'd read too much into my silence. She cleared her throat, as if asking for an explanation.

"He was pleasing to speak to," I said.

"He certainly looked pleased."

I prayed for my dark skin to hide the blush that crept up my neck. "Oh no, don't mistake me. He is but recently arrived. I was being kind."

"I believe you. But some men need very little encouragement, especially poor men looking to make a living."

I frowned. She'd made concessions for me, defended me when Don Bernal had made assumptions about my character. But now she did the opposite to Nicolao. Why?

We walked past the cobbler and tanner shops with their displays of cured hides and saddles, past the apothecary with its scent of dried roots and vinegar. Farther down the street, men rolled barrels of stone and mortar. Their grunts were barely audible beneath the metallic beats of a hundred hammers. Streets lengthened every day, and whole new neighborhoods emerged replete with green, cobbled plazas and towering white churches.

I couldn't let the matter go. "Are you saying I mustn't be kind to Señor Lopes, because he's poor?"

"Now, don't misunderstand me, Catalina. Of course you must always be kind to the poor, just as our Lord Jesus was, but I must speak plainly, as a friend." She tucked her arm through mine. "You're a flourishing, talented young lady with a powerful father. A man who can give vast lands away with a drop of ink. How you're still single is a mystery to me."

Oh dear, I thought, *how did we get on to this?* Good thing I knew the answer to her mystery. "That's obvious, is it not? No one wants me, lands or no lands."

"Rubbish. I have it on good authority that your father receives at least two proposals for your hand a week."

I burst out laughing. Two proposals a week! People must've been starving for gossip if that's the tale they were telling. We turned left and crossed the open square in front of the east-facing cathedral. A small herd of bleating goats munched on the tufts of soft grass growing around the cobblestones. The wind blew dust and the earthy smell of horse dung.

I shook my head and swatted a fly away. "Your authority must be mistaken."

Isabel squeezed my arm. We were outside the palace. "I believe your father knows, as you should know, that you ought to be demanding. My best guess is he's waiting for a nobleman to come knocking, looking to exchange his title for your considerable dowry. I expect you could fetch at least a hidalgo, if not a lord."

"Or better yet, a rich cacique," I said. "Oh wait, they don't exist. Just like these proposals you speak of."

Isabel's lips pursed. "Doubt all you like. Just make sure you don't lose your head for your heart, trust me."

I laughed again. "I do! But the truth is, there's no man I can lose my heart to."

She raised an eyebrow. "Well, I'm glad of it." She kissed my cheek goodbye. "If only to spare you the pain of marrying beneath you."

I turned around and greeted the guards with a nod. I mulled over the strange turn our conversation had taken, her advice, and the way her voice had caught at the end. She rarely spoke of Judge Ramirez, only when asked. For a moment I thought perhaps this was why she worked so hard to look composed, why she constantly spoke to others about their problems and ailments. Perhaps it was her attempt to make them forget about the ceaseless rumors surrounding her husband. Or to at least give the impression that she was unaffected by them. I felt a pang of pity, and thought perhaps I'd make something to cheer her up.

I walked through the thick arched doorway and into the main courtyard, went around the fountain, and headed up the steps into the long, dark hall.

There, I was struck by a wall of sound and the stench of roasting meat mingled with sweat and spilled aguardiente. Under the weak glow from the iron chandeliers hanging under thick wooden beams were men, everywhere, talking and arguing in booming voices across the two long tables. Encomenderos, government officials, and clerks rushed from corner to corner, capes swishing out from behind, holding on to their swords and bits of parchment to keep them from flying. Servants chased after them with trays of bread and liquor.

It was chaos, running the country.

Father insisted that I inform him of my return, so I had to enter the mess. As I walked between the two long tables toward the back of the hall, where Father's office was, several men turned to look at me. I bowed my head when one of them greeted me in passing, and wondered if he was one of the alleged proposals. He smiled bright enough when I gave him a second look. I turned away with an incredulous smile of my own, and felt a prickling sensation on the back of my neck, like someone else was watching me. I looked up to the right of Father's door, and we locked eyes. He stared at me with that familiar scowl of his.

Son of the Jaguar.

Lord Juan.

I waded through the blurred crowd, heart thumping wildly. He was not alone. The second, lesser king of the highland Maya, Don Juan Cortés, "El Grande," was with him. He was just as tall and haughty, but not as handsome, and older. Both wore earrings, Lord Juan a pair of obsidian circles, and El Grande what looked to be some kind of polished animal bone. They were not the only Maya in the room, not by far, but unlike me, no one would've mistaken them for servants, even in their humble cotton robes.

I curtsied to both. "My lords."

They nodded. The silence stretched for the space of four panicked breaths. Lord Juan shuffled and cleared his throat. I'd never seen him look this uncomfortable before.

A smile tugged on El Grande's cheek. "Pardon my brother king's manners, my lady. He appears to be a little tongue-tied. We've not been formally introduced. Juan Cortés, at your service."

I offered my hand and he placed an airy kiss above my knuckles. "Don Cortés, I've—I've heard so much about you."

"And I of you," he responded with a playful glance at Lord Juan.

"I'm sure reports have been greatly exaggerated," I said, trying not to glare at Lord Juan as I imagined all the awful things he might've said about me.

"I thought, perhaps. But to be sure, of your beauty and nerve at least, I can see there were no more embellishments than simply calling a rose, a rose." He gave me an elegant nod.

I was too stunned and confused to do more than stare. There was no situation in my mind in which Lord Juan would've paid me one compliment, let alone two. I glanced at him. He looked like he would've liked nothing more than for the earth to swallow him whole.

Could it be true? El Grande's sheer enjoyment of his response was plain on his face. Was he lying then, to tease him?

"Thank you," I finally said, just to say something, "and are you here to see my father?"

"We've met him already," said El Grande. "The cacique has been named minister of native affairs. We came to settle the terms."

"Oh!" My brow tightened, and I blurted out, "I thought you'd previously declined this position?" I remembered well, for Father had raged on about how much better off he would've been, as the position exempted him from paying tribute. He'd called Lord Juan a rabid ninny, if I recalled correctly.

El Grande's smile broadened. "I believe there's some . . . additional incentives that have contributed to the change of heart."

I hesitated, unsure of what he meant, and whether I should offer congratulations. To me, it was sheer irony to appoint a king to a position he would've had all his life had it not been taken away from him in the first place. I decided against it.

"Will—will you be settling in Santiago, my lord?"

El Grande crossed his arms and gave his brother king such a brazen look, I blushed in his stead.

"I'll split my time between Santiago and Santa Cruz," said Lord Juan. "I have ongoing business with the Dominicans there." I nodded, remembering Father had said the monks paid him sometimes to give them advice on K'iche' customs and language.

"He'll be a regular visitor to the palace soon," said El Grande, and I sensed the prod of his words, seeking some kind of reaction from me.

"I—would welcome more frequent news of our friends." My voice quivered. I wanted to say, *Tell me how she is; tell me where he is. Tell me anything about them, please, I beg you.*

"You seem to be making plenty of friends here," said Lord Juan with a flick of his head at the back of the hall, where he'd seen me smile at the Spanish gentleman. But the thought of Cook had made my heart sore, and I couldn't rise to the bait.

El Grande clicked his tongue in rebuke. "Heartless! Can't you see how she suffers?"

Lord Juan looked away.

"Please, how is Cook?" I whispered.

A shadow crossed Lord Juan's face, shame perhaps? "She's working for the Pulido family in Santa Cruz. Your father gave her a good reference."

I gasped at the flood of relief that surged through my chest and shoulders. When our eyes met again, his face had softened.

"Would you like us to relay a message back to her?" asked El Grande.

I reached to grab his hands, but stopped myself. "Oh, my lord, thank you, yes. Thank you. Please apologize to her on my behalf. I've not been permitted to send word." I lowered my voice to the tiniest whisper. "I'm constantly watched. A maid, Maribel, spends all day with me." I quickly listed all my other restrictions. They shared a concerned look.

"So you see, I'm unable to write *anything* without help." I gave Lord Juan a significant look and hoped he would catch my meaning, that if we were to resume writing the *Popol Vuh*, I would need his assistance. I raised my voice a little and said, "So yes, please send Cook my warmest regards, tell her I think of her every day and pray every night for her good health and happiness, and for Noble River, and that I wish so badly I could see her—" My throat shut. Tears streamed down my cheeks.

"Ah, my lady. Please do not weep," said El Grande.

"Forgive me, it's been a difficult time," I mumbled.

Lord Juan took out a handkerchief. Our fingertips brushed when he handed it to me, sending shivers up my arm. "I shall give your message to Cook in person," he whispered. "I am keeping the books safe, and I promise to return to you soon, to assist with such matters."

I clasped the handkerchief and started when it made a crumpling sound. It was obviously covering something thin and hard, like folded paper.

"We must take our leave," said Juan El Grande with a knowing smile.

I shoved the handkerchief back into my sleeve and thanked them again. The big, lumbering doorman, a guard called Victorino, barged into Father's office when he saw me.

When he reemerged, he said in a low, dull tone, "You've been summoned."

I ignored the way he looked me up and down and entered the office, cursing the idiot for not mentioning that Bishop Marroquín and Captain Lobo were inside. The bishop stood perfectly still, except for a hand rubbing his goatee. The lord treasurer was pacing around the room. His ruffled sleeves wobbled with every step.

"Señorita," Lobo said with a curt nod. He glanced at the way Father's huge dog wagged his tail at my entrance. Father gestured behind him to the corner of his office, where there was a high-backed wooden chair. I sat and Maloso put his head on my lap. Father sometimes asked me to sit in on meetings with men he disliked. Whether to comfort him, or discomfort them, I was not sure of his purpose, but I stayed and listened.

"You were saying, Francisco?"

"Dear man, your favoritism—it's dangerous," said the bishop. "It emboldens the *Indígenas*, gives them aspirations and makes them shameless. Those two, especially, we would not want them to rebel like their fathers did."

"I've already written to the emperor. Their powers are merely symbolic, and in any case, Alvarado made sure they'd never forget what happens to traitors."

I gripped the chair. What did he mean? What had Alvarado done to them?

"It's not enough!"

"To see your father executed in front of you?" Father's voice was deadly quiet.

My breath caught in my chest. My stomach clenched. That great, rancid, unhealed wound inside me threatened to unravel, until I caught the bishop's concerned gaze.

It couldn't have been a worse moment to betray my feelings, so I forced myself to swallow and sit up straight. The bishop shot Lobo a placating look, then took a breath.

"Alonso, at the very least tell me you read the letter I brought you, from the friar Bustamante?"

"I don't recall it specifically."

"He warns that your reforms have obstructed the conversion process."

Lobo cut across the bishop: "Yes, and all the neighbors complain of less order, and more thievery, and such drunkenness and carnality I'm ashamed to utter it in front of your daughter. We ought to be saving the *Indígenas* from this behavior!"

"Or perhaps we ought to be enslaving all the loose Spanish women and drunken Spaniards, yourself included. By Mary—there'd be such an excess! You'd come so inexpensive it'd solve all our problems."

I choked back a laugh, feeling a rush of affection toward my father.

"How—how can you be so cruel to your own people?" said the bishop.

Father slammed his hand on his desk. Maloso growled. "Damn it, Francisco! The only reason *my people* hate me is that they can no longer give themselves airs." He looked straight at Lobo. "Without *Indígenas*, they're just boorish adventurers who are as crude and savage as the people they claim to want to civilize."

The bishop remained stock-still. Captain Lobo shook like congealed fat on a cut of cold meat. "I shall write to the emperor, I swear. I shall tell him of your disloyalty."

"Be my guest!"

Lobo stormed off, but Father kept yelling. "Add whichever punishment takes your fancy—something novel so the emperor will enjoy it!"

The bishop closed his eyes, took a deep breath, then nodded at me before leaving the room. As soon as the door was shut, Father shrank down to his seat with a weary sigh. He rubbed his eyes and his stomach, which I knew pained him, though he denied it. He looked so small I couldn't help standing and placing a tentative hand on his shoulder. He stopped for a moment, his body eased, and he leaned his head against me.

"Ah, little bird, you're my only comfort in this land of beasts."

"Oh, Father." My throat tightened again. Maloso whined. "Will you be in too much trouble now, with the emperor?"

Father barked a laugh. "Not quite. His Majesty has said it himself, I'm his one bastion when it comes to his New Laws. I've never failed to uphold his word. That's why he's promoted me, over and over again, from clerk, to advisor, to judge, and now president."

He patted my hand and we were silent for a long moment. The caresses faded and turned into quick finger taps, and then Father said, "Did you run into the caciques?"

"They were kind enough to say hello."

"You spoke to them, eh?" He twisted to look up at me.

"Only in passing—what did the bishop mean, when he said you favored them?"

"I favor no one but the Holy Emperor and our Lord Jesus Christ, as you well know."

"You like him, though, don't you, Lord Juan?" I ventured.

"Like him?" His white, bushy brows knotted, as if the thought of liking anyone was too abstract a concept. "He's tolerable, I suppose.

Useful." He stroked his chin. "You can say I admire his fortitude. He's endured things that would break the strongest of men. And he's a true nobleman, unlike the riffraff setting sail from our Spanish shores. How I wish we were welcoming persons of quality, but *no*! We must make landlords out of soldiers of fortune and bucktoothed laborers who can hardly string two sentences together—makes me sick."

"Well—why not give the land back to the caciques, then?"

His eyes widened in astonishment, then a shadow of fear crossed his face. He glanced at the door as if to make sure it was shut properly and whispered, "Are you mad? Don't ever say such a thing, do you hear?"

"But—*you* just said—"

"It's His Majesty's land now, and rightly so. If he wishes to settle it with imbeciles, it's not up to us to question him. If those imbeciles make a colossal mess, it's our job to fix it for him. If he wished to give the caciques some land to rule in his stead, that would be fine by me. But unless it comes out of *his* royal mouth, it's treason. Some would hang you for it, just to spite me, so never say anything like it again, understood?"

I gulped down the knot in my throat, the hurt and fear from his tone and words, which soon turned to rage. Why was I never allowed to say anything, do anything, *ask* anything, without being torn down? With a trembling voice I said, "All right, Father. I won't share my thoughts with you again."

He called after me, but I ignored him and stomped back out into the noisy, stinking hall. I turned right and went down the echoing corridor that led to the private stairway up into the residential wing of the palace. I hitched my skirts and almost broke into a run down the long inner balcony, but there were people below in the courtyard. I did not wish to draw any more attention to myself, so I walked as fast as I dared to my chambers in the opposite corner. I opened the heavy wooden door and bolted it shut. Tears swam in my eyes, and I nearly tripped on the colorful woven carpet at the foot of my four-poster bed.

I took out Lord Juan's handkerchief and a piece of paper fell out.

CHAPTER 8

Santiago de los Caballeros, Guatemala
Summer 1552

Two pairs of knitted silk stockings were draped over the arms of the single wooden chair in my room. I threw them on the bed and dragged the chair away from the small writing desk, which was only ever used to display flowers. I pulled the chair toward the large arched window, unfolded the piece of paper with trembling hands, and gasped when the tiny letters written in Cristóbal's careful hand shone back at me.

> *February 19, 1552*
> *Dear cousin,*
> *Pray forgive me for not writing you sooner. I had no means of ensuring my letters would reach you safely, until today. A good friend has found me board and bread with a Kaqchikel family. It was difficult, after dear Godfather's banishment. "Upon pain of death," he said, I was to leave Santa Cruz and not return for a year and a day. Your father said he would be taking you with him to Santiago and I was not to go there either, ever again. I tried to explain that he was mistaken about us, that indeed I loved you, as a sister, but I would never presume any-thing more. He said anyone who presumed more would*

be sorry, for you were never to marry as long as he lived! So you best take care, cousin, for you will not find in him a willing matchmaker, should you ever feel so inclined.

Alas, all arguments were in vain. He had enough love left for me to spare my life, but I was thrown out with only the clothes on my back. He even took back the sword he'd given me for my twentieth birthday. I must admit, the ease by which he got rid of me was a bitter blow. He tossed me from his life like a moldy loaf of bread. I thought—I thought I'd meant more to him. I think I always knew, deep down, that his kindnesses were mostly a favor to your mother, but I'd allowed myself to think otherwise. To be fair to him, he sheltered me from much harm and injustice. And such injustice there is, cousin, you would not believe. If you could see what I've seen since leaving your side, it would make you sick.

But pray, do not pity me, for while I'm now in a poor village near Panajachel, I am safe. My hosts have a large milpa where they grow maize, summer squash, and beans, and I'm enjoying tending the land, though it is hard work. Their son, Pablo, who is the same age as me, has become a dear friend and confidante, but pray do not worry, no one can take your place. He's teaching me their language. You ought to hear their stories.

The father, Jun Kaaj, was taken not just in war, but in a slave raid when he was a young man, his face branded with iron. He was made to work as a tameme for your father's predecessor, who afterward sold him to his first cousin. When your father became president, he was freed, but not before being branded again with the word "LIBRE."

So you see, each time I behold the blotched scars on his cheek, I realize how fortunate I am, to have escaped a fate that fell upon so many of our brethren, and how one must never fall into despair, but persevere, and right as many wrongs as one can along the way. Nearly half the year has passed already before this mildest of punishments is lifted. Until then, we must all endeavor to stay in the best of health and high spirits, for we have great duties yet to fulfill, great stories to write.

I pray God keeps you and your father well, and hope to meet you again soon.

Oh, blessed relief! I hadn't realized the burden I carried, though Cristóbal was right; it was nothing compared to Jun Kaaj's. I pictured the terror of those glowing irons as they neared his face, his cheeks sizzling for the second time in his life. Emblem of slavery and price of freedom too. I closed my eyes and prayed, *Please, Lord, give me the courage to do what is right, give me strength like Jun Kaaj, boundless hope like Cristóbal, and bless Lord Juan for this great kindness.*

The poor, poor man. A shiver ran through me at the thought of what Alvarado had done to Lord Juan and El Grande. If I'd known how much we shared . . .

His face appeared before me, tender, the way he'd looked at me in that brief moment after he gave me the news of Cook, the way he seemed genuinely embarrassed when I'd heard he'd complimented me. Could it have been true? I colored with pleasure and realized that to deliver our letters, he must've walked miles and miles, all the way from Santa Cruz to Lake Atitlán.

The place of tranquil waters, where the rainbow gets its colors.

I gasped, but the shock I felt from hearing her voice again soon turned to a strange gladness, and then, to my surprise, relief. No terrible memories swept over me. There was a heavy sadness, true, but the grief did not swallow me whole, and I did not crumble.

I shut my eyes and smiled at her from within, then whispered, "Hello again, Mother."

I couldn't help my spry step, my easy smile. Cristóbal's letter and Juan's promise to return, *to me*, were like two amulets that glowed from deep in my heart. I knew help was on its way; Juan was on his way. We would meet to write the *Popol Vuh* soon. It wasn't going to die. I was going to keep my promise, and all would be well.

Over the next few weeks, Nicolao joined Don Bernal's household, and although I tried to keep a cordial distance for Isabel's sake, we became friends. We often paired up in games of primero, and I helped him teach Diego his letters.

One morning, I was out in the bright inner patio again with them. The boy was being most unruly, and flatly refused to sit down and study. Nicolao explained he'd overheard talk of plague spreading in the northwest.

"Doña Clara didn't exactly hold back. You know, spreading rumors of people waking up with a chill one morning, falling dead by nightfall, selling amulets and talismans for luck."

I shuddered. "She didn't happen to leave any spare ones behind, did she?"

Nico laughed and stepped closer to me. "Surely a clever woman like yourself doesn't place faith in any such trinkets."

I laughed. "Everyone needs some reassurance every now and again."

"True, true." He stepped even closer. "Perhaps you will allow me to reassure you then, my lady? If you ever have need of it, I hope you know you can speak to me?"

I gave him a bright smile. Too bright, maybe. I ought to have been more careful.

Still, a part of me was pleased, a part of me enjoyed his attentions, though I wished he were someone else, someone who apparently valued my beauty and nerve, perhaps. It was pure vanity, I knew, but it was harmless.

"You are most kind, and I am grateful for your friendship." I emphasized the last word, just to be clear. I turned and sat on the polished bench by the blue tiled wall.

Nicolao sat on the other end and cleared his throat. He murmured, "My friendship, yes, of course."

There was a flutter in my gut then, a caution. As if to confirm it, he turned to gaze at me. Out of the corner of my eye I saw it, the dash of longing.

I tensed and made an excuse to leave. All the way home, I cursed my vanity, for the flutter in my gut had turned to dread. I remember thinking I ought to have listened to Isabel.

It turned out, I was right.

Don Bernal stood, en garde, holding an imaginary sword in his hand. "We'd not gone far when our scouts spotted about three thousand *Indígenas*, carrying their two-handed swords and wearing crowns of feathers. Their swords were as long as broadswords and made of flint and obsidian, which cut worse than a knife."

The puffed green breeches over his white stockings swayed with each thrust and parry. We'd moved some of the furniture in the drawing room out of the way and arranged the four plush armchairs so they faced the old conquistador. Don Bernal was framed by the open window and the plastered walls painted with honeysuckle and pomegranate motifs.

Nicolao sat on the chair next to mine, elbows on his knees, watching with thirst in his gaze. Isabel was to the right of the lively storyteller. She looked a little pale, and her eyes were puffy and red, but she had declined to say if anything was amiss. She'd neatly stacked the pile of Don Bernal's documents to her side, and got to writing. Her quill scratched furiously atop the broad wooden desk.

"We sent the prisoner we'd captured the previous day, and asked them not to attack. You know what they replied? That they'd make peace with us by filling their bellies with our flesh and honoring their gods with our hearts."

"Pray, slow down, Don Bernal," said Isabel.

"I'm sorry, dear, but I tell you, they did wonders with their two-handed swords." With great effort, he paused and waited. A breeze brought in the smell of muck and dust. Somewhere below in the street, a horse neighed, and he blurted out, "They even managed to lay hands on a good mare, and cut her head so it hung by the skin of her neck."

I gasped. "Poor thing!"

"Oh yes, it was a horrid sight. But God, in his great mercy, aided and protected us and, with our good swordplay, they eventually retreated. We even managed to rescue the rider from the enemy. They were dragging him away half-dead."

"Did he die?" I asked.

"Not then. Ten of our men were wounded, but none perished."

A puff of laughter burst out of my mouth. "Come now, Don Bernal, surely you're not saying three thousand battle-hardened Tlaxcalans didn't manage to kill a single Castilian!"

He stared right at me, as if by some miracle his sight had fully returned for a brief, shocking instant, yet rendered him temporarily mute.

Isabel gave a small cough and said, with a look of annoyance, "Dear, you know Don Bernal needs to maintain the utmost concentration. I'm not sure it's appropriate to interrupt in such a manner. But while we're on the subject, I personally do not think it odd. After all, we had the advantage of God's favor, and our weapons and armor were clearly superior."

Her condescending tone galled me. Who was she to reprimand me so? And surely she did not want Don Bernal to write such ludicrous nonsense. Who would believe it? I knew there were Spaniards who thought *Indigenas* were as meek and helpless as lambs, but most verged toward the other extreme and thought they were all savage man-eaters. Of course, neither version was true. But if the majority of people thought *Indígenas* capable of so much bloodshed, would they not read this passage and respond with derision?

I studied Isabel's open, slightly perplexed expression and realized I was wrong.

I swallowed a bitter taste and looked down at my hands to hide the mess of emotions that must've shone plainly on my face. For I was shaking with anger and hurt and burning with embarrassment, which bewildered me. I couldn't understand why I should feel embarrassed at all, but I did.

Before I could begin to figure it out, Nicolao interjected. "Drink, sir?" From his tone, it was obvious that he wished to change the subject. He gave me an inquiring, encouraging smile. I shook my head. Isabel's quill continued to rasp against the parchment.

"Wine, m'boy. The cask from Valladolid, in the cellar."

Nicolao stood up. The moment he was out of the room, Don Bernal turned to me and said, "Dear Catalina, let us forget our small disagreement, for I must ask for your help in a matter concerning your father."

"Oh?" I sat upright. My heart leapt in fear and confusion.

He cleared his throat. "Though my enterprise to the New World has left me rich in memories, I am but a poor man. I cannot pay for Nico's services, but I've promised him an encomienda in return."

I stared at him, unsure of what exactly he expected me to do about that.

"You do see, don't you, darling child? Despite the small influence I yield, only your father has the power to grant land with tribute rights and, as I'm sure you know, he's never loved me. So, I would appreciate a good word about Nico from your part, if at all possible."

I glanced at Isabel, who shrugged lightly as if to say, *What choice do you have?*

I squirmed in my seat and bowed my head, for there really was no other choice if I wanted to keep some of my freedom, though each passing day felt more like a punishment. "It'd be a small favor to repay your many kindnesses."

Don Bernal beamed and pressed his hand against the middle of his gold doublet. "Oh, bless you! I shall speak to him tomorrow."

"The gall!" Father roared. His voice resounded like a cannon blast. Maloso let out a couple of barks. It was midnight, and we sat in the empty hall of the palace, just Father, the servants, and I among the two long tables and the moths flittering around the candlelight in the damp summer air.

I shook my head and feigned disbelief. I had to try to soothe him, or he'd never listen.

"A wolf in a sheep's cloth, I tell you. All these conquistadores and adventurers, they're something else." He grumbled some more and dipped his mutton into a spicy tomato-and-onion salsa, took a sip of wine, reached for the bread basket, and tore a steaming loaf. I knew what he'd say the moment he swallowed.

"Why's it so hard to make good bread in this land?"

Right on cue. "The doñas say it's the water, Father."

"Nonsense. Anyway, what do you make of this Nicolao?"

I shrugged. "He's very polite and accomplished. He's a very good guitar player, and knows the classics by heart."

"Does he?" Father loved Homer.

"I've heard him reciting the *Odyssey* to Diego. His accent is impressive."

"Hmm. He's unmarried, though, and Carlos's fervent wish is for the encomiendas to go to families and married settlers first."

I nodded and looked away, as if deep in thought, but I'd rehearsed this in my head already. "He's a poor but educated man and claims to be a humanist, so he might be more likely to uphold the New Laws. I'm sure he'd be married in no time, if he had the means to afford a wife. But you know the emperor's heart best, Father. Why not meet him and judge for yourself?"

Father grunted. We continued to eat in pleasant silence for some time.

"Have you any news from Spain?" It was a gamble of a question. If Father had received a letter from our relatives, his mood would soar threefold. If he hadn't, well. I should've known better by then.

"Not for some months," he said, but he didn't flare back to anger. Instead, he pushed his plate away and shrank into the chair.

"I'm sorry, I—"

"I've had word from the other one." His face pinched as if her name were a red-hot pincer, pulling at his tongue.

Beatriz, who'd broken both our hearts when she'd abandoned us for that silversmith in our greatest hour of need. Unlike Father, however, I'd forgiven her. She'd been brought to the New World from Spain, torn from everyone she'd ever known, and plopped in tiny Santa Cruz. I knew she'd been desperately lonely, and had craved Father's affections, but he was who he was. Mother, I think, had been his one exception, the one person who'd never failed to draw a smile from his face, though it had never seemed to matter much to her. Beatriz couldn't have failed to notice this, how much he cared for my mother. I raked my memories for signs of jealousy, but it was difficult, for they hardly ever spoke to one another.

I couldn't blame her now, really, for seeking sanctuary in another's arms. Yet, even after the smith died, Father wouldn't see Beatriz. I thought it too harsh, and begged him to let it go. He said he couldn't forgive her, that he didn't want her to influence me with her sinful ways, and banned me from asking any more questions. It was only after her second husband was killed in a mudslide that he agreed to help her, for she now had two children and no income. Father gave her money and arranged the match with her current, third husband, Sancho, a conquistador twice her age. He granted Sancho a large encomienda, and I think he even put her name on the deed. Last I heard they were happy and had a daughter together.

Since she was a forbidden subject, I kept my face a veil, my voice soft. "Oh?"

"The plague has claimed Sancho and her two girls."

"No!" My hand flew to my trembling lips. "Poor angels! Oh, poor Beatriz!"

Without warning, I began sobbing into my handkerchief, lost in flashes of memories. Beatriz picking a peach from a tall branch and handing it to me. Following her around when Mother had one of her episodes, days on end when she'd lie in bed tossing and turning from feverish nightmares. Beatriz reading to me, then shouting at me to leave her alone, though I wouldn't really. I'd watch her, weeping for her own mother.

Oh, I didn't know her pain back then, but I knew now.

I cried until I felt the change in pressure, the rush of wind before a looming storm. Father was watching me. I hiccuped and tried to rein it all back in, to blow the clouds away, to change their course. But Mother's voice was still in my ear, singing me to sleep. Her voice begged for a solemn vow from my childish lips, to protect our people's sacred book.

"Forgive me."

"Mourn the children," he said. The chair scraped the floor as he got up. "But believe me, that wretched woman, that sister of yours—she's not worth your tears."

"But why?" Perhaps there was more to the story, something he wasn't telling me, something else she'd done to earn his complete disapprobation, but I couldn't imagine what it could've been, and I felt too upset to guess. All I could say was, "It was so long ago, can't you just forgive her? She must be so desperately sad. Please let me write to her?"

"No! I forbid it and I'll not have you questioning me. Come, Maloso."

He turned and walked away, and I almost shouted after him, like Bishop Marroquín had done, *How can you be so cruel to your own people?* I looked down the long, empty table and choked again when I thought how full it could've been.

Two weeks later, after morning Mass, Father and I emerged from the cathedral into the main square. There had been no more mention of Beatriz, so things had been more peaceful. On the other hand, my elation after seeing Juan and reading Cristóbal's letter had begun to fade. I scanned the crowd, searching for signs of either of them. I thought of them constantly and dreamt of them. Of Juan, mostly.

I'd dreamt of him the night before.

It was a strange, recurring vision of a hunt in the dark woods. At the start, I was always alone, with only my horse beside me, scared and lost, until I found a forest clearing.

Then Juan would step into the light, dressed in a king's finery. The golden pelt of a jaguar hung over his shoulders, and quetzal feathers adorned his brow.

I'd run to him, relieved, but froze when I spotted the sacrificial dagger in each of his hands, black jagged glass like his eyes. I knew they were meant for me.

Immediately, I'd reach for the jade arrow strapped to my shin and let it loose to strike his bare shoulder. The pelt around him would roar and leap to life, transformed in midair. He'd run at me, no longer man but beast.

With my heart hammering, I'd spring onto my horse and spur it to a full gallop. Beneath my thighs, its powerful legs pounded the earth and tore through the forest, but no matter how hard I urged it, every time I looked back the jaguar drew closer, eyes burning into mine.

There would always be an obstacle, a fallen tree, or a large boulder. The horse would leap as the jaguar lunged and reached my torso.

He'd lift me back and away into the air, wrap me from behind with his now-human arms. His hands felt me and searched deep into my body.

We'd fall into a black void, and it was pain and pleasure all the same.

I could hardly bring myself to look in the mirror the following morning as I got ready to attend Mass with my father.

The only words I had for these sensations, for the heat I felt when I woke, came from sermons on lust and sinfulness, not unlike the one the priest had prepared for us that day. I frowned at the lively, colorful descriptions of the inevitable fiery doom awaiting me and vaguely wondered if God made concessions for sins occurring during your deepest sleep, all the while feeling disturbed and restless.

I was beginning to make mistakes, to murmur the passages of the *Popol Vuh* out loud. I did it then, sitting next to Father, then flinched in horror and looked around to see if he or anyone had heard. Too much time had passed—we had to write the *Popol Vuh*. I had to take matters into my own hands. Perhaps I could somehow convince Father to take a break, to head back to Santa Cruz.

I made up my mind to speak to him after church, but as we emerged from the cathedral to the main square, someone called out my name. Father and I both turned. Isabel and Judge Ramirez descended toward us. Behind them, Nicolao smiled at me, cheeks aflame. He looked down and prompted little Diego to help guide his father down the steps.

"Suppose you'll be wanting to visit that goat's hovel today."

"If it pleases you, Father," I said. "Isabel's always so grateful."

"Small joy I can bring that poor, devoted woman," he mumbled. "If Ramirez wasn't so damn loyal to the New Laws, I'd have him flogged for lechery."

"Oh no, is he really that awful?" I whispered.

"A rabbit has more self-control—good morning," he said to the couple.

The pang of pity I felt, and the full, warm embrace Isabel gave me, drove me to forgiveness. It was true, she had behaved so rudely to me that day at Don Bernal's, but she was also my only friend in town. Surely she hadn't meant to make me feel so . . . inferior. Perhaps she'd been upset at Judge Ramirez. I thought it was right to give her another chance.

"Good morning," said the judge. I nodded, cold and dismissive.

Nicolao cleared his throat. "Don Alonso, I must take this opportunity to thank you again for the honor you've bestowed on me."

Father huffed.

"If there's anything at all I can do to—"

"Yes, get married, have children, and pay the royal fifth. Ramirez, we've business."

Don Bernal gave Father a stiff nod of the head. The judge kissed Isabel's hand and walked after Father.

"We'll have the pleasure of your company today, Doña Isabel?" asked Nicolao.

"If Don Bernal requires my assistance?"

"Indeed!" said the old man, who offered his arm. Diego ran ahead of them, shouted, "Look, Papa!" and jumped over a large puddle.

"May I walk with you?" Nicolao's voice was odd—high pitched and strained. I nodded but frowned at the obvious question. We walked a few steps without saying a word, away from the crowd and into the quiet street that led to Don Bernal's home. He slowed down, as if to gain some distance from our company ahead.

I was about to ask him if something was amiss, when he whispered, "Don Bernal told me how you spoke in my favor. How you commended me and praised me to your father, and I want to tell you how grateful I am, how much I feel in your debt, my lady."

"Oh!" I breathed out and smiled. "Of course, it's no—"

"Don't." He winced. "Don't say it's nothing."

I stared at him. "Is something ailing you?"

He took a deep breath and looked ahead. We were far enough behind to not be overheard. The blood drained from his face, which made him look so pale the spots on his face were incandescent. I considered running to the apothecary, but I couldn't move. Dread rose in my stomach like the black clouds of ash my mother had taught me to fear.

"Only this. That ever since we met, I've hoped and prayed to God for a sign that you care for me as much as I care for you."

Oh no, no, no. "Oh, Señor Lopes, you misunderstand me, I—"

"Call me Nico, please, Catalina, if I may be so bold." He reached for my hand, but I took a step back.

"I'm—sorry, Nico, Señor Lopes." I shook my head; I didn't know what to say. His chin trembled and he looked at me with such desperate longing, I couldn't bear to say more for fear of crushing him.

"Do you—do you not care for me?"

"I, I do! But—"

"Please, do you love another?"

"No!" A pair of caramel eyes, Juan's eyes, flashed into my mind, and I blushed with guilt. Nico smiled, relieved, misled.

"Then I have reason to hope my prayers have been answered?"

"No! I mean, it's not that simple!" Oh God, what could I say? I blurted out the first viable excuse that came to mind. "Father does not wish me to marry."

He laughed; a great big guffaw came out of his mouth, and I flushed, indignant.

"Oh, darling! Do not be angry with me. I laugh for I feel as if I could fly."

I glowered at him and crossed my arms. "How so, sir?"

"Because! Because the woman I love admits she cares for me!" He threw his hands up and crowed again. I took another step back, thinking he'd gone mad. He sighed at the look on my face, and his hands reached up as if to caress my cheek, but he stopped himself.

"Oh, I shall wait," he said. "For as long as it takes. For your father to change his mind, or for God to claim him home. I shall be as patient as a martyr. I shall wait for you."

CHAPTER 9

Santiago de los Caballeros, Guatemala
Autumn 1552

The next few weeks were unbearable. I pestered Father daily and begged him to have a rest, to return to Santa Cruz and to take me with him. He needed it for his health, I said, which was true. His stomach pained him almost daily. However, I was also desperate to get back to the *Popol Vuh*, and I really, truly, urgently wanted to get away from Nicolao.

I had no reasonable excuse not to continue joining Isabel in her visits to Don Bernal, but Nicolao was always there. He acted a desperate fool, constantly trying to catch my eye, asking me a thousand questions, inviting me to help him in his lessons with Diego. Really, all he wanted was to steal some time alone. He wrote terrible verses into tiny notes and pressed them into my palm whenever he kissed my hand goodbye, which also lasted much longer than necessary. So much for his talk of being a martyr. All he achieved, really, was to make me think more often, and feel more keenly, about someone else entirely.

Isabel noticed my cool, distracted demeanor and asked if all was well, but I didn't want to tell her the truth. I worried how she might respond. I finally told her Father needed tending to. At first, it was only partially true, but soon, it became an all-consuming fact, for he fell terribly, terribly ill.

◆ ◆ ◆

I sat on the edge of the mattress in Father's cavernous bedroom. The fire crackled in the background, throwing strange shadows over his large wooden desk, his rocking chair, and a painting of two desperate mothers fighting over a child in front of King Solomon.

The windows were shut and the curtains drawn, blocking out the moonlight and any potential breeze. Beads of sweat rolled from my forehead to my neck as I leaned over a man so altered, I questioned if it was really him.

Perhaps he's not. Perhaps the lords of Xibalba have sent a mannequin of their own. Perhaps Bone Scepter has hollowed him and Blood Gatherer has dried him out. He was always too strong; he was never strong enough.

Hush, Mother.

He groaned and his eyes pinched in pain. His beard was matted and tangled, and stank of sweat and fever. Maloso lay by the foot of Father's huge bed, and his droopy eyes looked as despondent as I felt. I'd done everything in my power to help, focused all my energy on him. I'd even forgotten about the *Popol Vuh*. Well, not quite. It was always somewhere, lurking in the depths of my mind, niggling my soul. Not that I would've been able to write a thing if the chance had presented itself then; I'd not slept in days. I was utterly exhausted.

My options had slowly dwindled. The apothecary and the three best medics in town had been useless. I'd banned them from entering with their bloody fleams and leeches. I didn't know who to turn to. I kept thinking of Cook, for she would've known what to do.

Mother chanted through the names of the demons of Xibalba, as if they were here, dancing among us, causing all this misery. *Demon of Jaundice, Pus, and Wing, Flying Scab, Gathered Blood, Claws, and Teeth. Demon of Jaundice, Pus, and Wing, Flying Scab, Gathered Blood, Claws, and Teeth.*

"Hush!" I covered my ears, not that it helped.

Demon of Jaundice, Pus, and Wing, Flying Scab, Gathered Blood, Claws, and Teeth. Demon of Jaundice, Pus, and Wing, Flying Scab, Gathered Blood, Claws, and Teeth.

A gentle knock stunned me back to reality.

"Come in," I said.

Maribel walked through with a tray of hot, steaming drinks, a desperately sad look on her face. She set it down by Father's table and surprised me by speaking.

"It's terrible to see the don like this, señorita. Do you think he'll turn good?"

"I hope so . . . ," I whispered. "I'm not ready to let him go." My throat knotted and my voice squeaked and cracked.

Maribel shook her head. "Is there anything I can do?"

I was about to say no, but then thought better of it. "If you can, please write a letter to my sister, Beatriz. Father's steward knows where she lives. She ought to know how poorly he is . . . that he might not make it. That I might . . . need her assistance if he passes."

The thought strangled me. I had no other family, no one to turn to. Who would care for me? What would happen to me, if he died? I beseeched Maribel with a look.

She nodded. "I will try."

I blinked, dumbfounded and dazed at my luck, then turned back to dab Father's forehead, expecting her to leave silently as she usually did. At first I didn't notice that she was still standing there, until she coughed.

I twisted slowly to look back at her, but I was too exhausted to say anything.

She glanced at the open door and at Father, then gave me an odd, terrified stare, as if she were readying herself to jump from a great height.

"I'm sorry, but . . . you wore a great treasure once," she whispered in K'iche'. "A necklace of jade."

My lips parted.

"It's poor timing, but . . . its owner, my true master, begs you to meet him by the graveyard next to the small hillside church, tonight. Will you go to him?"

I looked into her eyes, bright and brown like a treasure chest themselves. My heart began to hammer. My back straightened, and I suddenly felt wide awake. So many questions flitted through my mind, but I knew better than to ask, and I knew the answers already.

Juan was the necklace's owner. *He* was Maribel's master, her king, and he'd sent her to help me because he wanted to meet me in the graveyard, tonight!

I nodded, thrilled by the thought of seeing him again, after so long. Her face immediately relaxed, and she smiled.

"I will create a diversion with the dog. The guards will be called away from their posts at the gate." Her voice and hands were trembling. "Your father's horse is saddled and ready. Once everything is settled, I will say you've gone to sleep for a few hours. I can perhaps buy you until matins, at best. You must return before then."

I nodded again. "Will you keep him company, please, Maribel? He'll need to drink more lemon water, and I don't want the doctor near him."

She nodded.

"Right then, Maloso, go with Maribel," I said to the dog. He whined, and his great big head turned from Father to her and back. But with a pull to the collar, he did as he was told.

While I waited, I took Father's dagger, went into my room, and pulled on my boots, hood, and a warm skirt and then sat for another half an hour next to him, shifting in my seat as doubts swirled in my head. What if this was a trick? How could I trust Maribel? I should've asked her some more questions at least, made sure my assumptions were true somehow. I berated myself for not doing this, thinking of Father's warnings.

Servants' tongues were double-edged swords, he'd always said. He never told me which maid betrayed my mother, but after she died, we never had any at the villa again. Cook and Noble River had done practically everything for us in Santa Cruz, although it had mostly just been me they'd had to look after, and I'd helped Cook a lot.

Tension twisted and hardened in my stomach. Until I heard the scream. My mind cleared. I hitched up my skirts and ran out the door with fire in my belly. Over the balcony I could see brown-skinned servants rushing out from their quarters belowground. Maribel was running toward them, shouting for help.

Then, what seemed like the entirety of our poultry—our many dozens of chickens, turkeys, roosters, and ducks—burst out of the second courtyard in a shrieking cacophony, flapping their wings in all directions, leaving a chaotic trail of feathers and down eddying through the air. Maloso was chasing them, lunging, barking his deep, thunderous bark, wagging his tail, and clearly fulfilling a glorious canine dream.

"Guards! Guards!" Maribel yelled.

I ran down the stairs and waited in the shadows for a moment while the guards sprinted through the hallway. Victorino, the tall, oafish blond one, was spitting and swearing.

"You stupid cow, what did you do?" He pushed Maribel so hard she fell to the floor. The terrified servants attempted to catch the birds, and he howled at them some more. I hesitated, feeling torn about leaving everyone in this awful man's hands, but I didn't know when I'd get another chance.

In the stables I found Caramelo, Father's horse. The stable boys were nowhere to be seen, but he was fully saddled. I hopped on and rode as fast as I could toward the graveyard on the outskirts of town. The clank of galloping hooves blended with the painful rush of cold wind against my eardrums. The few people I encountered on the vacant streets were a blur, even under the bright moon.

In no time at all, I arrived at the church, a small lime-coated building that appeared to be painted orange, but in the sunshine was bright yellow. The graveyard next to it was also small, reserved for less distinguished Spaniards, but as it was next to a field of grass, it was peaceful and quiet. I strained my eyes and there he was, next to a sculpture of an angel, holding the reins of an old mule. I gasped in surprise, feeling a rush of delight. Because on top of the mule sat the one person I wished to see even more than Juan.

My darling Cook.

Beaming from ear to ear, I hastened toward them. "Oh my goodness!" I breathed. "Oh, please, my lord, help me down."

Juan reached up and before I realized what I'd asked for, his hands were on my waist, and we were close enough that I could count every one of his long, moonlit eyelashes. My arms were on his, warm and powerful. The world seemed to blur for a moment, except for his eyes, which sank into mine. He swayed forward, as though pulled toward me by an invisible force, but then he blinked, and I came back to my senses. It was only an instant, but it was enough. I'd learned everything, and so had he.

I muttered an awkward thanks and stumbled to Cook, wrapped my arms around her trunk, and placed my head on her lap. I inhaled her earthy scent, a mixture of cinnamon, hearth, and maize. She stroked my face and I looked up at her round, lined face, at the strands of black and silver hair that peeked out of the long thick braid falling over her shoulder. She looked older, weary, sickly even.

"Oh Cook, are you not well? Was it an awful journey?"

She huffed, pouted, and shook her head.

"I can't believe you're here," I whispered.

"When I told her how much you wished to see her, she insisted on coming."

"Well, it is a balm to my heart, and your timing is impeccable. Father is so unwell. I think you may be the only person left in this world who can help him."

"In that case, perhaps we move on, my lady," said Juan.

I wiped my wet cheek and turned to him. "How can I thank you? Twice now, you've brought me closer to the people I hold most dear, and if Cook can help my father . . ."

His jawline twitched.

"Truly, you—must know what this means to me—"

Our eyes met. His voice was soft when he said, "I would've come sooner, but I was severely delayed. There was plague in Santa Cruz, and it was not safe to travel."

"Oh no." I turned to Cook. "Is Noble River well? Your grandchildren?"

Cook nodded in a reassuring way.

"My lady, we mustn't delay. Do you need help to get back on your horse?"

I knew I should, but I wanted to be with him longer and speak to him more, so I said, "Oh, no thank you, I'll walk with you. If you don't mind escorting us a bit farther?"

"Of course." He nodded. "I'll take you to the gates. I know a shortcut."

We walked in uneasy silence for about half an hour, side by side, out of the graveyard, toward a copse of trees. And even though Father was sick, and I was exhausted, every time Juan opened his lips, or looked my way, or whenever our arms happened to touch, the fire of life blazed brightly through my core down to the tips of my toes. Sometimes I felt Cook's eyes on us. Whenever I looked back, she was staring into the distance, but I knew I didn't imagine the trace of a smirk lingering in the crook of her cheek.

For the longest time, I struggled to think of what to say. So much turmoil had passed between us. Finally, after what seemed like an age, I asked him how Juan El Grande was.

"Don Cortés is well and healthy, thank you for asking," he responded, sounding relieved. Perhaps he'd been racking his brain as much as I had been.

"You said once you two were like brothers?"

"Indeed, he's like a true brother to me. Well, he's near forty, so more like a second father." He paused and added in a whisper, "He practically raised me, in his own home, after our fathers were . . . after they passed."

I stole a glance at his face, his facade, devoid of the feelings his voice betrayed, feelings I knew too well. I wanted to touch his hand, but a shyness had stolen over me.

He cleared his throat and said, "You made quite an impression on him."

It took me a moment to remember whom he spoke of. I managed a smile. "The feeling is mutual. I don't see why Father's never warmed up to him. I find Don Cortés perfectly amiable."

The corner of his lip curled up. "I believe your mother also used to hold him in high esteem. Perhaps too high for your father's liking."

My mouth fell open. "How—what?"

"Oh, they were friends, nothing more," said Juan. After a pause he added, "He said you were much like her. That you had her fighting spirit, though I think you could hardly avoid it. Your father is a fighter too. I'm sure he'll get better."

My throat latched shut, and my vision swam with emotion. "Father said the same of you. That you had fortitude, and were a true nobleman."

For some reason, a shadow crossed his face. He muttered in K'iche', so low I barely caught it, "I'm but a wisp compared to those who came before me. Compared to my father and grandfather, who had the courage to give their lives for their people."

This disclosure gave me pause. "You don't need to shed blood in order to fight," I countered, and we fell silent again, returned to looking at the uneven ground.

A short moment later, we reached a stream and had to stop because the animals were pushing for a drink. Lord Juan also stooped to collect some water in the rough palms of his hands, splashed his face and ink-black hair, and took a long sip. I tried not to stare at the droplets trickling down to his chest and reminded myself that my father was dying, for goodness' sake, and Juan's chest was the last thing I ought to be thinking about.

"Have you news of my cousin?" I asked.

"Oh yes, finally. I meant to tell you. He's been difficult to track down."

My eyes widened. "Oh? Why's that? I thought he was based in Panajachel?"

"He's been on the move, which also caused my delay. But I'm hoping you'll do us the honor of meeting with us in the next few days." He gave me a fleeting smile.

It took every ounce of self-restraint to bow instead of jump, and say, in the mildest of voices, "Of course, sir."

Finally, we would be meeting to write the *Popol Vuh*! He'd not forgotten his promise to me at all! He'd been trying to help, but hadn't been able to get ahold of Cristóbal until now.

"I shall send word as soon as we return to Santiago."

Too soon, we emerged from the forest. In the time we'd spent under its canopy, a thick expanse of clouds had rolled across the sky, blocking out the moon. We sneaked through the shadows into town, which was strangely deserted. We failed to come across even one miserable, flea-ridden street dog.

When the palace gates were in sight, and we could hear a chorus of voices rising from inside its walls, Juan leaned close to me and whispered, "Catalina, I think I must leave you now."

The way he said my name made the hairs on the back of my neck stand on end. I could feel his quick breath on my cheek, but I was too afraid to look.

"It's been very good to see you." His tone was tender.

I gulped. My voice squeaked when I responded, "It's been good to see you too."

He cleared his throat. "It won't be long before I return."

I armed myself with a trace of courage, met his eye, and whispered, "That happy moment cannot come soon enough."

His intense, furrowed gaze searched all over my face, hungry, as if he were trying to find a shred of deception. His breath quickened, as did mine. Everything but his eyes became a haze around me . . . until Cook let out a blatantly loud cough.

We flinched and took a step back.

"I—I shall pray for your father, my lady," he grumbled.

I nodded, unable to speak.

Before he left, he looked at me one last time, and pressed his hand to his heart.

CHAPTER 10

Santiago de los Caballeros, Guatemala
Autumn 1552

Rain began to pour down as I led both Caramelo and the mule carrying Cook to the right outer wing where the horses were kept. The noise of a large crowd inside the palace sent my heart into a frenzy. I berated myself for lingering so long. It couldn't have been more than an hour or two at most, but I ought to have just grabbed Cook's mule and galloped back to the palace to help Father.

Instead, I'd behaved like a stupid, simpering fool, loitering around Juan like some drunken, lovestruck hussy. What would he make of me now? How would I ever face him again? What if I was too late to save Father? And why in Mary's name were there so many people here?

"What's happened?" I yelled to the groom. "Is it Father? Is he dead?"

"Miss, where did you go? Some doña came by, found out you were gone, and called all these people," he said. "There are men arming themselves now to go find you."

"But my father, is he still alive?"

"Yes, miss, but the poor master is not well at all."

I tugged the tired old mule into the stable. "Come on, you! Hurry! Cook, what do you need? Tell me what you need."

She made garbled, hoarse sounds, awful sounds, but I understood her hand signals.

"Water," I said, and she nodded and signed that it was for both drinking and bathing. "Vinegar, oil, rags." She nodded again and shooed me away.

"Help her off, gently now! Take her to my father, and help carry her things," I said to the stable boy, who stood gaping in horror at the dripping Cook. No wonder she never made a peep. "Do as you're told!" I turned and ran through the courtyard. I managed to avoid being spotted by some young ladies gathered around the fountain, but when I entered the hall, I was assailed by a bunch of courtiers. "It's her! It's Lady Cerrato!"

"Excuse me." I tried to push my way through as I scanned for a flash of blue livery. There was a scullery maid pouring ale into wooden mugs at the back of the table.

"Agustina, where's Maribel?"

Captain Lobo and a group of cackling doñas I knew from sight at church pushed her out of the way before she could speak. "Fetch the lady some mulled wine!" one of them yelled at Agustina. "Poor sweet, we need to dry you out or you'll catch your death. Take a seat."

"No, no, thank you, I—"

"Why ever did you run off?" said Captain Lobo, whose breath stank of aguardiente.

"Hush, Javier, she needs something to eat first," said his wife, Doña Imelda, who grabbed my arm with her cold, skeletal fingers. "Look at her—you! Bring cheese and bread, quick, quick."

"Don't forget the wine, and several glasses for us as well."

"No, thank you! Please, I cannot—"

"Are you hurt?"

"Catalina!" Everyone looked around. Nico, fully armed and wearing a gleaming breastplate and cape, ran toward us. His eyes were red-rimmed and his chin trembled. My fists balled in frustration, and I tried again to extricate myself from the woman's grasp.

"Darling—thank goodness," Nico said, drawing meaningful looks from everyone else.

"Excuse me, Captain Lobo, Señor Lopes, I must go to my father."

"For the love of God, she needs to see her father," Nico said.

"I need water, and—oil, and vinegar." I shuffled away.

I thought I saw the flash of Isabel's face by the kitchens, but before I could take a second look, Captain Lobo said, "Don't you worry yourself, sweet, Doctor Rivera's been called. He arrived a few moments ago, I believe."

"What?" I pushed past them all, knocking the treasurer down. My heart drummed in my ears. If the doctor bled him, Father would surely die. I'm sure that's what they all wanted, but I wasn't going to let that happen. I wasn't going to let these vultures have him.

Nico ran after me into the corridor. "Catalina! Catalina, dearest, wait!" He grabbed my wrist, but I snatched it away. His face burned carmine.

"I'm not your dearest! But as you claim to be my friend, I would ask you, please, to fetch me water, oil, and vinegar."

He frowned but nodded, and I ran away, up the stairs. I tried not to cry, but I had to focus on Father, and trust that Nicolao would get the things I needed.

Father's door was the first on the right. Cook stood outside with the stable boy, who kept attempting to push the door open. Without a thought, I rammed my entire body into the heavy wood and shattered whatever was behind it into the floor with a loud thud. There was a shriek from the maid in the corner.

"What in the heavens!" The doctor stood over Father. He held a shiny brass fleam in one hand and an empty bowl in the other. I was just in time.

"Don't touch him," I growled.

"I tried to keep him out, señorita," Maribel sobbed.

"What hysterics! Your father needs quiet; the humors in his veins—"

I pulled out my father's dagger and ran at him. "Out! Out or you'll be the one to bleed."

The doctor squealed and dashed out the door. I ran to Father. He was unhurt, but looked just as bad as when I'd left him. Cook sighed and began to take things out of her wet bag—herbs and potions. I recognized the milky white liquid in one of the jars: essence of lotus. The fire was burning, good, but the stable boy goggled at the scene.

It must've been a shocking sight to a child. Father, whom he loved, looking like a preserved cadaver in his large, filthy bed. Maribel, curled up in the corner, bawling her eyes out. Tongueless Cook, hunched over in front of the fire, a sinister being underneath the flickering shadows bathing her aging body.

I had to raise my voice over the maid's wails. "Child—quit staring and fetch more firewood. Maribel, please stop crying. You've done well. I just need you to go to the kitchen and bring back oil, and we need lots of water, enough to draw a bath, and—"

"Vinegar and rags," said a quiet, feminine voice from outside the door.

"Thank mercy!" I ran to Isabel and helped take the things we needed from her arms.

"Where did you go? I was worried about you," she whispered. "Why did you not come to me for help? I've tended many sick people in my life; I am glad to be of help."

"Sorry, I just went for a ride to clear my head, and ran into Cook." It was a terrible story, but it was all I could come up with in that moment.

Isabel seemed dubious at first, but the moment she looked at my father, her face darkened. "Never mind. Quick, let's get to it."

I nodded. The mob gathered in the courtyard below, muttering and pointing. But Isabel didn't ask another question. She closed the door and rolled up her sleeves.

About a week later, on the feast of Saint Luke, Maribel and Agustina came into my room early to help me dress. The cocks crowed and the church bells rang for morning Mass.

Maribel whistled an old K'iche' tune while she tied the ribbons of my sleeves to my gown. How she'd changed since that night. I'd hardly gotten a word out of her before. Since then, she'd more than atoned for all that silence.

"Agustina's going off to get married today, my lady!"

"Oh, congratulations, Agustina." We discussed some of her plans, though the girl was shy and barely muttered two words. Maribel did most of the talking, but I wasn't fully listening. My thoughts were all about Cook, who'd been too exhausted and a bit sickly since her journey. I'd ordered Maribel to give her the best available room in the servants' quarters, and she'd assured me they were taking care of her, and that she was getting her strength back.

I had to think of a way to help Cook return to Santa Cruz, when her health returned. Perhaps Judge Ramirez could assist us. He often traveled north. I was sure Isabel would put a good word in. She'd been very helpful that night, and I was terribly grateful to her.

She'd also advised me to lie quiet for some time, to let all this gossip blow over. So I'd hidden away in my room or in the library, observed daily Mass with Father in his chambers, visited Cook, and prayed and prayed to become invisible once again. It wouldn't do to be noticed, especially as I knew I'd be meeting Juan and Cristóbal to write the *Popol Vuh* any day now. I wanted to ask Maribel if she had any news, but Agustina was in the room. I bit my lip in frustration and bounced my knees. It had been far too long.

I wish I'd spoken to Juan more, looked at him more, touched his arm when he spoke of his father. I wished many other things too, though I didn't know how to articulate them.

All I knew was that I needed to be near him again.

Maribel finished braiding back my hair and stopped to look me over. With great care, she adjusted my hairnet and frill. Agustina collected some of my dirty skirts and stepped out the door. Maribel and I both glanced at the door and at each other.

"Any news?"

She nodded. "Tonight, my master begs you to meet him down in the cellar, at midnight."

Into my hand she pressed a small wood carving, round and almost flat, like a large coin. On its surface was the bust of a jaguar with an arrow piercing its breast.

There wasn't time to study it further or learn more from Maribel, because Agustina barged back into the room, huffing.

"Begging your pardon, miss. Your father wishes to see you."

I paused as soon as I entered through Father's door. The curtains were drawn, so it took me a moment to realize that Isabel was standing by his bedside.

"Aha." Father's voice was a wisp, a dry autumn leaf. But at least his skin had gained color, and he was sitting up on his pillows.

"Morning, Father." I kissed him and Isabel and sat next to him with my hands folded on my lap. Somewhere outside a couple of dogs barked. "Is—everything well?"

Father shook his head and pointed at Isabel, too weary to speak. I held my breath, my stomach twisting. Someone had accused me of something; that was it. Doctor Rivera had complained about me, or someone had spotted me with Juan. Maybe Cook's fever had worsened. Or they'd put two and two together, and realized the chickens had been let out on purpose so I could escape.

My lower lip trembled. I steadied my voice and asked, "What's wrong?"

Isabel waved her palms in a reassuring motion. "There's nothing to worry about, dearest. I had to come speak to your father. You see, Don Bernal tells me there's a rumor circulating that you're secretly engaged."

My jaw came loose. This, I had not expected. Isabel spoke, but I did not hear. The shock had left me momentarily deaf.

"Of course, I thought so," she said. "I knew it was a lie. He's been bothering you for quite some time, hasn't he?"

I was still too surprised to speak.

"Catalina—this Nicolao. He's been paying court to you for weeks, has he not?"

My senses sharpened as I felt Father's eyes, marred with fatigue, but still measuring me. I covered my face. "How, I mean, yes—but I told him no, Father, that he was confused. I said you had other plans for me."

Isabel placed her fists on her waist. "I assure you, Don Alonso, your daughter has behaved with perfect decorum and propriety during our visits to Don Bernal. This tutor has lofty ideas. He ought to be put in his place. Catalina is a noblewoman, whereas we do not even know this man's family. Who are they? *What* are they? I'm appalled by his daring!"

Father wheezed something and Isabel fell silent.

"Leave it with me," he repeated.

"What do you think he'll do?" I asked her when we emerged onto the balcony.

"Well—your father is a very good man, despite what everyone thinks. A just man. I'm sure the punishment will be mild."

"Punishment? No! Isabel—why didn't you speak to me first?"

"When you refused his advances, what did he do?"

I thought back and blushed. "Well, I told him Father did not wish me to be married. But—he laughed and said he'd wait for me."

Isabel's lips drew thin and her nostrils flared.

"Oh—I'm telling this all wrong." My thoughts were all over the place. "I just don't want anyone to be hurt because of me."

She sighed and rubbed my arm. "Catalina, look at me. Whatever happens to Nicolao is his own doing. He ought to know better than to lie, especially when such a notion could harm your reputation."

I scoffed. "What reputation?"

Isabel weaved her arm through mine. "Come now, dear, let's not get into a silly fight."

Isabel stayed the whole day. I had to pretend to yawn so she would leave. When she finally went, I paced my room and tried to make decisions, but I couldn't seem to pacify my mind, my nerves buzzed so. I'd been waiting for this for a long time.

Was Juan here, so close to me, already? Would we be writing the book in the cellar? It was too risky. We were probably going somewhere else, but where? How should I make my way unseen to the cellar? I shook my head from all this worry and tried to focus again. By the time I'd decided it was best to keep my slippers on rather than change to boots, the quiet knock came.

I leaned my ear to the polished wood. "Who is it?"

"It's Maribel, my lady," she whispered.

My hand had almost pulled the bolt when there was a shout from the courtyard below. A deep voice carried up: "An urgent message to Lady Cerrato."

"See what it's about," I said.

I pictured Maribel as she leaned over the balcony. "Keep the noise down," she hissed, "the señorita's gone to bed, and our master's unwell. What do you want?"

"Please—the old woman's taken a turn for the worse. Our lady must come right away if she wishes to say goodbye."

My hand slipped from the door to my side. A black, molten sensation rose inside me, clouded my vision, and buckled me over. All I could do was try to breathe.

"Miss? Miss?" Maribel's taps were insistent.

I couldn't find the strength to stand straight, but I managed to unlock the door.

She rushed in and gasped when she saw how I swayed. "Oh my lady! Oh my goodness." She helped me to my chair and fanned my face with her handkerchief. After a few breaths, I waved for her to stop.

"What must we do? There's no time. The *ajpop* is waiting," she whispered in K'iche'.

I closed my eyes and wished for divine intervention. The pressure mounted in my chest and choked my throat while I waited and prayed, *Mother, Jesus, Hacauitz, tell me what to do.* But this time, of course—no one did.

"Señorita? What must we do?"

What choice did I have? The *Popol Vuh* was too important.

"T—tell Cook that I—" That I what? That I loved her? But how would she believe it, if she heard it from a stranger, as she took her last breaths alone, with no family. Surrounded by stone walls built for the *other* kind of people, the kind who'd ripped her tongue out and left her speechless with shame. I burst into tears.

"I'll go, miss—I'll tell her," Maribel said. "I'll explain."

"No—take me to her. I can't leave without saying goodbye." I stood and faltered. I couldn't seem to find a buoy in that terrible riptide.

Maribel reached out her hand. "Let's go then, my lady, we mustn't dally."

I took it and she guided me to Cook's room belowground, although I cannot remember the journey, or any details about the room at all. I can only see a candle, and her small, delicate body, barely breathing underneath a white cotton sheet, her long peppered hair framing her pinched face.

She never opened her eyes. Not when I told her how much I loved her, or when I said how grateful I was for every day I'd had with her, for everything she'd done for me. Not when my tears fell on her forehead, as I kissed her one last time, and realized that I was losing the one and only person who'd never made me choose a side.

She'd seen everything I was, all my contradictions . . . Spanish and K'iche', eagle and quetzal, oppressor and oppressed.

She'd seen all of me and loved me without reserve.

I leaned over her and cried.

Too soon, Maribel touched my heaving back and whispered, "My lady, I'm so sorry, but you must go. Make your way by the dark edge of the courtyard. None of the household servants will disturb you—they're going off to celebrate Agustina's wedding. We planned it so they won't be back till dawn. The dog's with your father too, so don't you worry. I've smothered all the torches leading to the cellar, so mind your step."

I clasped her hand and sobbed. "Watch over her for me, Maribel. Stay with her until the end, like a daughter would."

CHAPTER 11

Santiago de los Caballeros, Guatemala
Autumn 1552

I walked to the cellar unseen.

There wasn't a soul, not an eye, not a rustle of wing or branch. Perhaps it was a small grace, a gift from the gods. Perhaps the billowing cloud in my heart had seeped out of me, enveloped my body in mist, and I could not be seen, couldn't be spotted.

The cellar door creaked. I vacillated before I descended the many steps into the pitch-black room, cool like the cave in which Cristóbal, Juan, and I had first met, but instead of a dank smell, there lingered a sweet scent of tobacco leaf, of cork, and cured meat. I grunted when I hit my head on one of the animal legs dangling from the ceiling, and I put my arm out to stop it swaying.

"Juan?" There was a shift in the air and a soft click, from a stiff hip or an ankle rousing, but I started as if a musket had been fired.

My foot was back on the first step. I readied to sprint when he called out my name. "Ab'aj Pol. We're alone at last, though we have little time."

I turned my head in the direction of his voice, but I couldn't see a thing.

"I want to tell you something I've told only one other person before." His voice was closer. He must've walked forward, but his feet had made no sound. My heart galloped.

"I want to tell you my true name. Do you wish to know it?" He stood in front of me now, invisible. He radiated warmth. I nodded. Somehow, he saw.

He leaned down and whispered in my ear, "My name is Q'anti."

A chill ran down my spine. His closeness, its meaning. Fer-de-lance, yellow-throat.

Snake, viper, fierce and deadly.

Look there, hummingbird. Step on one of those, and you'll not live to see the morning.

"My mother said I would have to be both jaguar and snake to survive this New World," he said.

"She was right."

"She died from the pox, when I was four." His voice sounded just as young. I couldn't help but lean into him. Into his solid chest. He hesitated briefly before wrapping his arms around me. For a time, we were just two motherless souls, breathing.

He mumbled, "The curse I placed on you, the hurt I caused you. The weight upon my soul is crushing me. Can you please forgive me? For everything?"

Something about his tone, the heaviness of it, as if the muscles of his mouth tested a foreign word, made me think this was the first apology of his life.

I whispered, "Maybe," and sensed the smile on his face, his chest as it expanded with joy. His arms tightened, and I thought they would never be tight enough.

"I will earn a yes. I swear to you. I—may I kiss you?"

I wished for nothing more than to feel the full warmth of his words. Those words I'd prayed for, without knowing, for weeks, months, a whole year. But I couldn't. Because the fog had returned, cold and heavy, and if he hadn't been holding me, I would've floated away, dispersed. I would've reappeared only as a weak, drizzling rain.

I felt him stiffen and draw away from my hesitation. The viper, quick to rile and defend. "You're still angry with me. I—I deserve it."

"Don't," I said, weary. "No, I'm not. Something's happened." I told him about Cook.

He sighed, held me a moment longer, and kissed the top of my head. A poor consolation for the both of us.

There was no more to say. No point in asking if I'd changed my mind. The *Popol Vuh* had to prevail. He took my hand, guided me to the back of the cellar, and bent down behind something large, probably one of the barrels of wine.

"Let me guess. A secret trapdoor."

His laugh was airy. "Come, sit here. Lower yourself down, it is only a small drop."

To me, it felt like I'd fallen off a cliff, but I managed not to scream. I stepped out of the way, and he lowered himself down. He dragged the hatch to a close and lit a torch. My eyes squinted as they grew accustomed to the light.

Once they did, however, I wished I'd been blinded. The tunnel might as well have been carved by a giant worm. It was pure earth. No brick, no polish. Just a tunnel of red soil, held up by a couple of wooden beams here and there.

"Oh no, oh no, no." It was my worst nightmare. I pictured the beams failing and the earth tumbling upon us, crushing our bodies alive and slowly suffocating us under its weight. My chest constricted. I struggled to breathe.

"Tonatiuh ordered it built. I used it today, to sneak into the palace."

He meant Alvarado, the conquistador. The mention of him distracted me. I'd heard rumors that the Mexicans thought the Spanish were gods, and Alvarado was nicknamed Tonatiuh, the Child of the Sun, because of his red beard and fiery temper.

Juan held my hand again and we walked forward.

"I'm sure he put it to excellent use," I blabbed. "Charity, probably. He'd sneak food out for the poor. Silver for almsgiving." Juan looked to check if I was being serious. I rolled my eyes and said, "Mother met him once, during Father's first trip here, right before their betrothal. He frightened her. She said his eyes could turn yellow like a devil's."

I suddenly remembered something else she'd said. Something I'd tried to forget.

We met at a party, she'd said. *Tonatiuh took me to a dark corner. Your father saw us and asked me to dance. Tonatiuh said, "You can have me or him."*

Your father was older, much older. But his eyes were kind, so I picked him.

"He had—a savage nature, that man," Juan said. "He enjoyed making others suffer, including those he claimed to love. Many K'iche' women, young girls, did not survive his passions. Their bodies were taken out of the palace through this tunnel."

I seized up, and he had to tug me forward. I spluttered, "That's— horrifying! Why? Why in the heavens would you tell me that?"

"Are you still preoccupied by your own fears?"

"Oh, I see. You're a right genius, aren't you?"

"I've always thought so."

I shook my head.

The tunnel led to an abandoned granary on the outskirts of the city, a place bordering the forest, where there was nothing but stalks of maize, conveniently tall and dense and close to the river. I tried not to imagine the bloated corpses of all those women, those girls, bobbing down the glimmering current. How young was young? I didn't ask, but now I knew that my mother could've been one of them. I shuddered and swallowed a cry. I didn't think I could withstand learning of any more atrocities committed by half my people.

The river gurgled and swallowed its secrets. We walked until we reached a narrow, shallow crossing, where I removed my slippers but soaked my hem and hose up to my knees. Then, ignoring all the wise, well-meaning warnings I'd received over the course of my life, we entered the forest. My mind conjured images of stalking beasts, of claws and fangs sinking into my neck. I couldn't believe I'd brought no weapon.

"Did you bring a knife? Or a musket even?" I whispered.

He huffed a laugh. "There is no need."

"Oh, are there no jaguars in these woods?"

"There are. But they'll not attack their own kin. They'll not attack me."

Oh, great. Wonderful. I picked up a sturdy-looking stick and he shook his head.

"Shake all you want. You'll thank me when I'm beating them off your deluded back."

The good thing was we didn't have to walk for very long. Only about a quarter of an hour or so, until the murmur of water turned to a whisper. A hooting owl flashed its wing, and we caught the scent of burning copal. There, on top of a mound, framed by two imposing ceiba trees, sat Cristóbal. His legs dangled, and his back leaned on a towering stela. I had to look twice, for he wore loose trousers held up by a woven sash and a white capixay, the old military vest of our K'iche' people.

The moment he saw us, he pushed himself off the edge, flew through the air, ran straight at me, and nearly knocked me down with his embrace. I didn't care. I squeezed him back, setting him like the Song of Solomon, as a seal upon my heart. A seal upon my arm.

"I missed you," I said. He groaned in pain. We backed away and looked at each other. There was just enough light to show the dark circles underneath his eyes. He frowned, noticing mine, which must've been worse, like the black pits of Xibalba.

"Why do you grieve?" he whispered. "Is it Godfather?"

I shook my head. He waited, but I couldn't speak.

Juan placed a hand between my shoulder blades. "Tonight, we shall dance in honor of the grand lady. She had a strong, loving heart, B'ix Kotz'i'j."

Song Flower. I stared at Juan, remembering the day we met, when he'd called me by my secret name. He guessed my thoughts and said, "'Tis one of the many gifts given by Tohil to the lords of the K'iche', to be able to recognize the name written in his people's hearts."

Cristóbal looked sideways at him. "I've never told you my K'iche' name."

"K'oxol, Sparkstriker," Juan said without hesitation.

Cristóbal's eyebrows rose. He shook his head, clearly impressed, then paused and gave me another hug. "I am truly sorry for the loss of Cook. She was a wonderful woman."

"If she's gone, perhaps she'll be here tonight," I said.

"Perhaps. Although we don't have much time." He turned, climbed up the mound, and lifted a sack hidden behind the stone slab.

"Let's try to get as far as we can," said Juan.

Cristóbal walked down and sat at the bottom of the mound and bent his head in prayer. I was about to say one too, but the items he took from the sack distracted me. There was a wooden mask carved in the shape of some kind of feline, which he quickly put back inside, a box with the old manuscript and the new one, and a wineskin.

"Here is the drink," he said. "I don't think we should have drums, though. We might be overheard." He handed me the wineskin.

The moment it touched my hands, I forgot everything, or maybe I wanted to forget everything. I poured it down my throat.

"Whoa!" said Cristóbal.

It was *balché' ki'*, of course, a mercy. It cleared my head, my heart, and the fog behind my eyelids. I laughed and pushed it into a stunned Juan.

"Here! Let's drink to Cook, to Song Flower, my second mother, and to the father of Hunahpu and Xbalanque. Let's drink, let's cheer to One Hunahpu!"

◆ ◆ ◆

I ran to the top of the mound and watched Juan. He was so beautiful as he turned his raven gaze in my direction and said, "Heart of Sky, Heart of Earth, the K'iche' speak to you and beg for your blessing. On this night of Jun Kame, the night of the owl of death, we beseech you to honor this account of our place in the shadows."

He drank and, with each gulp, the moonlight faded and goodness seeped from my pores—virtue, kindness—it all poured into him. I, on the other hand, sank down to where there was no trace of light.

The darkness did not bother me, though, for my eyes were made of night. I watched as my hands lengthened, and my nails became sharp blades of obsidian. My fingers were linked to every living being and could've stopped the strongest heart or withered the thickest trunk with merely a snap. Oh, how I smiled, as I became the most powerful being in the universe.

I became the lord of Xibalba, the bringer of destruction.

I became One Death.

Gently, I walked down through the nine levels of my realm. I slipped through shadows, past sharp canyons and deadly rivers, composed not of water, but of blood, and scorpions, and infection. Yet, there was beauty too. Creatures of darkness were revealed in their full glory—crystal moths and fireflies, jaguars and pumas with beams for eyes, and the rarest flowers, which bloomed only by twilight.

The roads shifted and changed. Their purpose was meant to beguile and confound outsiders, to make them forget every memory, to put them into a fitful sleep that lasted a thousand years. One misstep and my body would've turned into a bat, a snake, or a glittering beetle. But I was the master of these roads, and I did not get lost. I approached my beautiful jade palace, the tallest pyramid of all. It was surrounded by the six houses of torture, where we often sent our most hated enemies.

My court awaited me, my brothers in death, part skeleton and part animal. These demons hailed my entrance, placed a crown of crows on my head, and wrapped my shoulders with a cape made of black jaguar pelt. They touched my body and marveled at my strength. "My lord," they said. "You are a mountain," they whispered. "Your guile, your cunning, is sharp like the eagle's talon. You are a wonder; you are glorious! Praise be! Praise be!"

For a long time, I was happy. Until I heard a noise. An odious sound that increased day by day and shook my realm. A bouncing, a thundering.

"What is that? Who is making that racket?"

The demons covered their ears. "Oh, great lord, these two boys, One and Seven Hunahpu. Every day they play ball on the road to Xibalba. They stomp and shout and show no respect, no shame. We get no deference from them!"

I hissed, "How dare they—this is our domain! We are the ones who make humans swell, who squeeze purulence out of their legs, who shrink them to bone and skull, ha! We shall have those boys, don't you worry, and we shall have their kilts and yokes, their panaches and headbands. Invite them down!"

I watched as the brothers descended through my devious roads and crossed my deadly rivers. They were not defeated, but I was unfazed, for I had such tricks and troubles awaiting them. For my first trick, I hid and placed a moving mannequin of myself in my stead. The boys entered the palace, smelling of honey and rain. They approached my mannequin and bowed, bidding me good morning.

The palace exploded into laughter. My demons and I emerged from our hiding places. "You two have bowed to a mannequin," I said, gleeful they'd failed this first test. But they had one more chance to prove they were worthy of their lives. I gestured to what looked like a bench, but was really a burning rock. "Do take a seat, for it is good you've come."

The boys took a seat and immediately shouted, leapt into the air, and rubbed their backsides.

"Fools! Fools!" I shouted, shrieking with laughter. "These were only the first of many tricks and tests, and you've already failed. We shall not suffer your stupidity, your insolence! No, you shall be sacrificed. Break them off!"

My demons charged. They tore out the boys' hearts and cut off their heads. Only a beautiful carpet of blood was left of them.

"Bury them, and put their heads by the fork of the dead tree out on the road," I said.

The demons did as I said, but quickly ran back, shouting, "My lord! My lord! The tree has borne fruit!"

I left my palace to take a look. The dead tree had bloomed. Thousands of fruits—beautiful, perfect gourds—weighed from every branch. A sense of dread pulled at my chest.

"No one is to pick the fruit, or go beneath the tree," I commanded, then closed my eyes.

When I woke, I was no longer One Death, but the beautiful maiden Blood Moon.

I stared at the tree, and something about its fruits called to me, their odd shape and their vibrant green and orange, so rare a color in Xibalba, where all was dusk and black and silver-blue. "It is a shame," I said to myself, "to waste all those fruits. Surely I should pick one."

So I weaved my way to the tree when no one watched. I danced around it and was amazed by its liveliness. I stretched out my hand, but a voice called out from inside the tree.

"You don't want it," said the voice.

"Who are you?" I asked.

"It is I, one of the murdered boys. My name is One Hunahpu. My head is hidden among the gourds, and I tell you, you don't want the fruit."

"Oh, but I do, I do want it!"

After a pause, One Hunahpu said, "Very well, stretch out your hand again, so I can see it."

I looked around, then did as he said.

A treelike hand entwined our fingers and pulled my hand to a cluster of gourds. A pair of brilliant eyes appeared on one of them and met my own. I smiled. He touched my palm to his lips and gave it a silent kiss. A drop of moisture remained on my skin.

Xibalba dissolved around me. The forest, the sacred ceiba trees, and the stela came back into focus. Juan was in front of me, and his eyes were sharp, hungry. He was himself, and I was me again, feet back on earth, breathless. He bit my wrist, and there was a flicker of pleasure and amusement in his cheek. He was toying with me. My nostrils flared.

"She looked in her hand and inspected it right away, but the spittle was gone." He continued reciting the story as if nothing had changed, but raised a brow. "It was a sign."

He let go and I looked at my hand, grateful my back was to Cristóbal.

"Now, go up to the face of the earth, fair maiden," he said. "You shall not die."

"And something generated in her belly, from the saliva alone," I murmured.

"Yes, this was the making, the conception, of Hunahpu and Xbalanque."

"That's enough," said Cristóbal, clapping his hands twice. "Can you hear me? Catalina, my lord—"

"We hear you," said Juan. I turned away, unsure what to do with myself.

"I apologize; there isn't time for more. I just need to finish this last bit." The quill flew in Cristóbal's hand. He mumbled, "Face of earth, keep word . . . not die."

"And something generating in her belly," Juan breathed on my neck.

◆ ◆ ◆

I had to walk away and sit next to Cristóbal, my shield. Even in my hazy state, I shuddered to think what would've happened if he hadn't been there. I wasn't ready for . . . whatever Juan seemed to be ready for.

I wouldn't even know what to do. I'd seen dogs at it, but surely that wasn't the human way. I thought I would've probably made a huge fool of myself, deprived myself of my greatest asset, as Father called it, and that had been one of his nicer lectures. The worst had ended with the story of Hippomenes, a leader of the Athenians, who'd discovered his daughter had been deflowered and, as punishment, shut her in a stable with a starving horse, who tore her to pieces and ate her.

"Are you cold?" Cristóbal asked.

I shook my head. "Just—tired, I guess."

"I bet. I had to scamper out of your way twice—you really went wild! I'm shocked *you* were chosen to be the Xibalban, without meaning any offense, sir."

Juan chuckled and leaned back on a tree. At the rare sound, Cristóbal's head snapped up. He shot a wondering look at me, and gasped.

"Your gown!" Cristóbal grabbed my arm and pulled it up.

My sleeves were rags, thread and silk, torn to bits. My skirt was filthy. "I need to get back. I need to fix this before morning!" I said.

Juan leaned forward. "I'll escort you back. Cristóbal will need to head back to the lake. It's a long journey."

"Can't he come too?" I asked, suddenly petrified of being alone with Juan.

Juan's face dropped and darkened. Cristóbal sat as still as the stela behind us, watching.

"I just—when will I see you again?" I said to Cristóbal. "We've not even had a chance to speak. I don't know if you're happy or not. Please come, no one will see you in the tunnel."

"Of course, I'll come," he said.

We packed up and rushed back. I lost my slippers as we crossed the river. We reached the tunnel, and Cristóbal stumbled through a series of breathless stories about Jun Kaaj and the lake. He'd learned how to fish. There was a girl in a nearby village who fancied him, but he wasn't interested and desperately wanted to avoid hurting her feelings. He'd taught Jun Kaaj's son, Pablo, how to wield a sword. I asked him a hundred questions and tried to stay cheerful, but it was a farce. Both of us pretended Juan wasn't hovering behind us, sulking up a storm.

When we reached the end of the tunnel, Cristóbal and I hugged.

"When will we meet again?" I asked.

"We shall send word to you," he said.

"No—it's been torture, waiting to hear from either of you, being unable to write. Tell me the plan, right now."

Cristóbal shifted and looked at Juan as though seeking permission. Juan nodded. "Nija'ib', I believe you're . . . traveling these next few weeks?"

"Yes, I'm constantly on the move, cousin. I cannot say why, but I won't be back in Santiago for at least another two months."

"Two months!" I groaned in frustration and confusion. It was such a long time, and he was obviously keeping something from me, but what, and why?

Cristóbal grimaced in apology.

I sighed, too tired to argue, and turned to Juan. "Will—will you be coming to the palace anytime soon, Cacique?" I hated the sound of my voice, pitiful and small.

"I've been given a reception room. I'll be moving in the next few months as well."

"Oh." I wished to hold him like I'd done in the cellar above. Just hours ago we'd been so close, and now he felt so far away.

"Best of luck with the dress," he said.

"Thank you." I lowered my gaze.

He lifted up the trapdoor, and Cristóbal gave me a leg up. "Don't walk in with those stockings." He wiped his hands on his trousers. "They'll leave a trail of mud."

I nodded and waved goodbye, trying to steal one last glance from Juan as I closed the trapdoor, but he'd turned away. I sighed and took a few steps before I remembered my hose and stopped to roll them off. Beautiful pair, taffeta tops and all, ruined. It was then I heard the rising murmur of Cristóbal's and Juan's voices. I knew I should've gone, and I was about to, but when they said my name, I simply couldn't resist. I tiptoed back to the corner and lowered my ear to the floor.

"She's the Daughter of Fire. The true child of Hacauitz. We belong together."

"With all respect, I think you'd be doing your people a disservice." Cristóbal's voice was so clear, he must've been standing right below me. I held my breath and tightened every muscle in place.

"In what way?"

"Her father is our only ally! The only leader who's ever helped us keep those rapists, those murderers, in check, and he's barely managing as we speak."

"But you've just said it—he's our ally."

"He would never consent, not in a million years. They see it as their right, for Spaniards to take our women whether they like it or not. But you know, for all intents and purposes, she's theirs, no matter how strong the flame of her mother's god, or how dark her skin. They'll claim her when it suits them, and it'll suit them in this instance. And they'll be outraged. An *Indio*! Courting a doña?"

"We need not ask them."

"But you need ask me. And Grande. It's a matter that concerns our nation. We are your council. Would Grande consent?"

"Aye, he would."

"Well, I wouldn't—I won't. You've not treated her right."

A pause. "She's forgiven me. She cares for me."

"You don't even know each other!"

"I know that she's brave and kind, and true." His voice shook. "There's no one else like her. I'll not have you get in our way—I've told her my true name already."

"Oh, very well, and I'm sure you told her you're betrothed too, engaged, I should say?"

"I—that was a mistake—in any case, we're not married yet."

"You're as good as. Have you no honor? How do you think Woven Tree will feel when you spurn his only daughter? You'll start a war with House Zaquic—a war we cannot afford."

"Why don't you spit out the real truth, Nija'ib'? You don't want me to have her, because you want her for yourself."

The notion was so ridiculous, I scoffed, then covered my mouth. Luckily, Cristóbal laughed at the same time, so they didn't hear me. I got down on my knees and pushed my ear as close as I could to the floor, but they must've walked away in a rush, because I could hear only their angry echoing tones. I lay on my back. My breath came in fast as I replayed their conversation. *Rapists, murderers.* I'd never heard Cristóbal's rage. I couldn't believe he'd called me a doña. I couldn't believe Juan's declaration, *We belong together*!

A million thoughts flew through my head, until there was only one, circling and stinging like an angry wasp. *He's engaged. He's engaged. He's engaged.*

I threw my arm over my face and lingered too long.

The creak of the cellar door nearly tore a shriek from me. Light from a candle flooded the darkness, revealing the stone steps. I spun onto my hands and knees and crawled away, feeling with my hands for a big enough space behind one of the many barrels.

"Señorita?"

I exhaled in relief at the sound and rose to my feet.

"Maribel," I began, and my voice echoed through the chamber, but one of the reverberations was wrong, off, low in pitch and angry.

"Thief! Stop right there!"

She squeaked and tried to block me from his sight, she really did. But Victorino raised his torch and the cellar was flooded with light. We locked eyes, and he smiled.

CHAPTER 12

Santiago de los Caballeros, Guatemala
Winter 1552–1553

When I woke the next day, I was in bed, wearing only a shift. The curtains had been drawn around all four posters. My pulse spiked and resounded in my temples. Vague memories of the night before drifted in my mind, voices and shadows.

I couldn't remember much except for the one glaring thing: Juan's engagement.

My head throbbed sharply like a drum. I groaned, unstuck my tongue from the roof of my mouth, and reached out for water, but my muscles were too sore and weak, like my heart. It felt like a wounded animal, a coati perhaps, or an egret, perforated by poisoned darts. My arm fell and I wept in silence.

Pathetic.

Of course he was engaged. He was a king. It was his duty to marry and have children. As many heirs as he could, to keep his bloodline alive. His native bloodline, which would probably be unacceptable to my father. Cristóbal was right. If it was rare for Spanish men to marry *Indígenas*, it was almost unheard of for it to be the other way around.

A spasm of grief seized me, and I suddenly wished Cook were there to comfort me, but that only hurt me more, for I felt the truth in my bones. She was gone.

Oh, I thought, *where is Maribel?* I needed to know what had happened last night. I needed to know Cook had gone in peace, that she hadn't felt any pain, that she'd been sung to and caressed, loved until the end. I called out, voice hoarse, "Maribel?"

Something scraped the floor, the foot of a chair or a stool, and heavy footsteps approached. "Who's there?" I said.

The curtains ripped open and I yelped, pulling the bedsheets high up to my chin. Father looked down. His gaunt face was blotchy, and his beard and hair stuck out at odd angles. He leaned on a walking stick with a silver handle, wrought in the shape of a ram.

"The princess finally wakes from her slumber."

"Father! You're not well! Go back to bed!"

"Why? So you can sneak off again?"

I froze.

"Victorino spotted that maid of yours going down to the cellar. We've had rats before, servants with sticky little fingers. So he followed her, and behold, found you instead. He came straight to me. Told me you were drunk. Drunk!"

I jolted. My head pounded behind my eyes.

"What have you to say for yourself?" He waited for me, and a vein pulsed at his throat.

I whispered the first sensible thing that came to mind. "I've been so scared with you being so sick and—"

"Do not lie to me!" He reached into his pocket, pulled out some kind of cloth, and threw it at me. It was so filthy I didn't know what to make of it until I spotted the ribbon tops. Taffeta. *Oh,* I thought, *this is bad. This is really bad.* I looked at Father and shook my head. Sweat broke out on my upper lip. I thought I would be sick, and not from the *balché' ki'.*

"What's that—you don't know? Those are your stockings. Why were your stockings not on your legs? Why were they torn and covered with mud? Why were you drunk in the cellar in the middle of the night? Answer me!"

"I—I—"

There was an urgent knock on the door.

"What!" he roared.

The door creaked, and I caught the sound of a guitar being strummed with unmistakable passion. Victorino's sluggish voice cut through: "Beggin' your pardon, m'lord, but there's a gentleman downstairs, causin' a scene."

Father's eyebrows stitched together.

"Best if you took a look."

He hobbled away, out onto the balcony, and I, overwhelmed by relief at his distraction and feeling an unwholesome sense of curiosity, also walked toward the half-open door. I pulled my mother's sarape across my shoulders and peeked through the gap.

My hands flew to my cheeks.

Nicolao was balancing on the edge of the fountain. His gaze was fixed on my room as he sang a well-known sonnet at the top of his lungs.

> *The virgin is on the riverside*
> *Culling the lemons pale;*
> *Thither—yes! Thither will I go*
> *To the rosy vale where the nightingale*
> *Sings his song of woe.*

A crowd gathered quickly. Some were clearly just attracted to his voice, which was rather good, while others nudged at each other and smirked up at the balcony. All were smiling except a woman in black who held the hand of a grumpy-looking little boy and, to my horror, Juan. Lord Juan. Who was betrothed, but not to me.

He seemed to think better of whatever he was going to do, and walked off. I looked at Father, who was gripping the balcony edge so tightly his knuckles had turned white. Maloso stuck his nose out of the gap and wagged his tail.

Victorino caught my eye and winked. Perhaps he'd figured out the chickens were a diversion, and this was payment. Perhaps this was another way to curry favor with Father.

Perhaps he was just a bastard.

Father turned, spotted me, and stormed back in. I tried to leap out of the way, but he gripped my arm and crushed it. I cried out, but he was like a bull, eyes bulging out of his face. Maloso barked and leapt from side to side. Maybe he thought it was a game.

"I see. I see what you've been up to, *putain*."

Nicolao's voice drifted up and Father paused as though bewitched.

> *The fairest fruit her hand hath culled.*
> *'Tis for her lover all,*
> *Thither—yes! Thither will I go*
> *To the rosy vale where the nightingale*
> *Sings his song of woe.*

"Oh, I'll make him sing a song of woe." He threw me down and slammed the door, but I heard him as clear as if he were screaming into my ear.

"Grab that clown—take him to the dungeons!"

I could've stopped him.

I could've told Father about the *Popol Vuh* and saved Nico.

But I did not.

For the next few weeks, I lingered in a state of anxiety. I felt as though lightning had struck and there was no stopping the incoming thunderclap. I had no idea when it would strike, but I could not stop it. I could only try to muffle the sound. So I did everything Father asked of me without complaint. I endured another visit from the midwife. I stayed in my room, not that I had a choice, as it was locked from the outside. I swallowed the tears of rage and powerlessness and spent my days staring at the colorful maize and deer patterns woven in the carpet by the foot of my bed, at the dropping marigold petals drying out on my desk, and at the way the green velvet curtains sparkled when the evening light burst through the windows.

No dogs were allowed, no Maribel, no news. Only prayer, needlepoint, and the occasional handpicked book containing cautionary tales of fire and brimstone for women who defied their families and dishonored themselves.

In my best calligraphy, I was made to write down Father's favorite passage by Vives to keep by my bedside and read aloud each night:

> *Chastity is the equivalent of all virtues. Women who take little care of their chastity are worth all calamities and worse. For many things are required of a man: wisdom, eloquence, knowledge of political affairs, talent, memory, some trade to live by, justice, liberality, magnanimity, and other qualities that it would take a long time to rehearse. But in a woman, no one requires anything of her but chastity. If that one thing is missing, it is as if all were lacking to a man.*

Father brought Bishop Marroquín to see me. My forehead crinkled in surprise and confusion, but I kept my eyes down, as meek as Mary.

He asked in a gentle voice if I wished to confess.

"Not today, Your Excellency," I said. "My body is intact."

"Ah, but how about your mind, your spirit? It is preferable for the stomach to be in pain, rather than the mind," he replied. "It is difficult, being young. But prayer will guide you through any pain and sorrow." We recited a rosary together, and even though he had been my only visitor in weeks, even though he'd been unexpectedly kind, I was unmoved. He wished me luck, and begged me to read the letters of Saint Jerome, and I did because, even though a part of me was angry, a part of me felt I deserved it all.

The bishop was right. My spirit was in turmoil, because I'd used him, Nico, that poor enamored man. My heart twisted every day when I thought of him, of how I'd thrown him to the dogs. I told myself I'd protected the *Popol Vuh*, and Juan, and Cristóbal. I'd created a fantastic diversion, but at what cost? I could bear my cross; I'd earned it. But poor Nico. No one would tell me what he'd endured, or would endure, but I knew it would be terrible. I'd rarely seen Father so angry. I truly thought if I was good, if I behaved exactly as Father wanted, then maybe Nico would be shown mercy.

I watched the Christmas procession from my bedroom window. Father and other persons of quality carried a colorful palanquin with a life-size model of the Holy Virgin and Child. The townspeople followed, *Indígenas* and Spaniards alike, dressed in their best. They sang, whistled, banged their drums, and burned incense.

I ate Christmas dinner alone in my room. It was a new low. Even in that horrible year after Mother's death, Father had been there with me. He'd been tough, relentless in his attempts to expunge any heresy left behind by my mother, any sins I might've learned at the hands of Beatriz. But he'd been there, and a storm is never solid. Rays of light had gleamed through, every now and again. We'd shared laughs in those dark times, tenderness too. Moments that I held on to fiercely, foolishly, to this day.

My main companion now was Agustina, who'd been assigned to attend to me. She was even more silent than Maribel had been before the cacique brought us together. Maribel had been dismissed, of course, sent back to wherever she'd come from—no one would tell me where that was and I never found out.

The only thing I was told, or shown rather, happened on New Year's Day, when Father ordered me to stand by my window. With a shudder, I realized this was it.

The thunder, his judgment, my reckoning.

My heart sank and I swayed when I spotted the whipping post that had been erected in the middle of the square. Throngs of people were gathered around it.

They jeered as Nicolao was brought out in a squeaking wagon. His hands were tied up to the irons and his shirt torn to reveal the creamy skin of his back.

The sentence was read out: nine lashes for drunkenness and dishonorable behavior. I felt sure the drunkenness bit was just for me.

Father stood behind me so I couldn't turn away. I wouldn't have, anyway. This was my fault, my responsibility. I would witness the consequences of my actions.

He made me count the lashes. One . . . two . . . three . . . the whip snapped, carved lines of scarlet, and flushed his skin purple. Nico groaned, from the pit of his soul. Four . . . five . . . six . . . a scream tore out of him. By the eighth, he was out cold.

All the while, I felt separated from myself, like I floated above my body. I heard my deadened voice. I watched the blood soak like spilled wine into his shirt and trousers, but I couldn't feel a thing.

Perhaps a month later, Father entered my room, Maloso by his side. The dog hardly knew what to do with himself; he whined, leapt at me, and tried to lick my face.

"Down," Father said. Maloso obeyed, but his tail wagged on.

I think I smiled, but I couldn't be sure. My cheeks felt foreign to me.

"That's quite enough, wouldn't you say," Father mumbled.

I didn't look at his face, not anymore.

"You're getting pale. I don't like it. You'll start looking like me, and I couldn't forgive myself for that. You may walk the palace grounds, but you are not to leave them."

I nodded.

"The cellar is out of bounds, obviously. I've made sure to change the locks."

I bowed.

"Catalina, look at me."

I glanced up at his chin only. His beard was neat and trim. He'd gained weight, though he still relied on the cane for support.

He sighed. "You've been ill. That's what you'll say, understood?"

Father helped me down the stairs, as my legs had weakened. I sat by the fountain edge, out of breath, and tickled behind Maloso's ears. Courtiers and clerks, servants and guards came and went. Some nodded or lifted their hats, but otherwise I was left alone.

Good, I thought. *Isn't that what I wanted?*

In truth, it was hard to want anything. Even the *Popol Vuh* or fantasies about Juan failed to stir up more than a flicker of interest. Ever since Nicolao had been flogged, I felt like desire had dissolved from my body. I felt dead to life, exhausted. All I ever caused was pain. I thought maybe it would've been best if I'd gone to sleep and never woken up.

Maybe that's why Mother had spent so much time in bed during her bouts of melancholy. She'd always pulled herself out of them, though, and always by the time Father returned home. I thought perhaps it had been love, but maybe it was just to keep up appearances, keep him happy, keep herself safe. I don't think she ever trusted him, even though he never hurt her or even raised his voice at her. She never trusted a Spaniard.

That morning, as I sat and stared at the books in the library, Isabel paid me a visit.

Her face blanched when she saw me. She kissed my cheeks and told me how much she'd prayed for my recovery.

"I've missed you. Truly. I was so worried you'd perhaps caught the same thing as your old Cook, bless her soul. I'm glad you're better. You've no idea what it's like to be left at the mercy of Doña Clara for company. You see, I've hardly seen Pedro. He's been so busy presiding over the trial of Captain Lobo, did you hear?"

I shook my head. The sudden mention of Cook had left me too shaken to speak.

"It was my husband who discovered it all, in fact. He found a mountain of stolen gold and jewelry in his cellar. It seems he made deals with grave robbers; can you believe it? There's been an uproar about it."

"Oh." What else could I say?

Isabel studied me. "What happened to you, Catalina? You can trust me. Was it the tutor? He brought it on himself, you know, and he's recovered by now, gone back to Don Bernal. Your father was merciful, didn't take his lands."

"Thank you, but it's the truth. I've been unwell." I gave her a small smile. It's all I could manage, but it seemed to reassure her.

"Well, I'm glad you're on the mend." She lowered her voice and looked at the library door. "Look, something arrived for you a few weeks back, at my house. A letter from a woman named Beatriz who claims to be your sister. She wrote to me too, saying she knew we were friends, and asked me to please deliver this to you, discreetly. Well, I am always glad to help a family come together, but I thought your only relatives were in Granada?"

I sat up and she handed me the letter. "Indeed, my father's family are in Granada. Beatriz, my sister from my father's first wife, lives here, but she and my father are estranged."

"Oh?" I could tell Isabel wanted to know more, but I'd begun to read.

February 3, 1553
Dear Catalina,
I pray you are well. I must first apologize for the delay in my response. I've had much on my mind since my husband and girls passed, though it is not as terrible as you may imagine, for I have God by my side, an encomienda to run, and my beautiful son still to care for. Thus, time passes and before you know it, here we are, old and grown and weary.

Speaking of old, I hear Father mended well, and I am glad, for I do not wish him any ill, nor you, ever. I have always cared for you, and have done everything with my best intentions for you, including staying out of your life, as Father warned me to do in his most gentle, loving

*way. So, I beg you, do not ask your maid or anyone else
to write again.*

*You are precious to me. Worse still, you are precious
to Father. Do not cross him. I would hate for you to end
up like me, with only your hand for currency.*

May God keep you in his ever-merciful arms,
Beatriz Cerrato de Cano

I read it again, this first and only letter she'd written me in however
many years. It was so short. She'd not even addressed me as "Dear sister." She didn't want me to write back. She wanted nothing to do with
me. I felt faint, light-headed, sick to my stomach.

My vision darkened. For a moment, all I could hear was my breath.
Then, I felt Mother's presence move through me. Just her presence, not
her voice. She left behind a fragrance, resin and yucca, freshly dug earth,
lingering in my body.

What did this all mean? I covered my face.

"Oh, dear, you're not well at all. I shall fetch a maid, and we can
talk about this another time." She grabbed the first maid who walked
past the library and got her to help me back to my room. I sat in bed
all afternoon, thinking about Beatriz.

So many questions flitted through my mind. Why hadn't she stayed
home for me after Mother died? If I was so precious to her, why hadn't
she ever written? It didn't matter that Father had asked her not to;
she had plenty of opportunities to reach me in Santa Cruz, when he
was away. Perhaps she felt Mother and I had usurped her in Father's
affections, and resented us for it? I suppose that made sense. But then
again, she'd been good to me, mostly. She'd played with me and told
me stories, and taught me with diligence and passion. It was all very
confusing and hurtful. With my eyes brimming, I read the letter again.

More questions. What did she mean by having only her hand for
currency? Did she think she'd failed me by marrying a silversmith? I
guess Father had always placed a lot of pressure on her to be the perfect

model of a Christian woman, to show Mother and me how to pray, how to act, how to love God and follow his commandments. Maybe she felt a silversmith was too lowly a choice for people of our stature? Well, I didn't care, as long as she'd loved him.

I couldn't understand her; something was missing, something I didn't know. But by the evening I'd had enough of trying to figure it out.

Agustina came by with a tray of hot chocolate, and I went out to the balcony to sip on it. Suddenly, I had that strange tingling sensation in the back of my arms and neck. I looked around and spotted a familiar figure walking toward the second courtyard. He'd not seen me, and I felt so muddled by the events of the day I wasn't sure if he was real or not.

"Is that the Cacique de Q'umarkaj?" I tried to keep my voice steady and disinterested, though a flutter in my heart made it past the numbing sadness and confusion.

The maid nodded. "Lord Juan has finally been given a reception room in the palace, miss."

CHAPTER 13

Santiago de los Caballeros, Guatemala
Spring 1553

The very next morning was so beautiful and brilliant, I felt something stirring in me, something like life and hope. I burned Beatriz's letter and sat on the fountain edge, listening to the tinkling water and the songs of warblers and flycatchers looking for their breakfast, while I waited to see if Juan would walk by again. For so long I'd been forced to sit and wait for things to happen, it took me a moment to realize I didn't have to anymore. It was so simple.

As simple as breathing, Mother said.

I stood and walked into the second courtyard, which I'd seen him disappear into.

Once I got there, I felt rather foolish. What was I meant to do, knock on every door until the right one opened? And what would I say to the ministers behind? *Oh, excuse me, just having a look, making sure you're doing your jobs and not dozing off like Father says you always do.* Or what if one of the guards stopped to ask what I was doing?

That had happened a few times. That oily barbarian Victorino, for example, always went straight to Father, in the hopes it would advance him, win him a promotion to captain, or earn him what they all wanted in the end—an encomienda of his own.

It should be fine, though. Father had specified I could go around the palace grounds, and I sometimes went that way to pick flowers for the chapel. I mostly visited in summer, when the yuccas were in bloom.

There were orchids then. I cut a few stems, but really I studied each door and thought of him. *Where are you, Q'anti?* There was a gust of wind, and one of my orchids flew out of my hand and rolled along the floor toward one of the offices.

I sprinted to pick it up. There was no one around. I reached up, opened the door, and entered. When I turned, he was there, eyes wide, sitting behind a huge mahogany desk.

"Hello," I whispered.

Juan leapt up and over the desk. Two strides and I was in his arms. He looked down at me with full, swimming eyes and stroked my cheek and the small of my back.

"I've been so worried. So worried," he said.

It took me a moment to understand him. I couldn't believe this moment was real, that we were holding each other once again.

"I tried sending word, but that new maid of yours was too scared to help. No one else would tell me anything, only that you were sick, and I thought, I thought . . ." I felt his hands as they trembled behind me. He cleared his throat. A gentle warmth began to blossom from deep within me, but I still couldn't speak. I could only gaze at him in wonder.

"Catalina, I have to tell you, I must take this opportunity, you must know." His voice was hoarse. His chest heaved as he struggled to find his words. He closed his eyes and leaned his forehead on mine.

"I—I love you." He looked at me again, and for the first time in months, I beamed.

He laughed, a beautiful, full, radiant laugh. I noticed for the first time a dimple on his left cheek, and I laughed too, wrapping my arms around his neck. There was no asking this time; our lips insisted. The orchids tumbled to the floor, and the numbness melted. In one go. It all melted away.

◆ ◆ ◆

"Wait." I gasped. "I can't breathe."

Juan kissed me more, twice, three times. I leaned away with a laugh. "I can't breathe!"

"Right." He shut his eyes like it cost him a gargantuan effort and we swayed in silence, cheek to cheek. After a long moment, he asked, "What happened, are you better now?"

"Yes, I'm better now." I didn't want to talk about what had happened. I didn't want to ruin the moment. I never wanted it to end.

"I worried, constantly. Truly, I thought—" He shuddered.

"No, no." I hushed him gently and stroked the line of his jaw. Our lips met again, soft like grazing petals, and I found it was my turn to tremble.

A few heartbeats passed until a familiar noise seeped into my consciousness. I couldn't quite make it out at first, until I realized it was the bells tolling. I groaned.

"Don't," said Juan, and he kissed me softly again, like he knew it'd stall me.

It did.

"I have to go." I placed my hand on his chest. "I must."

He sighed and shook his head. "I'll check the courtyard is clear, then."

"Wait—" My insides twisted, like an orange, grown and ripened, then cut and wrenched for every drop. "When—how will we meet, and what of the *Popol Vuh*?"

"Nija'ib' has not yet responded to my summons, so the book must wait, unfortunately. But as for us . . ." He frowned, looked at the floor, and picked up the wilted flowers. "I'll leave a sign. An orchid or two, floating in the fountain. You'll know I'm in that day, and I'll be hoping to see you here. If it's safe for you."

I nodded, but I couldn't bring myself to smile, for I felt as if a jury had handed me my sentence. I'd learned my fate, and it was a terrible one. To wait, and to hope each and every single day to see a flash of white drifting along sparkling water.

◆ ◆ ◆

A week passed, and there was no sign. I checked the fountain every few hours during the day. At night, I held the carving he'd made, the one of the jaguar with the arrow, which I kept hidden in the same spot as Cristóbal's letter. I rubbed it with my fingers and pressed it to my heart, hoping it would bring me dreams of him.

I was checking the fountain again, on the afternoon of the feast of Saints Perpetua and Felicity, when Father emerged from the hall. I was shocked when he spoke to me, which he hardly ever did anymore.

"Good, you're here. I've a message from Ramirez. We're going to his house, both of us. Something about Captain Lobo."

I grabbed my drawstring purse and followed him through the square in silence, wondering about my sudden freedom. We didn't get very far. We'd reached the palm trees in the middle when we were nearly run over by a horse carrying a frenzied Judge Ramirez.

"He's escaped! The bastard's gotten away. He's run into the cathedral, quickly!" Ramirez shot off. Father wobbled as fast as his cane would allow him. Unsure of what to do, I followed him.

We entered the dimly lit cathedral and froze. A woman was screaming at the top of her lungs, and shouts echoed through the great domed ceilings. Captain Lobo hurtled from the east wing toward us. He tore through the rows of pews and knocked down a sculpture of Moses. Judge Ramirez chased after him. Bishop Marroquín, plum robes billowing behind him, bellowed something about sanctuary. The treasurer's wife, Doña Imelda, ran after them all with her skirts hitched up above her knees. A couple of slack-jawed parishioners ogled at the scene.

The judge overtook the conquistador, who bent over and panted. His soiled clothes stank of sweat and urine. I moved to the wall.

"I'll not go back into that hole," wheezed Lobo. "I shouldn't have to. I'm—a servant of the Crown!"

Judge Ramirez didn't hear him. "For months I toiled away . . . I left my wife, whom I'd not seen in years, to search up and down the country, trying to find who was behind all these robberies, and it was you all along! You'll pay for what you've done."

Doña Imelda threw herself at the judge's feet. "Pedro, have mercy for my sake!"

The bishop placed himself in front of Ramirez, huffing and puffing, and opened his palms. "Calm yourself, Pedro. The man has claimed sanctuary."

"Your Excellency, this ruffian has no scruples. His gang of thieves stole from everyone, no matter how high or low. Look, Catalina—is this not yours?"

From his pocket, he pulled out a heavy green necklace and threw it at me. I caught it and gasped. It was my necklace. Juan's jade treasure.

"This *was* stolen from me, over a year ago!" I tucked it away, deep into my purse.

"Indeed—one Luis, a guitar player, confessed to the crime, assuring me that he was commissioned to do so by our dear lord treasurer, a great lover and collector of antiquities."

"Luis played at my sixteenth birthday party!"

"He didn't know they were stolen," shouted Doña Imelda. "The robberies must've been the work of someone else. The maids gossip about a bandit named Ocelot, what of him?"

"The Ocelot rumor is rubbish. Several witnesses have attested to your husband's involvement. He'll return to the dungeons where he belongs."

Lobo made a run for it again, but tripped over himself. Father leaned as if to help him up, but Ramirez grabbed his cane, whacked the conquistador over the head with it, and knocked him out cold. Doña Imelda shrieked and draped herself over her husband. Ramirez threw the cane down, and it clattered by her feet.

"You disgust me."

"Enough, Pedro! You'll not dishonor the house of God." The bishop grabbed Judge Ramirez's arm. "And you shall not take him; I'll not allow it."

The judge drew his sword, face contorted. Bishop Marroquín took a step back, toward me. I grabbed the bishop's habit and pulled. The blade missed his chest, but scratched his arm.

"You struck me!" Marroquín shrieked. He tumbled to the ground and knocked me back with him. I broke the fall with my wrist, which radiated with pain. I shook it off, then knelt by the bishop, who held his wounded arm close.

"Let me see," I said.

He didn't listen; he just stared at Ramirez open-jawed, face pale and clammy, trembling all over. I repeated myself and patted his hand. He started and let me have a look. It was only a shallow wound, so I tore a strip from the habit and wrapped it around his arm.

There were more shouts. The judge was attempting to light a harquebus. Father said, "I'll order two guards to watch him day and night. Come, my friend—don't shoot them. My daughter is here."

The judge glanced at me, and lowered his weapon.

"Argh! He stays here with two guards until his trial. But if he gets away—I'll claim both of you in his stead." He looked at Father and at the bishop and strutted out of the cathedral, cape swirling behind him.

Father sighed and turned around. "Someone help this hysterical woman."

Doña Imelda was bawling into her husband's broad back. Two ladies rushed forward and made encouraging sounds, tried to get her to release his soiled shirt, to stand and let them take her home, but she clung to him more and howled instead.

"Your Excellency, are you hurt?" Father asked Marroquín, who shook his head.

"Catalina, help the lord bishop back to his quarters. I shall go to the palace and pick some guards."

"May I help you, Your Excellency?" I offered my hand. Marroquín looked at me. He studied my face long enough that I squirmed.

"You—you saved my life?"

"She did! I saw her, Your Excellency. She pulled you away and fell to the ground when the sword was coming down," said one of the women helping Doña Imelda.

I instinctively cradled my sore wrist to my chest.

"Oh no, are you hurt, child?" the bishop asked.

For some reason, I shook my head, but Marroquín's face crumpled with pity. "Oh my, you are, which means I'm doubly in your debt."

"Please, sir, it's nothing. And anyone would've—"

"Not quite, especially not—" He reached out and squeezed my arm, then paused for a moment and said, "I want you to know, if ever you need anything, anything at all. Come to me, and I shall personally see to it. I swear on my office, as an apostle of Christ."

I stared for an instant before I bowed and kissed his ring, for this was a magnanimous offer, and only a fool would've argued or made light of it.

"You honor me," I whispered.

The bishop let me help him up. "Thank you. The nuns will tend to me now."

I understood I'd been dismissed, so I bowed again, and he excused himself. The women continued to try to help the inconsolable Doña Imelda.

"Save yourself," one of the women whispered with a wink. "Enjoy your triumph."

I took a few tentative steps out the door. I blinked in the bright, warm light and felt oddly exposed. I was walking in town, on my own, for the first time in my life.

Perhaps I imagined the stares from the townspeople as I crossed the busy square. The gentle glances from tiny Maya ladies who sat and weaved colorful cloths by the cool shade of palms and blooming jacarandas, or from the vendors selling summer squash, avocados, and raw cobs of corn. Men—tanned potters, burly smiths, and carpenters covered in sawdust—stared around appraisingly, and fair-skinned women giggled as they took an afternoon turn.

At the arches of the palace entrance, I ran into Father. He'd selected Lobo's guards. Victorino the brute was one of them. He leered at me, and a shiver slithered down my back.

"Good—you're back," said Father. "I'll see you at dinner."

I nodded and walked forward to the fountain, to do my thrice-daily check, and braced myself for crushing disappointment. But no, there they were. Two delightful white orchids bumbled on the surface and waved at me.

I fought the urge to run. Instead, I drifted along the garden to the corner arch, and attempted to look as morose and boring as I imagined I usually looked. There were a couple of ministers sitting and talking on one of the benches that bordered the second courtyard, so I made my way back to the fountain and waited. I wished I had something useful with which to occupy my hands.

I considered going into the library to grab a book so I could pretend to read, when the ministers emerged from the arch and walked into the hall. My heart jumped to my throat again as I made my way back, picked a bunch of red ember flowers, and waited, two, three breaths. A pair of grackles whistled from the treetops, but no one was around.

I walked steadily in the direction of Juan's door, then stopped and waited again, feeling every bit the common thief. A quick knock and I ran in, laughing with relief as I spotted him by the window. The next moment, he had me pressed against the door.

"Where have you been?" I murmured.

"Doing rounds." He paused. "Don't be angry, I thought we'd have more time, but I've just been asked to call on the monastery." He covered my protests with kisses until only a shuddering breath escaped me.

"Fine." I pushed him gently and tried to steady myself. "In that case, I have something for you." I took out the necklace from my purse and beamed at the stunned look on his face.

I had to reach out, open his palms, and lay it across them. With a devilish smile I said, "Don't you want your precious necklace back, sire?"

He huffed a laugh and hung the necklace around his neck. He tucked it safely inside his shirt before he took my hands in his. "You . . . you make me feel like a king."

"You *are* a king." I smiled, but his expression changed, to that of pain. "What's the matter?" I placed my hand on his cheek, but he turned his face away.

"It's a lie, that's all. Alvarado took this necklace from my grandfather right before he tortured and burned him. A few years later, when my father rebelled, he scalped and hanged him in front of me. He did even worse to Grande's father. They were the last true kings. I'll never have strength like they did. I'll never have their valor, or their power. I'm poor, broken, and empty." The bitter words flowed out of him. For a short moment I could do nothing but stare. I was so taken aback by his revelation, his pain.

"I told you I wanted you to know me, and the truth is, I'm no king. I'm nothing at all."

I stomped my foot. "That's not true! That's what they want you to believe, and I'll not allow it. You are not nothing; you are everything! Everything, you hear me?"

He shook his head. I leaned in so our foreheads touched. "You are strong," I said, and kissed his cheeks. "You are cunning. You're a survivor." I grazed his eyelids, tasted the salt on his neck. "You are beautiful, and powerful. You are Son of the Jaguar," I whispered in his ear, and bit down on his lobe for good measure. That brought a small smile to his face.

I rested my head on his shoulder. "Please don't ever speak like that again."

He sighed, and we held each other and began to sway. We couldn't have been in greater danger, if someone had walked in and seen us, and yet, in all my life, I'd never felt more sheltered, nor wanted a moment to last for all time. Until then.

"I don't want you to go," I said.

"I'll be back before long." He kissed my brow. "Perhaps even tomorrow."

"Promise me."

He hesitated, so I pressed against him, knowing he'd feel the shape of my curves, my breasts. A cheap trick, but it worked. His eyes widened.

"Tomorrow then, I promise."

CHAPTER 14

Santiago de los Caballeros, Guatemala
Spring 1553

When morning came, it took me twice as long to get ready. I stood there and stared at the collection of gowns strewn on the bed and thought how old and dreary they all were. My best one had been ruined when I'd gone to the forest. I'd found two of the buttons in my hearth. Maribel must've burned it that night, which meant I was doubly in her debt. If only I knew where she'd gone, but no one was willing to tell me. Only Agustina assured me, after daily questioning, that Maribel was safe, though that was all she'd say.

At last, I picked the red-and-gold gown and made a mental note to beg Father for a new one. Agustina had to braid my hair four different ways until I was finally happy. Half of it tumbled to the side. She interspersed my plaits with ribbons of red and gold silk.

I dabbed myself with rose water and Agustina tied my best lace frill around my neck. It was too late to take a quiet breakfast in the hall, so she brought a tray to the sitting room adjacent to my chambers. It was loaded with my favorites, cut papaya inside an alabaster bowl, two steaming green tamales wrapped in corn husks, served with black bean broth spiced with Jamaica pepper.

I ate the last bite of my tamale, and finished getting ready by sheathing my dagger around my calf. It was the one I'd taken from

Father the night I'd gone to seek Cook, with its gold-and-leather handle and three rubies at the cross guard and hilt. I never went anywhere without it anymore.

I was just about to leave when Agustina knocked again. "Señorita, sorry to disturb, but there's people waitin' in the library." She stared at the floor, voice softer than a breeze.

"Oh? Who?"

"Um, I think that lady friend of yours, miss, and the Lord Don Bernal."

"That's odd." Don Bernal never called unannounced. I hoped it wouldn't be long.

"Would your ladyship prefer that I tell them to return later?"

Poor thing, she looked terrified at the prospect, so I said, "No, thank you, Agustina, I'll meet them now, but come and get me shortly. Make some excuse." She looked even more terrified. "Tell them my father wants to see me, please."

She nodded. It was a warm day, so I stuffed my hand fan into my purse and left.

"Ah, there she is," said Isabel when I walked through the door. She rose to kiss me.

Don Bernal also stood and bowed. "I know I'm half-blind, but I'm sure you're looking exceptionally lovely today, dear."

"You're absolutely right, Bernal, she's positively glowing," said Isabel.

I fanned my face. "Thank you, you're too kind."

We sat and I picked up the bell. "Would you like me to ring for wine?"

"No, no, it's quite all right," said Don Bernal.

"Isabel, how is Don Ramirez?" I asked. There had been an uproar since the scene at the cathedral. Every snippet of conversation I'd overheard was about how the judge nearly killed the bishop. People had been staring at me again. Men lifted their hats and women bowed their heads whenever they saw me. Some had come to shake my hand and thank me. Father, on the other hand, had told me he wished the cut had been a lot deeper, for maybe then Marroquín would've felt more keenly for the *Indígenas* bleeding out every single day.

"Well! I keep telling him, we owe you the greatest debt," said Isabel. "Without you, he'd have murdered a beloved servant of God and who knows where he'd be."

"Sporting a rope around his neck for sure," muttered Don Bernal.

I fanned myself again. "Oh no. I'm glad nothing bad has come of it, Isabel, but you don't owe me a thing."

She gave me a rare smile. "In any case, I've thought of a way to repay you, haven't I?" She looked at Don Bernal.

"We're here to beg your assistance, my child," he said.

I cocked my head in response.

"I tried inviting Doña Clara in your stead, to call on Don Bernal with me, but she was . . ." Isabel paused to find the right word. "Most unhelpful."

"I couldn't get a word in, could I!" Don Bernal said. "She kept twitching and whimpering during all the battle scenes. So—we've decided to bring my memoir to you."

Isabel beamed. "Since you enjoy it, I thought it was a brilliant plan, what with you being unwell."

"And with the slight inconvenience of Nicolao's presence in my house," Don Bernal said.

They both looked at me like that was the best news I could ever have hoped for, so I gave them what I believed was a grateful smile. "My—my goodness, you are so thoughtful!"

"Well, we thought we'd start straightaway." He tapped on a leather case I'd not seen before, next to his leg.

"What—today?"

"Why yes! It's been far too long. You're not busy?"

"Of—of course not." I smiled through my teeth. I really hoped Agustina would find her courage and not abandon me with them.

"Splendid. Shall we move to the table, so Isabel can write?"

We got up. I offered Don Bernal my arm and he took it. We took a step, and the knock came. Agustina walked in, shaking and stuttering apologies.

"Your f-father w-wants you," she said.

"I'm dreadfully sorry," I quickly said to Isabel and Don Bernal. "Do you think we could meet another time? Perhaps tomorrow?"

After a brief pause, Don Bernal clasped his hands. "Oh, of course, of course! We were too presumptuous to think you'd be free. Isabel, I guess, could you guide me home?"

"With pleasure," she said.

"Thank you again for the lovely surprise," I said, though my chest eased with relief.

"You're doing us the favor, dear," said Don Bernal. Isabel nodded.

◆ ◆ ◆

When they were gone, I ran into the second courtyard.

Juan was standing below the avocado trees, by the flower beds. He looked me over and a shyness stole over me, warming my neck and cheeks.

He walked to my side and whispered in K'iche', "Don't look away. I love it when you face me, even when you have a bold spell."

I laughed. "Is that what you call my temper?" He nodded and I said, "Well, I suppose it's kinder than being called hysterical, like Doctor Rivera did when I threatened to stab him."

"It's a fine line, isn't it?" He sighed. "I wish we could be alone."

"Well, why don't we go to your office," I whispered.

He shook his head. "And then what?"

I stared at him, confused.

"How long will we get away with this? No, look at me."

I frowned at him, but his face was too tender. He leaned toward me, as if there was nothing more he'd like than to hold me.

"This isn't what I want for us." His voice shook. "I want—to be able to see you every day, like this, in the light of day. I want to take that thing off your neck and get rid of those puffed-up sleeves, and feel the skin of your arms and legs and hips, everything. I want to have a child with you, many children. If you wish it. Children with your brains and spirit. Legitimate, true heirs to guide our people. I want to love them and love you, and be the family we never had."

I couldn't see him properly through my tears, and it took every ounce of self-control to stay put and look around to make sure we were alone. Then, with my heart in my throat, I kissed him, pouring everything I was, and everything I had, into him.

That was my gift to him, my answer. It lasted but a breath or two, but when I opened my eyes, he looked as dazed as I felt.

We stood in silence for several moments. A dove murmured and cooed, and the reality of things started to sink in. I took a deep breath.

"How will we do it? I just don't know if Father would be willing. He doesn't want me to marry. He told Cristóbal as much."

"We could run away."

My eyes widened. "Where? Father is too well connected. He'd look for us."

"I've helped many to escape before, disappear into the Lacandon Jungle."

The name itself sent gooseflesh creeping down my spine. The Lacandon was wild and dangerous, and not just because of the animals. The Spanish called the people who lived in its shadows *los inconquistables*, the unconquerable. Most who entered never returned.

"We'd never see anyone again." I thought of Father and Cristóbal. "We'd never finish the *Popol Vuh* together. It's too important to me, and even you said we had to."

Juan took a moment. He nodded. "Aye, I did. Did I ever tell you about my vision?"

I shook my head.

"That moment we discovered the book was ruined. I saw a hummingbird flying down to where the three of us were kneeling. It flew around each of our heads, licking our foreheads with its tongue, before flying away."

"You never said. What do you think it meant?"

"It was a message. The gods wanted me to know that we had to work together." He paused. "So I shall have to face your father, then. But even if he consents, I don't know who from the church would marry us."

I gasped. "I do! In fact, we could go straight to him! Bishop Marroquín!"

"How's that possible?"

"He swore I could go to him for anything, anything at all, and he would help me. He gave me his word, as an apostle of Christ. But he'd probably do it anyway, to spite Father."

"Were there others there, who heard him?"

"Yes, there were witnesses."

"This could work!"

"If he married us, no one could or would say a word against us. We wouldn't even have to ask Father. We'd be free to write the book at our leisure."

The church bells pealed in the far distance. Juan said, "I must go back to Santa Cruz first. I might be a month, no more than two. I just need to . . . settle some business."

He didn't know that I knew exactly what his business entailed. He needed to untangle himself from Woven Tree and his daughter. I wished I could say I felt remorse, but it would've been a blatant lie.

"Will you run into Cristóbal?" I asked.

"It is possible, yes. I've finally tracked him down." He glowered at the floor.

"Tell him to write to me again, please. But tell him he must address the letter to Her Majesty, Lady Rojas." I smirked.

His face brightened like the sun in midday and made my heart soar. I touched my fingertips to his lips and turned away. When I looked back from the archway, he was gone.

CHAPTER 15

Santiago de los Caballeros, Guatemala
Summer 1553

More than two months passed. He'd said he'd be back by then, but perhaps we'd been too optimistic. Cristóbal had said it could end in war. I ought to have asked Juan for paper and ink to keep for my own purposes. I ought to have written to my cousin, to ask him to think of my happiness, and to help Juan with Woven Tree. But the Lord knew my head had been bouncing among the stars, and now it was far too late. Sometimes I pictured us living in the jungle, his body sparkling as we bathed together under a clear waterfall. In those moments, I thought we ought to have run then and there and left everything behind.

Isabel and Don Bernal visited often, too often for my taste. That evening, we all sat on the stiff-backed wooden chairs around the long table near the main library window. Behind us were shelves stacked with a few priceless leather-bound books and countless paper scrolls. Father's birthday was coming soon, so with needle and black thread I was embroidering a new shirt for him. Nothing too fancy, just a few twirls around the collar and sleeves. No flowers or vines, and definitely no color.

Don Bernal's leather case lay open in front of Isabel. The manuscript pages splayed out in front of her. She'd just sharpened her quill and dipped it in ink.

"So Moctezuma let you into Tenochtitlán on the eighth of November, 1519," she said. "You were describing the city."

Don Bernal closed his eyes. For a moment he was quiet, a smile of deep pleasure formed on his lips, and when he spoke, it was in a whisper. "When we saw these great cities, these beautiful stone temples towering from the heart of the lake itself . . . we were astounded. It seemed like an enchanted vision. Some of our soldiers asked if it were not a dream."

Isabel wrote. I dropped Father's shirt on my lap and stared at Don Bernal.

"It was all so wonderful, I don't know how to describe this first glimpse of things never heard of, or seen, or dreamt before. They housed us in spacious, well-built palaces of magnificent stone and sweet-smelling cedar wood. They took us to see their orchards and gardens, choked with fruit trees. They used long canoes to move through their causeways. Everything shone with lime and was decorated with marvelous stonework and paintings."

Don Bernal opened his brimming eyes and spoke to me. "I tell you, I stood looking at all these wonderful sights and I thought, *No land like it will ever be discovered in the whole world.*" He paused, covered his face, and shook his head. "But oh, how it pains me, it shatters my heart. For everything I saw then is overthrown; nothing is left standing."

My own eyes filled up. I gulped down the tight knot that blocked my throat and looked at Isabel. She also dabbed her cheek with a handkerchief.

I wanted to ask, *Why? Why did you destroy all this beauty, all this wonder?* But it was a stupid question, and I already knew the answer.

They had to ensure, they had to leave no shadow of doubt that a new age had begun, and since the Mexican Empire was the greatest power in the New World, they were sending a message to every other state too. A message written in blood and rubble.

We are the lords now.

"In truth, we were wary, as the people of Tlaxcala and many others had warned us that the Mexicans would kill us as soon as they had us inside." He smacked his forehead. "Truly, think about it, what men in all the world have shown such daring?"

"Indeed, Don Bernal, it borders on madness," said Isabel.

Don Bernal laughed. "The next day we marched until we were met by many caciques in very rich cloaks. The causeways were full of them. They told Cortés we were welcome and as a sign of peace, they touched the ground with their hands and kissed it. Then, the greatest Mexican lords went ahead to meet Moctezuma, and bring him in a rich litter."

"What was it like?" Isabel asked.

"You wouldn't believe. It had a marvelous canopy of green feathers, decorated with gold, silver, and pearls, all of which hung from the border, and the Lord Moctezuma himself, by Moses! He wore sandals of gold and precious stones. The other lords laid down their cloaks when he descended so that his feet would not touch the earth. None of them dared to look him in the face."

The door banged open and we leapt in our seats.

Father barged in with a couple of clerks, barking orders. "And then write to Ramirez, and tell him I shall not tolerate another burglary! This Ocelot person and his accomplices must be found. Tell him I shall personally deal with them!"

He spotted us and waved the young men out. "Back again, eh, Bernal? Where have you got up to? Have you reached the part where the Mexicans send you cowering to the hills?"

Don Bernal took this first strike in good nature and inclined his head. "Not yet, Alonso. We've only just reached Tenochtitlán."

"Ah, you poor souls don't know what's coming for you, then. A good and well-deserved whipping! To be honest, I'm not sure why you're bothering to tell this story, when Gómara already beat you to it."

Don Bernal's lips pinched as if he'd swallowed a lime. "I'm sure you're wise enough to spot a fairy tale when you read one."

Father's eyes sparkled, so I jumped in. "Sir, would you prefer venison or turkey for tonight's roast? I should like to inform the cook."

He ignored me and walked up to the table, laid a huge hand on the back of one of the empty chairs, and pointed the silver ram of his cane at Bernal. "You know who ought to have written a version of the conquest? Isabel Moctezuma, God rest her soul. Now *that* would've been an interesting read, eh? Did you know she set all her slaves free?"

"I'd heard," said Don Bernal, eyeing the ram with distaste.

"That's a statement if there ever was one. But no, there are idiots out there still trying to convince me that *Indígenas* prefer slavery to freedom."

Isabel shifted. "You're not serious, Don Alonso?"

"Serious? The amount of pestilence I hear would make cadavers of us all. Do you know what Lobo said to me when I went to check on him at the cathedral? He said it was wrong of me to separate *Indígenas* from their masters, because the Spaniards loved them like true sons, and what son wanted to be torn apart from his father?" He laughed.

"Truly, Alonso. He might be a bit rough around the edges, but that's a conquistador you mock." Don Bernal sat up.

"Then he said to me . . ." Father banged his cane on the floor in between gasps. "He said, 'I wouldn't have sold any of my slaves. That's how much I loved them. I wouldn't have sold *one*, not for a thousand pesos!'"

I let out a giggle. Isabel covered her smiling lips. Father guffawed and wiped his eyes.

Don Bernal got up and stormed out. "I've had enough."

"Ah, Bernal, don't be such a fussy old woman." Father rushed after him, still laughing.

"You have no respect for those of us who've bled so you can live in paradise!"

As the door closed, Father shot back, "Paradise or not, Lobo would chop off his own cock for a thousand pesos, don't deny it!"

Isabel and I looked at each other with wide eyes.

"Oh, I do apologize," I murmured. "Father is so unrefined."

A smile still played on her lips. She was in the middle of asking me to join her in tending to the sick at the convent tomorrow morning, when Father walked back in. His moustache twitched the way it did when he felt particularly gleeful.

"Sorry to break up your writing party, Isabel," he said. "But Bernal is such a dignified old hen, I simply can't resist ruffling him."

Isabel's lips pursed, though her eyes were lighthearted. She collected the papers and said, "You mustn't antagonize him so, Don Alonso. He's the governor, after all."

"Tut-tut. There's only one title I mind." He pointed above the window, where the imperial two-headed eagle of the Habsburgs was painted. "Anyway, *hija*, I need you to do something for me."

I swirled back around and blinked. "Yes, sir?"

"I need to discuss a private matter with you, regarding our family."

"Oh, did Beatriz write you a letter too?" Isabel asked.

I shot her an anguished, furious look. Father's head snapped between us. His brows set, and his face darkened to a dangerous shade of plum.

Isabel's eyes widened, and her pale cheeks flushed at the realization of the mistake she'd made, although she kept her composure. "Oh, Don Alonso, please do not be angry with Catalina. It was my fault. I delivered a letter from Beatriz, but I had no idea you were estranged, though it is my belief we must always forgive our family. For are we not all frail of character and in need of each other's grace and mercy?"

"Indeed." He gave her a wooden grin and spoke through his teeth. "It's the Christian thing, the honorable and right thing, to be as merciful as your nature permits. Now, if you will excuse us, I have much to discuss with my daughter."

We climbed up the staircase and walked into Father's room. He dragged his chair closer to the fireplace, sat down, and threw another log inside. The white cedar perfumed the small sitting room like sacred oil, and made the temperature nearly unbearable, but Father couldn't seem to stay warm ever since his stomach fever. I stood by the open window and looked down at the main square. I tried to still my nerves by gulping in the scent of fresh rain and observing the night. It was cloudy and getting dark. Only a spattering of people strolled about, carrying lanterns in their hands. The wet cobblestones refracted the shifting light in a hundred directions, like emerald eyes on a fly.

I didn't know what to say to him. For months we'd barely spoken. We ate in silence, except when he asked me about Isabel and Don Bernal, and I gave him curt answers.

We did not speak for ages. Father stared at the fire until it became too much for me. My throat was dry and itchy. I wiped my clammy palms on my skirt, looked around for the jug of water, and poured myself a glass.

"Would you like some water?" My voice was soft, but I may as well have shouted.

Father finally caught my eye, and the severity of his reproach sent a barb of pain to my core. "Father, please," I begged.

"Beatriz," he cut through, "has done nothing for this family except tear it apart. Why are you so adamant in wanting to speak to her? You of all people."

It was such a bewildering thing to say, I ran a hand over my face, unable to control my pent-up frustration. "She's my *sister*! Your *daughter*! Why are you so cruel to us? Keeping me like a prisoner, casting her aside, scaring her into never having a relationship with me. For running away? Father, she was young, and in love! It's not such a great crime!"

He goggled at me like I must've been dropped on my head as an infant.

"My God, you really don't see it," he whispered.

I blinked at him, confused at the look of pity and despair on his face. Then everything came together. As if a bucket of freezing-cold water had been thrown over my body, I stood still, soaking in a growing sense of horror.

It finally made sense. Why she'd abandoned us right after Mother was taken and never contacted me, why he'd been unable to let it go. Why he'd kept us apart.

"It wasn't a maid who betrayed her," I whispered.

Father groaned and rubbed his eyes. "No," is all he said.

I stared and stared as the truth sank its teeth into my throat. The memories of her last day engulfed me, one image after another. I had no strength to keep them at bay. My entire body began to shake, and an almighty pressure rose and built from my stomach, to my chest, to my head, until finally I let out a scream, a primal scream containing all the rage, the horror, the betrayal. I had screamed like that only once before—that day, that awful, godforsaken day, when the hooded men shoved her, standing, into a gaping hole in the ground.

The day they buried her alive in front of me.

I grabbed the clay jug and smashed it on the floor, then I threw all the glasses against the wall. They broke into a hundred pieces, but my fury wasn't spent. I rounded on him and shouted, *"You lied to me!"*

"What in the bloody hell else should I have said?" he shouted back, but his expression wasn't angry; he looked as shattered as the glass. "You loved her—you were only a little girl! And I thought it would be obvious from her actions, her flagrant escape, her shameful elopement to that—that base, common, good-for-nothing smith!"

My chest seized, but a part of me still couldn't believe it. "Why did she—*why?*"

Tears sprung to his eyes. He wobbled over to his desk and opened the drawer. Under a layer of scrolls, he took out an envelope containing a torn piece of paper, stained and browned with age. "The note she wrote the day she left."

I snatched it away, but my hands were shaking too hard, my eyes were full of tears, and I couldn't read it. I slammed it on the table. "What does it say?"

He was wheezing and pale, but he grabbed the bedpost for support, took a breath, and recited it by heart.

"Father, I picture you coming home to this devastation, and my heart bleeds. Only God knows the sorrow I feel, and yet, I am angry with you too. For you did not listen. You did not listen to me when she chopped the heads off those birds and burned them. You did not listen when she visited those ruins, or when I told you how she was always whispering to Catalina at night." His voice, a hollow tremble, faded past me. Everything looked blurry and distorted, like heat rising from the ground.

"I know this won't make it right, but I truly thought the priest would merely send Raxal away. I disliked her, true, how could I not dislike a stepmother so near my age, but I never wished her harm. I only wanted Catalina to be safe. I never thought they'd kill her—"

I covered my ears, tore at my hair, and screamed again, then pulled the dagger from around my ankle and stabbed the letter, over and over, screeching, "Well, they did kill her! You—killed—her!"

Father grabbed me from behind and wrestled the dagger out of my hands. It fell to the floor with the other fragments of mangled paper and broken glass. He pushed me to a chair, and I doubled over. Spasms ravaged my body. A keening sound escaped my throat, and it went on and on. He knelt by me and spoke, though I couldn't understand his words. He shushed me, and stroked my hair for a long, long time, maybe hours, until my breath evened out. I leaned back and looked at him through my tears.

He seemed so old, and his gaze was so stricken, that I grabbed his hand. His mouth opened and closed a few times, and I waited and waited for him to speak his truth, to explain, to share his grief with me, *our* grief. This one great loss that only he and I felt. Together, I knew we could bear it. We could heal this rift between us, if only he'd open up to me.

We both breathed, six, seven times.

He couldn't do it.

I felt like a door was slammed in my heart, as he retreated behind that great angry wall of his. His jaw clamped down, and his bushy silver eyebrows drew together.

He patted my arm and got up. There was a long pause where I just stared at the floor, gutted, bereft of both my parents.

"I ought not to have lied to you, and perhaps I've been too hard on you. I suppose, the truth is I don't want you to be tied to this land, for you won't be in it much longer. I shall return to Spain in two years, when my tenure is over. The emperor has granted my wish at last."

His voice washed over me. It took me a moment to register what he'd said.

"You want me to go with you?"

He grumbled in assent. "That is what I wished to speak to you about today. Our Spanish relatives are ready to receive us, and a great homecoming it shall be. When we return, I'll make a great match for you. Your noble birth is recognized in Castile, and so is my considerable service to the Crown."

I looked down again so he wouldn't catch my indifference, but I felt the weight of his silence. He expected gratitude, so I gave it, and tried to keep the lead out of my voice.

"You just need to keep out of trouble, hear me? Let's forget this ever happened. Let's just . . . start over tomorrow."

I nodded, or at least I thought I did. My head and my heart felt so heavy, my body so weak, I thought I would topple over to the ground. The whole night, the betrayal upon betrayal, the way the conversation had turned—everything weighed down on me as if the earth had shaken and the palace had collapsed on top of me. At some point I asked to go to bed, and he helped me. He kissed my hand and left. Afterward, I lay there with heavy lids, exhausted, yet unable to sleep. For hours I blinked slowly at the ceiling until, at last, I was pulled under, though I did not rest.

Instead, I dreamt of Mother.

I could see through her eyes, feel through her living heart, for she was alive, though not well. The hour was late, deep into the moonlit night. She had wrapped herself in a hood and walked to the ruins with only a long needle and a small earthen jug in her hand. For weeks her mind had been too clouded with grief and anxiety. Something terrible was coming, and she had to ward it off. Only one thing had that power.

Blood sacrifice. Bodily pain to eclipse the anguish in her soul and bring her clarity. It had been too long, too many years. Perhaps this was why she'd not heard from Lord Hacauitz in months. Beatriz and Catalina were asleep and safe in the villa. Her husband was away.

The risk was worth it.

She stood in front of her god's pyramid and said one prayer for the spirits of her murdered family, and another for her brilliant daughter, the light of her world.

Then, she bit down on her protruding tongue and, using her nose as a point of reference, drove the point of the needle clean through.

A low, garbled groan escaped from the depths of her taut body. Her tongue swelled and throbbed, each time sending a barb of agony that reverberated from her earlobes to her toes. So much blood poured out it only took a few beats before the jug was filled.

With tears drenching her face, she poured the blood on the base of the pyramid.

It was then that a set of arms clamped down on her shoulders. Two large monks. Had they been following her all along? How could she have missed them? She tried to fight back, but they lifted her up and carried her away in a whirlwind of vapor and smoke. There were fresh tears, and not from the pain in her mouth. She spent the rest of the night curled up in a stinking cell, terrified and cold, thinking of her baby, her baby. What would happen to her?

In the morning, with barely a trial, she was sentenced to death.

The hole was dug. Hacauitz returned one last time, to bring her strength and comfort, and with him came an ocean of fiery rage.

Wave after wave thrashed and pummeled her, the choices taken from her, the stories taken from her, her parents and brothers, her true love, her dignity, and her life, all taken from her. She stood tall and speared all those putrid Spaniards with her gaze, silently cursing every single one of the foul invaders, picturing their blood flowing like rivers and waterfalls. Anyone tainted by their poisoned seed would be purged from this land, her land. She wished it so; it would be so. Until she saw her little bird approaching, screaming, and took it all back.

She would not waste her last wish, the most powerful wish of her life, on *them*. She would never curse her daughter. Her last power, last thought, would be for her, about her, a blessing.

Hacauitz, hear me, she thought. *Protect my daughter. Help her to find love, meaning, and joy. To live a good life, surrounded by kindhearted people. To have strength and courage beyond bounds.*

She focused on that with all her might, trying to stay upright and keep the tears at bay despite the fact that her baby was howling in horror, trying to get to her. El Grande pulled her back. They should've run away together, all those years ago. At least he was with Catalina. Seeing him by her side brought some peace in that last moment, before the hooded men approached from behind.

"Close your eyes!" she shouted, then closed hers too.

By the time I woke, it was past midday. I was drenched in sweat and tears. The curtains around my bed were wide open. Agustina scuttled around, attempting but failing to be quiet. For a short time I watched her picking out my clothes and placing them inside a large trunk, but

I said nothing. I had been ravaged by the truth the night before, and it had left me feeling depleted and empty. Finally, when I could see she was not going to stop until everything I owned was inside that trunk, I sighed and asked her what she was doing.

She started and dropped a sleeve. "Señorita, are you unwell? You were crying out, but I could not wake you! May I fetch you some breakfast?"

I sat up. "No, thank you. What are you doing with my things?"

"Oh—the Lord Don Alonso says you're going away first thing tomorrow. He asked me to help you pack, miss. I didn't mean to disturb you."

I didn't respond. She helped me get dressed. I opened the door, blinked at the late afternoon light, and wondered how it was possible for the world to look so beautiful, when at its core there was only death. Like the fire that eventually would burst out of those volcanoes . . . in the end you were left with nothing but a smoking path of gray nothingness.

A clear path.

It came to me then, that I was made of that same fire. I was molten rock. I was the daughter of the great god Hacauitz, and maybe I'd been a fool, but that ended now. Only one thing mattered, to write the *Book of Council*. I'd write it alone if I had to, and I'd blaze whoever stood in my way.

I spotted Father walking out of the library toward the hall, Maloso in tow, so I called out. He waited for me to walk down the stairs and into the courtyard. I bowed and he kissed my cheek. The dog sniffed my feet and pushed his nose into my hand for an ear rub.

"Where am I going, Father?" I sat on the fountain edge, noting with a glance that it was devoid of orchids. Juan wasn't there like he said he would be. Perhaps he'd married Woven Tree's daughter after all and couldn't bring himself to face me. I shrugged to myself. If he couldn't burn the world with me, so be it.

I looked Father square in the eye and patted Maloso on the head.

He cleared his throat. "Well, after our conversation last night, I thought why not speed things along? You should go to Spain early, stay with our relatives, with my sister. She can introduce you to society in Granada."

I nodded. If I argued, he'd just dig in his heels, so I said, "I suppose there's no point in me wasting my time here any longer, when I could be building connections over there."

"Exactly!" He let out a breath. "I'm glad you see my reasoning. We'll be apart, of course. Two years is a long time, but you'll have a better time there, and your aunt will be glad to have you."

"I've always wanted to meet her." I pictured my aunt like I always had, a female version of Father, broad, towering, and imperious. She'd be my new mountain, my new cage.

Father smiled at me. "It's all settled, then. I've made the arrangements already. The coach will come tomorrow morning. I'll go with you all the way to the port in Veracruz."

"That's a relief. I wouldn't wish to go alone."

"I wouldn't dream of it!" He stroked my cheek with the back of his hand and I leaned into it, half expecting him to jump back, for his skin to be charred and blistered.

A young clerk popped out of the hall and said, "Don Alonso, we need you."

"Wait—may I call on Isabel, Father? To say goodbye?" He hesitated and I frowned. "She's been a good friend to me. To us."

"Of course, you're absolutely right. Victorino!" He snapped his fingers.

The great blond boor lumbered toward us and saluted Father in a most obsequious way. Maloso growled and I scratched under his jaw. I would miss him.

"Take my daughter to see Lady Isabel, if you will."

I curtsied, took my leave, and threw a last wistful look at the fountain before I turned around. As I marched out of the palace, I made a silent vow.

I would never set foot through those gates again.

CHAPTER 16

Santiago de los Caballeros, Guatemala
Summer 1553

Victorino and I stood outside Don Bernal's towering front door.

The street was busy. A one-eyed Tz'utujil man was selling birds in the corner, toucans for company, turkeys for dinner. Another vendor walked around with fragrant cobs of chargrilled maize in a woven basket. Their scent made my mouth water. A Spaniard carrying a pet spider monkey on his shoulder made his way toward them and ordered three.

"This ain't the lady's house," said Victorino from behind me.

"It's common knowledge that Lady Isabel and I call on Don Bernal often." I banged the brass knocker, the roaring lion.

Victorino didn't answer, but I felt the tension between us tighten. I shrugged it off and waited, noticing the clinking of far-off pickaxes chipping at stone and the rising cadence of a flute mid-chorus. The maid opened the door and blinked at me before staring at Victorino with a frown of confusion.

I cleared my throat and gave her a pointed stare. "May I come in, Carmen?"

"Oh! Of course, Lady Cerrato, my apologies."

"Thank you." I stepped over the barrier and heard the clunk of Victorino's boot advance, so I turned my head and said, "You may wait outside."

His hand blocked the door. He eyed me with utter mistrust, cocked his head at the maid, and said, "She's meant to be visitin' Lady Isabel— she ain't 'ere, is she?"

My heart skipped a beat, because I knew for a fact that Isabel was at the convent this morning, but luckily the maid only glanced at me once before saying, "She's in the drawing room, my lady. I'll take you up right away."

I glowered at Victorino. "Wait outside."

He grumbled and slammed the door shut.

We walked across the outer courtyard until we reached the house. At the entrance, we stopped to cross ourselves in front of a beautiful oil painting of Our Lady of Guadalupe, surrounded by fresh roses and burning incense. I asked the Virgin for strength and clarity, because I had only a vague, half-formed plan in my head of what I ought to do next.

"You're after Master Nico, aren't you, miss," Carmen said matter-of-factly, as though in answer to my prayer. She looked up at me with a clear, sharp expression. Her rare, amber eyes reminded me of an eagle's.

I nodded. "And I'm so grateful for your help. I wish I could give you something, but I haven't got—"

"Never you mind, my lady. We've all heard of that *tz'i'*." She used the K'iche' word for dog, and her lip curled. "I wouldn't dream of leavin' you alone with him."

I pressed my hand to my heart and thanked her in K'iche'. She nodded and escorted me to the empty drawing room.

"Don Bernal is taking his nap. He'll be awake in about half an hour or so." Her voice wavered, and I thought I saw a flash of something like pain, but I must've been imagining it because a moment later her clear expression was back on her face.

I thanked her again, and she ran off in search of Nicolao. I walked about the familiar room and ran my hand over one of the upholstered chairs, which was patterned in gold and green silk leaves.

All those moments spent in this room, listening to Don Bernal, felt like a lifetime ago, another me. I'd been a candle then, a petty flame sustained by a flimsy column of white wax, my light and movements constrained by Father's hands. Now, I could've lit up the sky, if I'd been born a man. But I had not. I was still Father's property, and even though I had no coin to repay even a maid's kindness, I now understood I had a little currency of my own. I had my hand, as Beatriz put it. Perhaps I ought to have thanked her for that knowledge.

Or perhaps all women learned this truth, one way or another.

His footsteps were quick, which I took as a good sign. I wasn't sure how to face him, so I didn't. I kept hold of the chair and looked steadily at the oak floor. He entered and I turned my ear toward him.

"It's really you," Nico said, voice ragged.

I nodded and peeked at him. I couldn't make out from his expression whether he was glad to see me or if he would've preferred to strangle me, but he'd grown thin and his beard had thickened. He looked older, more jagged.

"Why have you come?" It was a good question, one I could scarcely answer myself. Thankfully, he kept speaking. "Carmen said you are here for me, but I don't believe it."

"I don't blame you," I whispered. "I've done nothing but cause you pain."

He laughed. "You mean the flogging?"

"And the public humiliation," I added. "Let's not forget that."

"No, let's not. But that wasn't you, was it? That was your father. No, what caused me the most pain, yes, the worst pain of all . . . was your silence." He walked toward me. "No letter, no message, no sign of your face. Not even a whisper to Don Bernal meant for my ears. I know you saw him."

There was only the space of a body between us, but it felt like a gorge. I knew I had to cross it somehow to get what I wanted, to leave Father for good, to stay here, in this land, where the *Popol Vuh* was. I looked into his eyes. "You wish for a sign?"

Nico's face twisted with uncertainty. He glanced at my lips. I stepped out, though it felt like falling. There was no turning back. I wrapped my arms around him and pressed my mouth, my whole body, against him, the man with the wings I needed.

It was awful.

For a moment it seemed like he'd lose himself to me. He kissed me back, and his hands grabbed my hips, my rear. He pulled me close, before he shoved me away.

"What are you doing?" he said, breathing hard.

"What I should've done months ago! I saw everything from my window." I was shocked by the honest spike of pain, the struggle to keep tears at bay. "Every lash against your back. I was so sick with guilt I could barely get out of bed."

He hesitated and shook his head. "Yet you couldn't write me a single note?"

"If I told you my father locked all the ink away, would you believe me? Because he did! And I was banned from leaving the palace. You of all people should know what he's capable of. But if you don't believe me, ask Isabel. She saw how sick I was."

Nico bit his lip. "She did say you were unwell."

"In any case, I didn't send word because I thought—I thought you'd never want to hear from me again."

"Why now, then? I don't understand!" He ran a hand through his hair.

"I guess I—I've come to say goodbye. Go—look out the window, there's a guard waiting for me. I'm to be shipped off to Spain in the morning."

His brow furrowed. He walked to the window and stayed there, with his back to me.

"He thinks—Father thinks I'm saying goodbye to Isabel. I'll never see her again. But I just couldn't go without telling you."

"Telling me what?" He looked at my reflection in the glass.

I took in a breath, but the words choked back. My tongue stuck to the roof of my mouth; my voice abandoned me. It was too great a lie. I covered my face. I was going to fail, and for what, for whom? For a man who'd first cursed me and then abandoned me?

Had he not changed, though? I thought he had. Then why hadn't he returned?

Nico turned, walked back to my side, and grabbed my arms. He'd mistaken my anguish and thought it was for him. "Tell me what, Catalina?"

I leaned my head on his shoulder. He had a pleasant smell, a mix of lavender and grass. A memory of Juan flashed in the back of my mind. The day he'd asked me to be his.

I realized I never said it, so I said it to him then. I hoped with all that was left of my scorched heart that the messenger gods, the owls and the eagles, the fireflies and the fish, would deliver my message to him, carry it through air and water, and whisper it in his ear while he slept. *Q'anti*, I thought. "I love you," I said.

The grip on my arms softened and he started to kiss my temple, my neck, and my jaw. It was only when he reached my lips that I remembered he wasn't, he'd never be, my Juan.

"If I go back to the palace now, Father will lock me in the cellar, and we shall never see each other again." Nico and I leaned on the writing desk. His focus had slipped once he'd forgiven me. His attention, his hands, kept sliding away, trying to loosen the lace on my bodice, reaching under my skirt.

I let him get as far as my knee before I stood and rushed away, looking scandalized. "Sir, you shall not take advantage of me," I said.

Nico's lips parted. "My love, I wouldn't dream of it!"

"I'm trying to tell you something very serious."

He stood straight up. "I'm sorry, pray forgive me."

"We must get married, elope, right away. It's the only way we can be together." *It's the only way I can stay and fulfill my promise.*

His brows knotted together. "Of course. You're absolutely right."

"Bishop Marroquín has pledged to help me. We must send word to him immediately, and we must find a way to get to the cathedral without Victorino spotting us."

"There's no need to go to the cathedral, my love. Don Bernal has a small consecrated chapel on the ground floor."

I clasped my hands. "That's wonderful!"

Nico ran toward me and lifted me in the air. "It *is* wonderful, isn't it!" He forgot himself and kissed me again, until I gently pushed him back.

"Nico, we must send word."

"I'll go. I wouldn't trust anyone else with this matter." He kissed my hands and left.

I watched him run out from the window. The sky was streaked light pink. Soon it would be dark. I was running out of time. Everything had to be ready for his return.

I opened the door and said, "Carmen?"

She didn't answer, so I looked around the drawing room and tried to find a bell. But there was no bell, so I coughed and sang out, "Carmen?"

"Who's there?" Don Bernal's garbled voice echoed from downstairs.

"Don Bernal! It's Catalina. I'm terribly sorry to have come unannounced." I poked my head out into the stairs.

"My dear! To what in the heavens do we owe this pleasure?" His tone was thick with surprise.

"Oh, sir! Surely you can guess?"

He could. "My child, well—congratulations! I thought you'd forgotten my poor tutor, to be honest." He started to climb the stairs, his breath puffing.

"No, I never did. But you know my father," I said with a slight quiver.

"That I do, that I do. Whatever has he said about the affair? I can't imagine he's happy."

I waited for him to reach me and took his hand. It was as rough and calloused as his voice, but warm. "Don Bernal, that's why I'm here. I need your help, desperately."

He sighed, his shoulders and neck sagging. For once he wore no frill collar, and the great glossy scar near his windpipe was visible, a remnant of the Mexican spear that almost ended his life and forever altered his voice.

"My dear, what can I do? I'm just a poor, blind man, too old to fight. Too old to—"

"Bear witness?" I smiled. "I think not. Nico shall return at any moment, with Bishop Marroquín."

His head snapped up, his eyes piercing mine like arrows on a target.

"And I must beg use of your chapel. Please, Don Bernal." I knelt and pressed the back of his hand to my forehead. "Will you help me?"

Not too long after, we heard the parley of male voices arguing outside. I rushed to the window and spotted four heads, dyed blue with the hues of dusk. They slipped past the heavy wooden doors.

"Let's get this over with," said Don Bernal with a strange, weary air. Perhaps he was arming himself for future battles with my father, for they were sure to come.

He led me down the stairs. The men were still arguing, and Victorino's insipid voice asked for me. He said it was getting late, and begged pardon from the lord bishop, who remained silent. Nicolao laughed and uttered something too muffled for me to hear.

Don Bernal guided me away from the main entrance, through the dark dining chamber. We nodded at Carmen, who was lighting candles. I thought perhaps I'd imagined it, but her eyes seemed red and swollen. It could've been anything, but I hoped with a pang of remorse that it had nothing to do with Nico.

Don Bernal took a candle and instructed Carmen to set the table and beg the cook to whip up a celebratory feast for tonight. He then walked out the back door, into the small patio where Nico and I had first met.

The parrots were asleep inside their cages, but bats clicked softly above in the sky. We walked past the caged birds to an arched door. He handed me the candle and lifted a key from a golden chain around his neck. At that moment, the bishop emerged from within the house.

His face was solemn. I gave him a reverent bow.

"Your Excellency," I said, still bent and with my eyes fixed on his feet. "I am not worthy to call upon your service."

He gave me his hand and I kissed his gold ring. "Rise, my child. Let us go in the chapel so you might confess your sins, and go forth into marriage with a clean spirit."

We entered the vaulted chapel, which Don Bernal lit and closed behind us. The domed walls were painted with a beautiful fresco of Jesus in various states of agony as he made his way along the *Via Dolorosa*. The gilded altar, covered with a red silk cloth and perfumed with dried sandalwood and figs, took up half the room. There were only two velvet cushions on the floor to kneel on, and so we did. We crossed ourselves and lifted our hands up to the exquisitely carved crucifix on the wall in front of us.

I took a deep breath in preparation for my confession when he murmured, still gazing up at the altar, "I swore to help you, and I intend to keep my word. But I must ask you to consider the consequences."

"I have, my lord. I know it is a great favor I ask, and that it puts you in a precarious situation."

"And what of your father?"

I bowed. "This will hurt him dearly. I wish it were not so."

"The tutor said Don Alonso planned to take you to Spain tomorrow, hence the urgency."

I nodded. He studied my face for a moment, then reached out and brushed my shoulder blade. Perhaps he meant it as a comforting gesture, but I felt the sinews in my back tensing in response, and my hairs stood on end.

Juan's necklace flashed in my mind. Bishop Marroquín had gifted it to Father. He must've obtained it, either as a gift or purchase, from Alvarado. He was complicit, then, in its theft, in the demise of the K'iche'. He might not have come to these lands wielding a sword, but he was no less a conquistador.

One of bodies, one of souls, Mother said.

"There are other paths, Catalina," he whispered. His warm breath wafted past my cheek. It smelled of red wine and something curdled, like a mix of goat cheese and pickled onions. "The nunnery, for instance. You'd be well looked after. You'd be safe and loved."

My shoulder gave an infinitesimal twitch, and his hand withdrew and rubbed down his silver goatee instead. His face was even, impassive, without trace of balefulness or leer, but the unease in my core remained.

"I thank thee for your kind thoughts and gracious offer, my lord," I said as politely as I could, "but I have made my choice."

"The tutor it is. Let's not delay any further."

He made a quick job of my confession, then got up with a slight groan. I stood also, and watched as he opened the door. Nicolao stood behind it.

He wore a fine green cape over his shining breastplate. His sword was by his side. He glowed with such eagerness I felt a stab of pity. I told myself it was not so bad, that most married without love, and at least I'd be good to him, I'd repay the favor in kind.

The bishop walked past me, back to the altar, and I extended my hands. Nico took them both in his, and the ancient rite began.

It was a blur.

Only the bishop's singsong Latin and the flickering candlelight stood out in my mind. I felt like I floated the entire time. Not from joy or pleasure, nor grief or sorrow. Thoughts of the previous night drifted through my head, Father's stricken face, Beatriz's letter, Mother's sorrow and anger, her dying wishes for me. It seemed so long ago. I vaguely wondered what Juan would make of this, but I was immune to any feeling.

The fire had burned out, and the only thing left was vapor.

It was only a few hours later, when we were all sitting back around the dining table, when my head was swimming from too much wine and the men's faces were flushed with triumph and ale, that Victorino finally barged in. Don Bernal shot out of his chair, quick as an adder, and the guard groveled an apology.

"It's late, m'lady." He ground out the last word. "I need to take you home, right now."

I indicated to Nicolao next to me, who'd also stood up, and said, "Pardon me, sir. I'd forgotten about you! But see now, I *am* home. My love, this is Victorino, a palace guard. Victorino the guard, meet my husband, Nicolao. He's a tutor, did you know that?"

Victorino stared as if struck by lightning. He swelled like a storm cloud.

In my haze, I found his shock terribly amusing. I laughed and raised my glass to him.

A mistake.

In a blink and a roar, he had me by the neck. He threw me to the floor, and my head smashed against something sharp and solid. The pain was explosive, blinding. It deafened me to everything but a searing, ringing white noise.

A hot and heavy weight fell on my chest. I wanted to scream, but I could only gasp out for air. *God help me,* I thought, before all turned black.

CHAPTER 17

Sololá, Guatemala
Summer 1554

My thoughts rose slowly, like stems growing out of dormant bulbs after a long, cold winter. Poor, weak stems, searching for the sun underneath their pile of red soil.

"Guh-grass," I whispered. "Buh-blanket, breeze . . . buh-butterflies, butterflies, butterflies. Sunset." I looked out far below, at the great body of water. Not the sea. The word escaped me, like a phantom. It played hide and seek around my sluggish tongue. I'd learned to let it hide, to distract myself and wait for it to come to me in its own time.

It was easier said than done. Sometimes I broke into a fury of frustration. The last time it had happened, I tore my room apart. The cost had been horrific, as for days afterward, I could barely get out of bed. The headaches had been so intense I couldn't hold down food. So I'd learned that I had to be patient.

A string of ducks flew overhead, making a racket. The scent of burning fields was in the air, the sign of a new harvest being prepared. I sat on a woolen blanket laid out on the grassy lawn, looking toward the cliff edge. Below was the great pool of water, surrounded by gray, misty peaks and smoking volcanoes. There was a clinking sound and muffled footsteps from the villa behind me.

Aha, there was the lost word. "Lake," I said, and repeated it four times more.

"That's right, sister. Lake Atitlán," said Noble River. He placed a platter of cold meats, cheese, and bread on top of the wool blanket, opened a bottle of red wine, and poured it into a silver goblet. Then he sat next to me and watched me eat. The doctor had said the wine was good for headaches, and that I had to drink two glasses a day.

Once I'd swallowed every last bite, we practiced saying words aloud. Things we could see. Flowers, clouds, volcanoes. Canoes, waves, pebbles, birds.

He had endless patience for me, Noble River, with his solid arms and warm chest. Just like his mother, my beloved Cook, he'd kept me clean and fed me with his own hand when I'd scarcely been able to lift my own. Sometimes when we were alone in the garden, like today, we chatted in K'iche'. The words came easier to me that way, but not like before.

"More news from the market," he said. "Another encomienda was raided last night; all the silver was stolen, all their jewels, books, muskets, coins, and candlesticks. The Spaniards have set a bounty of five thousand pesos on the man's head."

"Who is man?" I asked. I understood everything, but speaking was another matter.

"Well, they say he's Maya, but he's yet to be seen or heard, let alone be caught in the act. At least that's what the Spanish say. I think there are those of us who might know, but who would turn him in?"

"Five thousand is much, a lot," I attempted to say.

He shook his head. "What he's giving us is priceless. You should hear the way the townsfolk speak of him. They say he's a nawal, a great ocelot spirit that leaps through the trees, summoned by the gods to humiliate the Spaniards and tear down their vainglory. Some say he's the ghost of Tekum Umam, the K'iche' general who was slain by Alvarado, come back to seek revenge. They say he rides on the back of his beloved quetzal, spreading the stolen treasure among the poor and downtrodden."

"Is good story," I said, smiling at him, feeling grateful for his presence, his help.

He had moved from Santa Cruz with his family to live with us, at my husband's humble estate. Apart from his wages, we'd also given him a large milpa, cut into the hillside leading to the lake, to keep for himself.

I waved at Noble River's oldest son, One Deer. He carried a crossbow slung over his shoulder and whistled old songs as he pulled weeds away from the clumps of pink amaranths growing near the far-right wall, a stone contraption as tall as three men standing on top of each other. After he finished weeding, he fed the pigs and chickens, and watered the cacao shoots Nicolao had planted.

After lunch, Noble River helped me walk to my room for my afternoon nap. Two hours, the doctor said I needed to sleep each day. Except I never did when I was supposed to. The moment Noble River left my room, I limped over to my desk and tried to write. These were the most trying times, when I was most likely to burst into a maddening rage. When I had all the paper, all the ink I'd ever desired, but the words wouldn't come. Those words I'd known all my life, the songs and verses, the myths and stories, as beloved as childhood dolls, slipped away, like silver fish darting into the depths of the great lake in the distance.

If only I had the original! Sometimes Noble River or his wife said something in K'iche' and bits of the story flowed out, clear as light, and I had to make excuses to be taken in all haste to my chamber. I'd heard them guess that it was because I'd not regained full control of my bladder, which I had, thanks to all that's holy. But I'd not bothered to correct them because it was a convenient excuse in more ways than one, like not having to share a bed with the husband I couldn't remember marrying, for example.

I looked down at the paper. My notes were scribbled in what could've been a seven-year-old's hand. Half of it was scratched out or written around blots of ink, and parts of it had been ruined by tearstains.

The maiden Blood Moon gave birth to Hunahpu and Xbalanque. They all went to live with their grandmother. Then a talking rat found them, and told them where their father's ball and equipment were. Their grandmother had hidden it, because she was afraid they'd share the same fate as her vanquished sons. But the hero twins were mischievous and bold. They found the equipment, swept the ball court, and began their game, playing until the lords of Xibalba heard them.

Three weeks, it had taken me to write that. Three weeks, and I knew I'd missed so much. I thought constantly of writing to Juan, to remind him I'd returned his necklace, and beg him to hand me back my mother's manuscript, so I could have a guide for my thoughts. I ought to have at least explained why I'd done what I'd done. But each time I dipped my pen in ink, my nerve failed. The same went for Cristóbal. We were so close. Sololá and Panajachel were only a few hours away from each other by foot, but I always hesitated. I couldn't bear to imagine what they must've thought of me, and I felt too afraid to find out.

A chorus of low, reverberating croaks from nearby toads reminded me of the messengers sent to deliver the message from Xibalba, and I wrote: *The demons sent a louse, but the louse was swallowed by a toad. The toad was swallowed by a snake, who in turn was swallowed by a laughing falcon. "You are to come in seven days," spoke the falcon.*

The twins hurried back to their grandmother, who cried.

It was bad. A terrible pain knocked on the side of my head, along the great scar that twisted from behind my left ear to the crown of my skull. I wished Mother would speak to me, tell me what to do, what to write, but it was no use. Her voice had completely left me. My eyelids sagged and drooped from exhaustion and grief. I hid the papers beneath the false bottom of the drawer, which I'd asked Noble River to make for me, and dragged myself to bed.

That night all the animals in my dream, from toads to swallows, pumas, mice, dogs, and lizards, even fleas, whispered to each other, whispered for help. There were only two words, screeched and hissed and growled in all directions.

Nija'ib', come!

I woke to a man's murmuring voice and a gentle pat on my shoulder. Noble River stood next to my bed. I rubbed my eyes and looked around my bedroom, except it didn't look like my bedroom. Where was I? Had I missed something? My brain felt cloudy and thick, as if too much cream had been poured into my hot cacao, when I'd wanted none at all.

"It's all right, sister," Noble River said in K'iche', as if he sensed my confusion. "You got married a year ago, but then fell and hit your head. You woke up two months later, and we've been helping you since then. You are now in Sololá, in your husband's house. Your brother is here to look after you."

He looked so much like Cook, with his round copper-brown face and full, downturned lips, warm eyes, and peppered hair. It seemed too strange for a moment, to think I was married. Where was this husband of mine anyway? But more important, where was Ma, Cook? I asked him, though the memory dawned on me the moment the words left my lips. Still, Noble River answered.

He took my hand and placed it over his heart. "Ma is here." He pressed it over mine. "And Ma is here too."

I sighed and thanked him, and in my mind I thanked her too, for sending her son to aid me. Later I would light a candle for her and burn some incense. I looked to the window and remembered my dream. I clasped Noble River's hand tightly, which startled him.

"Brother, I need you."

His brows knitted together.

"My cousin, Cristóbal." I lowered my voice.

"The troublemaker," he said, and knelt beside me.

"No, he helped. Like Ma helped with—secret, important, for K'iche'."

His eyes flickered from my writing desk to the door. He nodded. "You know? Ma told you?"

"This is why I have come," he answered, "for sister to heal, and for the *Popol Vuh*."

For a long moment I couldn't speak. "Please. I need Cristóbal, for *Popol Vuh*. Can you search for him, in Panajachel?"

There was a knock on the door. He got up and opened the curtains. The whooshing sound almost hid his last words. "Your husband's due to return soon. Order fish, so I have an excuse to go to the market there."

His wife entered the room. She carried a load of folded linen and other clothes in her arms, and she set it down by my desk. Her white blouse, patterned with little red birds, was cinched by a leather belt into a woven blue skirt that fell to her ankles.

She helped me dress. My clothes were simple, more like hers, easy to move in, easy to breathe in. A long black cotton skirt, and a silk shirt, embroidered with colorful flowers and Spanish lace. If I'd taken out the lace and worn a tzut cloth over my head, I could've been mistaken for pure Maya. Or perhaps not. Even when I sat, I was a full inch taller than she.

They had a routine for me. Each day, after breakfast, I walked four times around the estate to strengthen my legs. Afterward, it was time for Noble River to help me read for an hour. Usually, I fell asleep, and he let me rest for a short time. Then, I went back outside for some fresh air and painted or knitted if I felt like it. I would've preferred to do needlepoint, but it was too difficult for me. I could hardly sew a button.

In the evening, we returned to the villa to have lunch and write my letters. I wrote to Isabel, or Don Bernal, or my father, who never responded. No one had to explain why; that part was obvious. Finally, we took another four turns around the house, had dinner, and watched the sunset before bed. I always fell to the bed, exhausted.

That day, I stood on the porch and watched as the sun faded behind the mountains and turned the lake pink. There was a commotion by the gate, but I, delighted by the flickering dance of fireflies over a wave of cricket song, remained in place. It was only when his voice reached me that I turned and peeked through the gap in the blinds.

Nicolao changed each time I saw him. His face became more angular, which suited him, and his skin became a shade darker and his hair lighter from all the time spent riding. His eyes were unchanged, hazel green and as warm as ever. He took off his riding gloves and hat, shook both One Deer's and Noble River's hands, and asked after the smaller children. They always looked forward to his visits, for he often sat on the porch during the evening and told stories from the *Iliad* and the *Odyssey*. He spoke of the brave deeds of Heracles and Achilles, or recited whichever Greek myth took his fancy. With bright faces they begged for more. They'd already grown to know and love these faraway gods a hundred times better than the ones in their own backyard.

That day he bought me a box of *bizcocho*, and the men a whole lamb to share. He'd once overheard Noble River say that lamb was the only good thing to have come from Europe, and it had become a running joke between them.

Nico asked the men where I was. I quickly turned and positioned myself away from the window, so he wouldn't know I'd spied on him. He approached me with caution, the way one would an injured kitten or a thundering lunatic. Lord knew I'd given him plenty of reasons to be wary, which is why I felt it was my turn to set him at ease, but not too much, for I was afraid he would ask for that which I was hesitant to give.

"Welcome back," I said with a smile.

"Thank you," he responded, and I didn't imagine the outbreath of relief, the way the creases in his forehead disappeared.

"Your journey, was good?"

"Very good, thank you. I joined a trio of encomenderos on their way to Chichicastenango, so I was not alone."

I nodded. We paused, and I looked back at the fireflies and tried to force more words out of the mud trap my head had become.

"I've brought you a letter from Isabel." He flapped his cape aside and took the letter out from the pocket in his doublet, the one closest to his heart.

I beamed and said, "How kind she is to write me always."

Then I felt a pang of sadness because I realized no one else wrote to me. Only Isabel did, and sometimes Don Bernal, though it was in her writing. But not my father, not even Cristóbal did. Maybe he'd not heard about my injury, but how could he have not?

I cast the thought aside, for it filled me with pain.

"Do you wish me to read it to you? Has your sight improved at all?"

"Yes, better," I said. "Everything's better, thanks. I can read myself now, easy."

He smiled, though it was a tad subdued, tinged with something that looked a lot like sadness. Perhaps he'd enjoyed the times we'd spent, heads pulled together, as we read my letters. Our only intimacy, and now I'd drawn the line even there. I felt that familiar thorn of guilt I'd come to associate with Nicolao. I told myself I ought to love him, to give him more, this man, this good man who'd given me everything I didn't deserve.

"Well, if you need help, please ask." He handed the letter back to me.

"You're kind," I said, and there was an ache in my chest, because it was the truth.

Nico helped me back into the house. "What news I bring! Mary Tudor has married Philip the Prudent. England is finally moving back into the Pope's embrace."

"That is relief," I said.

"Indeed, there have been celebrations everywhere." We walked arm in arm all the way to my chamber, where we lingered.

Ask him in, I thought, *get it over and done with. Who knows, you might enjoy it, and you like him well enough—trust him even.* I took a deep breath and opened my mouth to say the words when he raised his hand to cover up a loud yawn.

He apologized. "My goodness, it's been a long trip. I'm exhausted."

"Oh—of course . . ." My shoulders dropped, grateful for the excuse.

Nico thanked me and gave me a sweet kiss on the cheek before he walked away. His chamber was at the opposite side of the house, past the dining room and kitchen. I entered my own. The warm imprint of his lips lingered. It was nice, but was it any nicer than what one felt for a friend? Or any warmer? It was certainly nowhere near as warm as one of Juan's.

Even the thought of one of those spoiled the competition, if there was any.

I reminded myself that there need not be. Feelings or no feelings, at some point, probably soon, I would have to fulfill my duty as his wife. Other men would not have been nearly so patient as Nico, so understanding. I was fortunate, truly blessed.

I could not take that for granted.

Noble River had kindly lit the candles around the room. His wife would be here soon to help me out of my clothes. I drew up a chair and opened Isabel's letter.

August 25, 1554

Dearest friend,

I cannot express the joy I feel whenever I receive one of your letters. I believe it when you say you're improving—I can see it in the stroke of your hand. Don Nico also paints a most favorable picture of your progress, for which we all give everlasting praise to our blessed Lord Jesus Christ. Oh my dear, I simply cannot bear to think of how we could've lost you! Thank goodness for Don Bernal, for his razor-sharp wit and even sharper sword. I know I say it every time, but I'm so glad he stabbed that barbarian. The things we've heard about him since—well, it won't do to terrify you. But let's just say, I am sure Victorino is in Hell, where he belongs.

Speaking of scoundrels, the jury has cleared our disgraced lord treasurer of all charges. Lobo claimed innocence to the fact the goods were stolen and used this Ocelot figure as a scapegoat. Pedro, of course, is livid. He believes a fair bit of gold was exchanged to ensure his release, and since they will be hanging the guitar player and other members of the gang, most neighbors feel justice has been served. "And anyway," I hear them say as if to excuse him, "Javier is a born gentleman!" What nonsense. We all know he is the son of a tanner. Anyway, he's back in power once again, as if nothing happened at all. An appalling precedent has been set. Even your father fears for the future of this government.

Speaking of your father, I have broached the subject of a reconciliation with you, but he is still rather unwilling to discuss it. It does not help that Bishop Marroquín asks him for news of you at every opportunity. I do hope he does it out of kindness, but I am starting to think otherwise. Regardless, for both your sakes, I shall continue to intervene. I know he misses you desperately, as do I. In fact, I wonder if you might feel up to a journey anytime soon? It would be wonderful to see you again. You are welcome at any time.

Anyway, I must be off. Don Bernal is hoping we can finish writing of the Night of Sorrows today, when the Mexicans defeated us in battle. It has been a most difficult account for him to describe, for most of his comrades were killed. Alas, it must be done.

Please write soon, although I am sure it is an arduous task. In the meantime, I shall continue to pray for

*your ongoing recovery and remain always, your most loyal
friend,*

    Isabel Saavedra de Ramirez

◆ ◆ ◆

Nicolao stayed for a fortnight. We had to delay Noble River's trip to the market in Panajachel because of all the lamb we had to eat. Nothing else happened, except for the day we all helped One Deer deliver some piglets, and another day when Nico and I went down the hill through our own secret path to the lakeside.

The children accompanied us. We watched them spend the afternoon jumping off a leaning palm and splashing into the water. Nico swam out far until we could barely see him. Strangely, I found myself gasping whenever a wave crested over his head. I shouted at the kids to stay in the shallows, and when he returned, I threw a shawl at him.

"What's the matter?" He dried his hair.

I didn't respond. I couldn't quite understand it myself, but I kept thinking, *What if he died? What would happen to us? Would we end up destitute and begging for a place to live, like Beatriz?* All the terrible memories of her flashed through my mind.

The night of Father's revelation was the last memory I had, and it was the first thing I'd remembered when I'd woken up, although the sick, twisted spike of betrayal had been quickly replaced by horror at the realization that I couldn't move.

If not for Nico and Noble River, I wouldn't be able to do half of what I could do now, and that was still limited. I couldn't even write the *Popol Vuh*. I needed Cristóbal, and I needed him now.

That morning, I ordered fish.

Noble River's wife gave me a strange look, but said no more. She helped me to the small rectangular breakfast table, wooden, like the four chairs around it and the beams on the roof. The hall was a modest size and full of light from the two sets of open doors, one of which led to the veranda with its lake views; the other was our main entrance. Nico had painted the walls a soft mustard color and hung several ceramics and woven K'iche' cloths as decorations. Our ferns and fig trees, in pots of cerulean blue, swayed with the breeze.

I dipped my bread into the hot chocolate Noble River's wife had poured for both Nico and me and said, "I sorry about yesterday."

He snorted. "Oh, you've done wilder things, believe me. Like when we were still at Don Bernal's and Carmen was helping me wash you, and you grabbed her wrist and tried to dance with her, right in the bathtub." He laughed. "You couldn't stand, of course, but you were singing at the top of your lungs. It sounded K'iche', but Carmen said it was gibberish."

My skin flared hotter than the cup of chocolate shaking between my hands.

His smile faded when he noticed the look on my face. "Oh. That's not amusing at all, is it." He shook his head and sighed. "Forgive me, I spoke without thinking."

He rose, kissed my forehead, and walked off. He spent his last day on his own, playing his guitar by the lake. Noble River was too busy running errands, so I sat alone on the porch and penned my reply to Isabel, which took hours. When Nicolao returned in the evening, his shirt was sticking to his chest, and the skin of his forearms where he'd rolled his sleeves was tomato red. I invited him to sit by me, and poured him a glass of water.

"Thank you," he said, and took off his straw hat. He didn't meet my eyes. With care, he leaned his guitar against the oak pillar, wiped his glistening forehead, and took a sip.

"I hope you not still unhappy from morning," I murmured, wanting to clear the air between us. "I'm fine. No need for sorry. I grateful for all you done for me."

He stared at the lake. "It was my duty to look after you."

I sighed and murmured, "Yes, but you done kindly."

Nico glanced at me with a small smile. "You are very sweet." He cleared his throat. "Now, I'm afraid I've wasted too much time down by the lake, and have much to do. Do you have any letters you wish me to take? I shall leave before dawn."

I nodded and handed him the letter for Isabel. "Will you be gone long?"

"Perhaps a month, it's hard to say." He searched my face, and I studied his. I think we were both looking for a sign, a stirring in the air between us, a sparkle, a closeness, but the only thing I felt was an uneasy flutter in my gut. I realized he was slipping away from me, and for some reason, this thought frightened me. I tried, clumsily, to lean in. Even though I did not love him like I loved someone else, I was with him now. I cared for him. I wanted to try for him. I thought maybe he would kiss me, but he pulled away.

"So much to do." He gave a nervous laugh.

"Oh yes, of course." I gave him a bright smile back, the type of smile that had once fascinated him, and wished him luck. He blinked, kissed my hand, and then he was gone.

The next morning, I had no time to think of the exchange, however, because Noble River barged in as the rooster crowed, smelling of fish and mud.

He shook me awake. "I ran to Panajachel this morning."

I sat up and rubbed the sleep from my eyes. "What time you left?"

"Same as the señor, listen—"

"You soaked!"

"It rained. Hush," he whispered. "I met a man called Jun Kaaj today."

I gasped and sat up.

"Yes, he said he knew about you, and about me too. That's why he spoke to me, and agreed to take me where your cousin was hiding." He grinned. "I was right."

"Right? What?"

"Your cousin *is* a troublemaker. He's the one they call Ocelot."

CHAPTER 18

Sololá, Guatemala
Autumn 1554

Cristóbal told Noble River that he would visit in several weeks, on the Lajuj B'atz', a meaningful date, for the B'atz' was the night of destiny.

We didn't know what to expect, so Noble River and I simply acted as normal as possible around his wife and the children. On the appointed night, I asked Noble River's wife to help me to bed a little earlier and gave her the rest of the evening off, which was not unusual.

When the door closed, I got out of bed and watched through a gap in the blinds as she headed back to the edge of the hill, where Noble River had built himself a decent-size lime-and-mortar house. Hours later, when I was sure the family was asleep, I opened the window, sat on the sill, and waited. I tapped my foot and strained to see the shadow of any unusual movement, to hear a swish or the whisper of a foot over grass or grit.

Instead, I nearly let out a bloodcurdling scream when Cristóbal appeared in the doorway to my chamber, bow and arrow slung from his back. He leapt to grab my arm before I tumbled out the window, and pulled me back inside, wheezing a laugh.

"Careful," he said, and tried to pull me into a hug.

I slapped his arms away. "You frighten me, stupid!"

"Language, cousin. I do not wish you to give my friends a bad impression."

I pulled the sarape tight around my bosom, suddenly very aware of my loose shift and bare feet. "Friends?"

He was too busy studying my room to answer straightaway. His eyes lingered over the three paintings of white orchids hanging opposite my bed, and his fingers trailed the handsome feather quill on my writing desk. He ran a hand over his chin and smiled in satisfaction as he studied himself in the looking glass.

"What mean, f-friends?" I asked again. If he noticed any of the difficulties I was having with my speech, he never made even a small sign of it.

"Well, only one's inside the house. The others are keeping a lookout." He poked his head back out and beckoned to someone in the hallway. A man who looked to be about the same age as Cristóbal, with a sweet, round face, materialized without a sound. He wore striped trousers and carried a sword by his side.

"This is Jun Kaaj's son, Pablo. He's my . . . right-hand man."

Pablo gave me a shy nod, which I returned. Cristóbal took me by surprise. He beamed at Pablo in a way I'd never seen, and teased him in Kaqchikel. The young man thumped him on the shoulder, then turned back to take up his watch.

"So, am I Ocelot's new victim?" I teased in K'iche'.

His smile vanished. He glared and sized me up. "Have you stopped paying your servants? Do you beat and rape them? Are you guilty of pillaging our treasures, of murder?"

I stepped away from his rage, bewildered and hurt. I hardly recognized him. He'd never spoken like this to me, never looked at me so cold and hard. "So you a judge now?"

"An executioner too." Cristóbal's voice had an edge I'd never heard. It gave me pause.

"I—I am sad to hear it." I reached out and touched his chest. "Just think, you were going to be monk."

He sighed, walked to the edge of my bed, and dropped down on his bottom.

"They're no better."

I sat next to him and looked down at my fingernails, unsure of what to do. We'd never not gotten along before, not once. It was almost as disorienting as when I woke up each morning and Noble River reminded me that almost a whole year was missing from my memory.

"It's just, well, there have always been slaves and nobles in our lands," he whispered. "We've always been at war with each other. K'iche' versus Kaqchikel, Mexican against Tlaxcalan. We fought for the gods, to appease them. For our kings, to glorify their power. But this, the greed, the savagery and injustice that exist now."

"Oh, cousin," I murmured.

"Once Godfather cast me off, I realized how much he'd shielded us. He's tried, I'll give him that, but those questions I asked you," he huffed. "I promise you, only one in a hundred encomenderos can answer *no*."

I nodded, my mind empty of words. I wished so badly that my two halves could, if not love, well, at least mind each other better.

Cristóbal shuffled closer and grabbed my hand. "Noble River says your husband is one of those rare men."

"I lucky," I mumbled.

"What, is that all? No gushing? No fanning?"

"Guess I just modest." A growing sense of discomfort was making me lose the little control I'd gained over my words, and my head began to feel fuzzy again, sluggish.

He studied me for a long time. "When I heard you'd married, I thought perhaps he might've stolen your heart."

I shook my head. "Heart was stolen already."

Cristóbal groaned. "Don't tell me Juan was speaking the truth." I gave him a guilty look and he grimaced. "Catalina, I thought you hated him! You *told* me you did! And when I last saw you both together, in the forest. Well, I could tell his feelings had changed, but you were so hesitant, so subdued! I thought you were being polite, so I—I fought against him, when he asked for you."

"What?"

He must've missed the flash of rage that crossed my face, because he continued. "I fought so hard, delayed him so much, I think he's more angry with me than with you."

I snatched my hands out of his. He blanched.

"I c-cannot believe. This your f-fault? I marry a man I don't know. I cannot walk, or speak without my head—bam!" I knew I wasn't being fair, that it wasn't his fault completely, but I was so angry with myself, with him, with this situation, I couldn't stop myself. It felt good to lash out, to vent my feelings. I gestured as if my skull were splitting in half, which was how it felt in that excruciating moment. "I'm in *pain*, bad pain, all the time!"

Cristóbal's jaw dropped, and his eyes filled with tears. "Please, I would've never, ever—"

"And you never write to me!" My voice cracked.

"I'm sorry, I couldn't, please—" He grabbed my hands again.

The rawness of his voice shamed me into silence. I closed my eyes, took a deep breath, and reminded myself he'd only been trying to protect me. He hadn't known about my real feelings. The throbbing in my head slowly edged away.

"Juan probably *so* happy now, with Woven Tree's daughter," I whispered.

"No. Woven Tree was too enraged. Even if Juan had asked for her again, which he didn't, he would've been denied."

I opened my eyes, but the spark of hope ignited and fizzled just as quick. "No matter. I married someone else and Juan will never, ever forgive me. Too proud. But, perhaps, he might still help me, or us, if you still willing."

He elbowed me in the ribs. "You dare doubt me?"

I couldn't help a small smile. "I hate to ask, but I cannot do alone. I—I've forgot so much; I cannot even hold quill until recently. Did Noble River tell you?"

He wrapped his arm around me. "I swear if that—that spineless, slobbering bastard wasn't dead, I'd kill him myself."

"Not if I got him first." I winked, and he returned it with a deferential nod.

"I'll go to Santiago and entreat with Juan, then. Have you a message for him?"

I shook my head. It was pure cowardice, but I couldn't help it. "When will you return? We agree to meet by a certain date right now, whether Juan comes or not. I tired of having this book hanging over me, and more tired of waiting for word from one of you men."

Cristóbal laughed. "Fair enough. Two weeks from now, how does that sound?"

I counted the K'iche' days on my fingers. "What's that, the Kan?"

"Indeed. A night to get rid of anger."

I snorted. "We will need all help."

The day before the Kan, Nicolao returned from Santiago. He claimed rumors were rampant that the Ocelot had been sighted near Sololá, and that he could not bear to leave us without his protection. Which is why, on the designated evening, I felt like the most disloyal harpy when I slipped some essence of white lotus into his afternoon drink.

A few hours later, I stood once again by my open window, waiting in the dark. Instead of a shift, I wore a simple brown dress under a dark hood and my sturdiest pair of boots. In my hand I held a walking stick Noble River had fashioned from an oak branch. My father's dagger was at my hip, but somehow it felt inadequate. I knew Cristóbal would never hurt me, but I had no idea who these new friends of his were.

I was even less comforted when three of them arrived under my window, slick as shadows and armed to the teeth. They wore gruesome wooden helmets that masked their faces. One was carved and painted like a skull emerging from the jaws of a snake, another like a feathered warrior, and lastly one that must have been an ocelot, bearing its fangs. The shape of the mask was rounder than a jaguar's, not spotted, but with four characteristic stripes crossing the protuberant eyes. The man I assumed to be Cristóbal touched his hand to his heart. He made a sign for me to come out through the window. I stifled several nervous titters as they lugged me out and half carried me down the hill to our little beach, where a long canoe awaited, along with five oarsmen, who also wore masks.

I glanced at a horned demon seated beside me, and I broke. A hysterical giggle built into an insane laugh that refused to die until we were way past the center of the gleaming, moonlit lake, where the Ocelot finally removed his helmet.

It was Cristóbal indeed. He glared as if he would've liked nothing more than to sacrifice me in one of the old ways, by binding my feet with stones and shoving me into the fathoms.

"Forgive me," I squeaked in K'iche', and wiped the mirth from my eyes. "This just—madness. I'm not laughing at you, any of you. You so tuh-terrifying that I don't *believe* I climb out of a window and into your arms."

"I see. Well, mind your irreverence does not displease the winds. A sudden gust could overturn us."

This pronouncement was delivered with such gravity that I bit down on my cheek to suppress another outburst. It was true that the lake could turn in an instant, but this manner was so unlike him. I was dying to tease him, but I caught the shaking head of the horned devil beside me, and clasped my walking stick to help me double down on my efforts. I didn't want to embarrass him in front of his companions any more than I'd already done.

I managed to stop, and for the next hour, the only sounds were the lapping of waves against the boat, the light trickle of droplets as paddles broke through the glistening surface, and the low, effortful huffs of the oarsmen panting in unison.

We neared an outcrop on the opposite shoreline, where the cliffside dropped straight into the water. "The Tz'utujil call this hill the Golden Door," said Cristóbal. "It is said to be one of the crossings into the underworld."

The canoe swerved behind a jutting rock, and we entered the mouth of a well-hidden cave. The air was cold and drafty, and with enough dank vapor it felt as if we were floating through a river of souls. Someone lit a torch, and I gaped at the height of the cavern and the rock formations like lances streaking down from the sky during battle.

The men continued rowing hard until the canoe scraped to a halt, and I was thrown onto the rower in front of me. Cristóbal helped me out of the boat, and I spluttered my apologies all the way up the pebbly bank.

"You should've given warning," I hissed under my breath.

"You deserved it," Cristóbal countered, much more like himself.

His men built a fire in the middle of the slope, and I looked around for some sort of staircase or tunnel along the curved wall. My breath caught as the light illuminated a gigantic painting of the god Q'ukumatz, the Plumed Serpent, the Heart of the Lake, with his turquoise undulating body slithering across the entire bend of the rock face, and his two heads instead of a tail, swathed in quetzal feathers. There was no other entrance.

"Won't the cacique get lost?" I asked.

"Indeed, which is why the Ocelot has kindly brought me along," Juan's voice answered. I whirled in its direction. My heart leapt against my chest.

Two men stood side by side. They wore the same capes tied around their bare sculpted chests. Bright-blue, knee-length skirts with red geometric designs were held at the waist by belts of jaguar pelt. Waves licked at their legs and at the little bells dangling from bands around their ankles. They were the same height and had a very similar build. The other must've been Juan El Grande—but it was impossible to tell which one was which. Both had identical masks, of hunters with patches of jaguar skin on their cheeks, and a waxing moon with sun rays for a crown.

I hid my disquiet and curtsied, using my wooden crutch for support, forcing my tongue to work right for once. "Won't you remove your masks, my lords?"

"They shan't, Catalina," said Cristóbal.

His men continued to set up the bank, our stage. Their feet crunched on the gravel. They muttered prayers and threw copal into the fire, scattered pine needles, and laid out handheld drums and rattles along the back wall. I spotted two wineskins and a rubber ball, as well as my mother's old manuscript and the new one. I caught one of the hunters watching me, but soon they both moved and I lost track of which one it was.

"Tonight, all four of us—both caciques, Catalina, and I—shall dance, for I have dreamt this must be so," Cristóbal said. "One of my men will scribe. The others, daykeepers and mother-fathers of our mosaic of peoples, will bear witness and preserve this knowledge, as is their right."

My muscles strained at the thought. The tension made it difficult to find my words, even in K'iche', but I managed to shake my cane and say, "I—I'm not as steady." I hoped it sounded as though I was afraid of falling, to the ground or into the fire even. But it wasn't only that. It was all these strange men, their gazes fixed on me, watching as I became what I became under the influence of *balché' ki'* and the otherworld. It was dancing with him again, when I knew he must've hated me so much that he wouldn't even show me his face.

"You will not be harmed; I give you my word," said Cristóbal.

I wasn't reassured. Even if he'd known what I truly meant, Cristóbal was a gentleman above all, so he found it easy to believe that other men were too. There was hardly a choice, though. It was this or risk drowning on my swim home. I removed my hood and boots but checked my knife was tight on my hip.

When I turned, the masked hunters stood by the fire with Cristóbal, and the others sat with their backs to the painting of Q'ukumatz, holding drums and rattles. The horned devil placed blank sheets of amate on a flat stone and sucked on a quill.

Cristóbal extended his hand to me. I walked to him, and he tied a beautiful panache of green and red feathers around my brow, one to match his own. He secured it around my braided hair with several pins, then held my hand.

"I won't let you fall." He gestured at my cane, which I put to the side.

We bent our heads and he said, "Heart of Sky, Heart of Earth, give us strength and courage, for you are our mountain and our plain. Plumed Serpent, bring us justice, truth, and peace on this night, which is yours alone. May our performance light the world, with your blessing."

The snake-skull man brought us a wineskin full of *balché ki'*, and we all drank in turn. The seated men drank too, except for the horned devil. My legs started to wobble, and I reached out to Cristóbal for support. One of the hunters' gazes burned my way, and I tightened my grip. My last coherent thought before the *balché ki'* took me was to never let go of his hand.

Except I did. Because I didn't need it. Because Cristóbal and I were becoming black fume. Our bodies billowed, sank past the roots of the mountain, circled in line with the beat of the drums. We were death and its warning, grinning at each other. We were mirrors. Xibalba was inside him, and Xibalba was in me. It fueled my body and powered my muscles. It sharpened my mind to a blade. Everything was clear again, steady, easy. My words, my memories, and my heart were strong and filled with dark glee.

I sat on my throne inside the glittering hall of the jade palace, in the deepest level of Xibalba. My demons surrounded me, wearing headdresses of feathered skulls and bracelets of starlight. But I was the greatest.

I was One Death, resplendent in my pelt of black jaguar, in my sandals of shade.

The court was tense. The firepits were alight, and blue-green flames licked the slick roof of the cavernous hall. Spirits darted in the shadows. They whispered and sniggered as they awaited our visitors. For we had sent a message to the children of One Hunahpu, who, just like their father, had dared to mock us by playing ball at the entrance of our realm. They'd disrupted our peace and never once offered us praise.

"Those tiresome twins," one of my demons said. His voice echoed, and an edge of deadly power rang behind each note. "It shall be good to put an end to them."

"They are near. Take out the wooden mannequins and hide," I commanded.

The twins arrived and we watched them while they studied the hall. Tall and strong, their skin was glazed a rich brown and gold, like copper melted in a furnace. One of them wore a panache with deer antlers, and the other had dark jaguar spots on his shoulders and back. Their gazes, true and steady, studied the mannequins for a brief moment and illuminated them with a candlelit glow. The air seemed to shimmer around them, and turned to vapor.

"We would prefer to greet the real lords of Xibalba," they said. They had not been fooled. We had no choice but to come out. The twins faced us, unflinching.

To our horror, they bowed and spoke our names.

"Good day." They named every demon, then turned to me. "It is an honor, One Death."

The demons were aghast, and hissed among themselves. I silenced them with a look, and smiled, pretending it was no matter, which was far from the truth. By naming us, the twins had diminished our power tenfold. The boys did not fall for our second trick either. They did not sit on the hot stone bench, but smiled and shook their heads instead.

"My lord! What does this mean?" the demons begged.

"Never mind," I growled. "It means nothing, for we shall continue to show them the delights of Xibalba, and they shall be humbled."

Skeleton guards took the twins through each of the six houses of torture. But they survived the sharp blades that zoomed through the air, slicing across bone and soul inside the razor house. They lived through the frozen wasteland of the cold house, and they even escaped the giant jaguars and bats, which had never failed to part visitors' heads from their bodies.

I grew more troubled. In private, my demons said to me, "How is this possible?"

"Don't you worry, we shall beat them at *chajib'al*." I winked.

The ball court was set up, a long, narrow passage between two great stands. The stone was swept and the ring was cleared of all cobwebs before the rubber ball was brought out. Every Xibalban came out to cheer us on—the spirits and the dead, those at peace and those fated to be haunted for eternity. They all watched from the heights.

"Remember," I told the boys, "if you lose, you die."

We played for what seemed like years. Seasons turned, oaks grew from tiny acorns and withered, as we sent the ball flying with our hips, our thighs, our shoulders. By the end, our score was greater than theirs. They had lost.

"Throw them down the great stone pit!" I crowed into the air.

"Wait," said the twins. "Just one thing—once we die, grind our bones and spill the powder into the river."

"Even better," I said. Everyone rejoiced. That night there were great celebrations everywhere. Phantoms rose like smoke and cadavers danced to the beat of our wild drums. The river bubbled in response to our cries, but we took this as a good omen.

Days later, when festivities had waned, the demons rushed to our thrones. "Great lord, have you heard? Two ragged vagabonds have been traveling the Black Road, performing great miracles."

"Indeed, they are great dancers and magicians."

I waved their nonsense away, but a demon said, "They make the dead rise again. They make them live."

At this, I turned in interest. "Who are these vagabonds? Are they really such a delight? Send them messengers, and tell them we wish to marvel at them."

The two old men arrived, hunched over and trembling, eyes wide with fear.

"We hear you are great dancers," I said. "Show us, then. Dance the Armadillo." They nodded and did as they were told. All of Xibalba arrived to admire their grace.

"We hear you are great healers. Set our home on fire, then put it out," said one demon.

So they set the jade palace on fire, with all of us inside it. But we were not burned. Everyone clapped and shouted in wonder.

"We hear you are great magicians. That you can wake the dead," I said. "Show us, sacrifice yourselves and come back to life."

They bowed. One of the disheveled men lay down, and the other took out an obsidian dagger, then spread his brother's arms and legs. With one clean motion, the standing one sliced his brother's head off and removed his heart. We gasped in shock. For a moment, all of Xibalba was silent. Then the standing brother said, "Get up." The head reattached itself, and the heart fluttered away from his palm like a bird, back into the chest.

Then, the brother rose.

I leapt in wonder. In all the long centuries of my existence, I had never seen such a sight; I had never craved to experience such power. To feel my own hand tear my life from me, only to be reborn again.

"Do it to me! Sacrifice me!" I shouted, and ran over, full of yearning. I knelt on the floor, and let my head roll off my shoulders. It was swift and painless. I waited.

Then, I waited some more.

There was still enough power in me to grant me vision, and what I saw, finally, was betrayal. The brothers changed before my eyes, their skin glowed brilliantly. They were lit from within—one silver, translucent, mystical, and the other gold and radiant, with flesh as hot as embers. Light poured out from every particle of their beings. They were the brightest jewels in this world . . . and they were not bringing me back to it.

"Who are you? Who are you!" my demons shouted.

"We are Hunahpu and Xbalanque, come to avenge our father, whom you killed."

The demons cried out for mercy, and though they were spared, they were cursed forever. "From now on, only the worthless will ever yield to you and pray to you. Only the guilty, and the violent, and the wretched," the twins said, and they broke out from the palace.

They left the walls to crumble, ascended to the sky, and lit up the surface of the earth for the very first time.

I watched them as my power faded from me. They were beautiful, though I hated them with every grain in my body. The golden one, Hunahpu, seemed to sense my rage, and glanced back at me. His eyes glowed with an emotion I couldn't decipher.

It was through his gaze that I was brought back to the cave. A human girl again, with a wild, human heart. I became aware that I was, of course, lying on the pebbles in the most unflattering way. Legs at an odd angle, and splayed flat on my back.

The oarsmen rowed with renewed vigor as the wind picked up and rocked the canoe like a cradle. I felt Juan's gaze burning into my back the entire way home, and I sat up straight. I was grateful for the hood hiding my face, even in this semidarkness. No one said a word until we arrived at my beach. Once again, Cristóbal helped me climb out.

"I'll help you up the hill," he said.

"I'd like a quick word with the cacique." I stared at the men in twin masks. One nudged the other, who sprung out into the shallows with a light splash. I turned and walked a few feet away, to a darker spot under the palm trees. The power of the *balché' ki'* had faded, and I was once again in need of my walking stick, although for now, my mind felt clearer than it had in weeks. I didn't know if that would last, and it both frightened and saddened me.

I didn't dwell on this long because Juan was following me, barely making a sound.

"Won't you take off your mask?" I whispered. To my surprise, he indulged me. He placed it under the crook of his arm, and wiped away the strands of hair stuck to the perfect, glistening skin around his jagged cheekbones. I lowered my hood and we stared at each other, unblinking. My body was a maelstrom of emotion. My heart drummed against my ears. I'd forgotten what I wanted to say.

"Well, if that's all you wanted." He turned on his heel.

"No—wait. How—how are you?" I winced.

Juan cocked his head around, incredulous. "How am I?"

I tried to think of something to say, but my chest ached with anguish. The sky was turning indigo, and the birds were waking. We didn't have much time. The pressure built inside my body; like a swarm of bees, it buzzed between my ears and behind my eyes. It was all I could do to keep from bursting into tears and humiliating myself in front of him.

"Spit it out, Catalina. I've a long trek back to Santiago."

"I never hurt you," I whispered. "M-meant to hurt you," I corrected. My tongue was a brick, and my words were stuck behind it. I knew what I wanted to say, but I couldn't get it out. I shook my head and blinked back tears of frustration. "Marrying Nico—I no other choice."

"There's always another choice," he snarled, and my pride riled against him.

"It was marriage or Spain. Does that not matter?"

"Oh, it mattered a great deal. But as they say, time heals all wounds."

My lip trembled. "So, that's all, then?"

"I guess so," he said with a shrug.

Maybe it was his tone, maybe it was the thought that he'd spoken the truth and I'd lost him—or the opposite, that he'd lied and was therefore refusing to acknowledge my side, my suffering. Maybe it was the beating ache across my temple, which reminded me of the grim reality that some wounds never went away, that I'd lost a year of my life forever. That I might never speak properly or walk straight again. That my old self was gone.

Whatever it was, it set my teeth on edge.

"Fine." I strode past him, ignored his mutter of surprise, and went up to Cristóbal, who rose from where he sat hunched on the ground. He held a rope tied to the tip of the canoe.

"Give me *Popol Vuh*." I stretched out my hand. He glanced in shock at Juan, and I looked back at him. "I want Mother's copy back. Now."

Juan crossed his arms. El Grande said, "That's impossible, my lady."

"Rubbish. You said you'd return it." I glared at Juan. "You gave me your word."

"*Now* you care for honor?"

"I waited for you." I had the satisfaction of seeing him blanch, but he didn't respond. I grabbed on to the rope. "I gave back your necklace, so hand me my manuscript. I'll not let go until you do."

"You're making a scene," Juan muttered.

"Cousin, please," said Cristóbal.

"You wish for revenge? Is that what this is?" I shook as I tried to keep my voice under control.

His eyes narrowed. "I'll admit, denying you is a delight in and of itself. But the truth is, we cannot return the old manuscript."

"Why? Wh—"

"Nija'ib', get back on the boat," Juan cut across me. "She can climb the hill by herself."

Cristóbal's face pinched in misery. He looked at me, and I couldn't hide the barb of pain as he stepped into the canoe.

"I don't understand," I said. "What you want with that moldy thing? It means nothing to you. Give it back!"

Juan jumped in and seized the rope from Cristóbal. "Let go. I'll not ask you again."

"What are you doing with it? Where you taking it? St-stop!"

He took out a knife and, with a swift motion, cut the rope. The oarsmen dipped their paddles and the boat glided away. I ran into the water, tripped, and fell on my front. My cane wobbled on the surface of the water. Juan leaned over as if to jump out, but he stopped when I grabbed the stick back and rose.

"Cowards, all of you!" I screamed. Tears of rage streamed down my face and dissolved into my drenched body. I kicked the surface of the lake and growled.

Cristóbal buried his head in his hands. Juan's eyes flashed before he broke into a twisted smile and said, "Time to freshen up for your husband. Time to warm his bed."

"Oh, I will!" I snarled. "Take a good look, my king! Next time you see me I'll be round with his child!"

I hiked up the hill in a fury. My boots squelched, my hood and hair were plastered over my face, and my dress weighed me down and dribbled. Even with the cane, I tripped and fell a couple of times on exposed roots and loose stones. The whooping, laughing grebes sailing on the surface of the lake seemed to mock me. By the time I reached the house, my palms were raked with scratches. I didn't bother with the window; I just tore in through the porch door into my room, wheezing and panting, but too angry to stop. I hurled my dress and crutch at the floor and marched in my wet underclothes straight into Nicolao's room.

He was curled up on his side, snoring slightly under a thin cotton sheet. The pale-pink dawn streamed through the half-open shutters and illuminated his young face. A gentle wind rustled the leaves of the potted palm tree near the window.

I took a few breaths to settle myself, then slipped behind him under the covers. He was wearing a smock, but nothing else. I stroked his arm and forehead and brushed his hair back, trying to be gentle with my hands, which were still shaking from my earlier rage. The muscles in his face flickered, and he shifted toward me, onto his back.

I leaned down and kissed his lips. He murmured something in a dazed but pleased tone. I thought he smiled. His eyes blinked open.

He gasped, jolted back, and pulled the sheets with him.

"Catalina! What—" He noticed my general state of undress and spluttered.

I laughed. "Take care, husband, or you'll fall from mattress."

"What are you doing?" He lifted the linen to his chin, as if he were the one exposed.

"Well, what do wives normally do?" I smiled and slid closer to him, but the alarm on his face stopped me short. "What is it?"

"I just—I don't think we—you're soaking, why?"

"I t-took a bath," I said with a shrug, and placed a hand on his knee.

"Stop." He grabbed my wrist and pulled it up.

A rush of blinding rage hit me again, more powerful than before, and I struggled to not slam my free fist into his cheek.

"Your palm's bleeding." He looked at my exposed shoulder with a frown. "You're covered in bruises!"

That pulled me up short. It was true, my shoulders were blooming puce, and my elbows and hips were sore, and surely as black as beans. It must've happened during the ball game, caused by the rubber ball, which felt like nothing at the time. My words got muddled in my head, but I had to say something.

"I too-took a tumble. No need for panic."

"No need to panic?" He got up and hurled the sheet at me. "The last time you *took a tumble*, you nearly died. Did you hit your head?"

"No, I'm fine!"

"You are not fine! You're not fine at all! How can you be so careless?"

"Why you so angry?"

He spluttered. "Wh—do you know what it was like to watch your skull crack open? To watch you fade? For weeks I prayed on my knees for God to wake you, and when he did—you didn't recall who I was. You couldn't speak." His voice cracked.

"Nico, I—"

"No! I cannot bear it any longer. My feelings—things have changed between us."

"But—we not spent time together—"

"You don't understand." He rubbed his hand over his hair. "For weeks, I washed you, nursed you, with my own hands. It—it changed things."

"Feelings can change back; can't—mustn't we try?" I reached out for him.

He shook his head. "Forgive me. It's too late. I cannot help it."

Tears streaked down his face. I gaped at him, torn between confusion and hurt. He had washed me, nursed me, and now he denied me? Or did he deny me because of it? He couldn't help what—not desiring me anymore? Even then, he didn't look at me as a man looked at a woman, his woman. I might as well have been his toddler sister, or a troublesome cat he was rather fond of, one missing an ear perhaps. And there was more, a type of guilt lingering behind his gaze, a guilt I knew all too well.

"You love someone else," I whispered.

Nico looked away. He didn't deny it. My throat strangled shut.

"Probably for the best—our marriage was not consummated, and it ought to stay that way," he mumbled, and went to his wardrobe. He placed a shirt beside me and took my hand again. "I will always care for you, and I swear you will lack for nothing. I will continue to support you financially, and I'll be generous, for I know all my riches come from you. But I think—I think we ought to seek an annulment."

A jolt coursed through my entire body, as though I'd been frightened right on the verge of falling asleep. Then I couldn't speak, couldn't move.

"I'll go and—and let you get dressed."

He left the room and for ages I sat there, staring at nothing, numb and hollow like a cask of wine drained to dregs. My husband was leaving me, my father refused to even write to me, my sister had killed my mother, the love of my life hated me, and my cousin was an outlaw. I had no other family, no friends . . . no one to turn to.

No, that was wrong.

I had one friend left in this world.

Isabel.

CHAPTER 19

Santiago de los Caballeros, Guatemala
Winter 1554–1555

It took me a moment to find my bearings when I woke. Isabel's guest room, with its plush blue furnishings and painted landscapes, was still foreign to me. However, every day it was easier for me to remember where I was. I needed less help every day, although I was not by any means back to normal. Noble River, who'd traveled with me, knocked and entered with a tray of sweet breads and a pair of dainty alabaster cups. One of Isabel's maids helped me dress.

Isabel and I took breakfast together with Judge Ramirez, who did most of the talking. From her narrowed lips and curt answers, I could tell she was bursting for him to leave so we could speak about the best clause to use to annul my marriage, but it wasn't until the bells chimed for eleven o'clock Mass that her husband finally left the house. Just as we'd walked into the sitting room and put our heads together, Don Bernal barged in, wheezing, led by a glum-looking Diego. His shirt was sticking out of his half-buttoned jerkin.

"My dears, I'm terribly sorry for the imposition." Don Bernal removed his feathered hat. His gaze found my general direction. "I'm terribly sorry. I truly am. Don't really know how to say this, the most dreadful news."

He paused to catch his breath, though perhaps to increase the suspense too.

When I didn't ask him for an explanation, he blurted out, "Carmen's run off—with Nico." He shook his head. "I suppose these things happen all the time—I'm practically astounded when a man has a reputation for constancy, and you can't blame him, really; she was an enchanting thing. So helpful and kind to him when you were unwell. But still, a maid." He glanced at Isabel and flinched. "Not to say those who stray aren't persons of quality, oh no, but men and women have different constitutions, of course. Even Doctor Rivera says these things can't be helped. Just the other day, he explained how men's blood is warmer, therefore—"

"Pray, excuse us." Isabel took me by the elbow and strode to the hallway. "We must go to your father. Only he has the power to force Marroquín to annul the marriage *a statim*. We must go at once—there's no time to spare."

I wrestled my arm out of her grip. "I do not wish to involve my father."

"Catalina, you'll be ruined."

"I've done no wrong." I lowered my voice to a hiss. "I told you we'd not even had—relations, for goodness' sake."

"That won't matter to the people of this town."

"I don't care about the people of this town, only you." A door slammed. Don Bernal had gone off. It would be only a matter of hours before all the neighbors knew.

"Well, I'll not see you brought so low." She turned on her heel and marched off, grabbing her billowing coat on the way out the front door.

"Where you going?" I grabbed my walking stick and rushed into the dusty road. The sky was a spectacular, everlasting blue, without a cloud in sight. The air was dry, for we'd had no rain in weeks. I chased her, but soon found myself leaning against a carpenter's shop wall, puffing and sweating. Isabel veered into the main square to the palace, but I was too weak to go on.

As I held the stitch at my side with my eyes closed, trying to catch my breath, he walked to my side and said, "Are you unwell?"

I jumped back and nearly fell, but Juan grabbed my arm.

"Steady there," he murmured.

I pulled my arm away and looked him over. He was dressed in a white cotton shirt and trousers, and his hair was tied back with a red ribbon that matched the coral pendant hanging from his left ear. I had to control my face, for I felt as struck by him as my sixteen-year-old self had that night of my party, when he'd spun me around the room and left me cursed and gasping for air. As for him, nothing much seemed to have changed either. He'd looked furious with me then, and he looked furious with me now.

We glared at each other, but the sun was in my eyes. They began to water, and I had to look away.

"I didn't know you were in Santiago," he said more gently, to my surprise.

Perhaps he thought I was crying. I huffed. I would not be thought of as a weakling. I made sure there was no one close by to overhear us, cleared my throat, stood up straight, and responded as tartly as I could. "Your eyes do not deceive you. I have been back but a day. It is good that we have run into each other, for there is much to finalize in our affairs, and I should like to be done with them as soon as possible."

I almost forgot the moment and cheered, because my words had come out effortlessly.

Juan scoffed. "I'm sure it is agony, being away from your husband."

So, he didn't know yet. Well, I wasn't going to tell him. I stabbed him with a look again and said, "Being reliant on you and Cristóbal to fulfill a promise to my dead mother is what truly agonizes me, though perhaps vow-breakers like you could never understand."

The fight seemed to evaporate from him. He looked tired, sad. He ran a hand over his face and sighed. "Indeed, a promise to the dead is binding, though no less important than a promise to the living."

I narrowed my eyes. "Then we agree. For once. So, listen—I st-stay with Doña Isabel, and Noble River is with me, whom I trust. I expect you to summon Cristóbal and send word to Noble River of our meeting in the next fortnight, if not sooner, and bring along my copy of the *Popol Vuh* with you on the appointed day, right?"

If he was irked by my commanding tone, I gave him no opportunity to say so.

"Have a pleasant afternoon." I spun around and walked off. When I got to Isabel's house, I pretended to slip into the villa. Once in the dark, I angled my head to spy on him. He walked down the road and to the right. There was only one street down that way, which led to the small church we'd met at before.

A blink later, I followed him. Even though there was little hope that I would see where he lived, I felt compelled to go. I caught sight of him, crossing the cemetery next to the church, and my spirits soared. I made my way surreptitiously toward the tombstones and hid behind the stone angel. There were bouquets of pink and yellow wildflowers dotting its base.

Once again, my breath came in ragged gusts, though I could not tell if it was from the chase, or from meeting him again, or from hiding in the shadows like a feral beast.

He walked slowly, with his head down, through a grassy field that extended into a large hill covered in woodland. Just when I could barely see him anymore, he disappeared into a tiny stone house there, on the hill, a hut so small I'd failed to notice it. It stood underneath a copse of trees covered in hanging strings of silver moss, which were swaying with the cooling breeze.

I watched the lonely little house for hours, wishing he'd emerge again.

He did not.

Two days later, my annulment was confirmed. On what grounds, I didn't ask. It couldn't have been that the marriage was unconsummated, for the midwife was usually called in those cases, and I'd had no such visit. Perhaps Isabel and Father had gone for the claim of infidelity on Nico's part, but I couldn't believe Father would want that set down for posterity. Possibly they'd made the doctor declare me a barren woman, due to my illness. If so, I'd never marry again.

Perhaps I ought to have been more grateful to Isabel, for using her influence over my father and interceding on my behalf, but a part of me was vexed at her meddling, once again, just like she'd done with Nico and Beatriz. But it was worse now, far worse, for she'd run to my father when I'd explicitly asked her not to.

"He says he'd like to see you again," Isabel had said. "He forgives you! This is his way of making amends. Won't you go to him? He misses you so."

Well, I did not miss *him* so. Not the person he'd become in the past few years.

My heart ached for the man who'd sat me on his lap and read stories to me as a child, but I finally understood . . . That version of him, that part of his heart, had been buried along with my mother and sister on that terrible day.

There was nothing I could do to bring him, or any of them, back.

I never shared my real thoughts and feelings with Isabel, however.

I'd realized once and for all that, despite her kindnesses, I was little more than Isabel's crutch, her favorite pawn. Her attempts at enlightening the native populace by displaying me as their model had wavered. Instead, I'd noticed since moving back that when we were together, she seemed to make herself small, so people stared at me, not her.

It wasn't difficult to understand why. I was the president's cast-off daughter, the heroine who'd saved the blessed bishop, the one who'd been nearly killed on the night of her elopement with a humble tutor who'd then abandoned her for the governor's maid. My scandals had become legendary, and Isabel preferred it this way, for they far eclipsed her own.

I had to feign interest, however, for she was keeping me fed and warm with a roof over my head. She was trying to bring me back into society, though I did not care for it. In fact, we had been invited to a small soirée Don Bernal had organized to honor the completion of his memoir. There would be drinks and a recital.

She'd gone ahead of me to help him set up. I didn't fancy attending, but I had to try to keep up appearances, for her sake at least.

When I arrived, alone, more people were gathered in Don Bernal's drawing room than usual. His writing desk had been moved out. All the wooden chairs from his dining area, even his garden bench, had been brought up and placed in a semicircle facing the back of the room, where there was a new, large painting of a resurrected Christ rising triumphantly toward the open heavens.

Doña Clara stood near the door and chatted with another lady I didn't know. They'd brought two of their enslaved Black women to show off. The poor girls, dressed up all in finery, stood in the corner and had to smile politely every time someone pointed and stared, which was nearly every second breath. I tried to weave past them without drawing attention, but Doña Clara clawed at my arm.

"My, my, if it isn't *Señorita* Catalina. At least, I hear you've remained thus?"

An odd, cough-like sound escaped me.

"What a stir it caused, to think that after being married for a year, one could remain so pure! My husband could hardly wait for me to cross myself at the altar before pulling up my skirts."

The other doña giggled. "Oh, Clara, you are wicked!"

"No, no, it's not her fault." She looked me over and eyed my cane. "She was quite unconscious for most of her marriage. I visited you, you know. I'm glad the Lord saw to spare you. We thought you'd be quite mad, if you ever woke up."

"Indeed. I'm not sure I escaped that fate," I said.

Doña Clara beamed with pleasure. She leaned in closer and whispered, "Tell me, truly, you really had no idea that worthless tutor of yours was hot for Bernal's maid?"

"Excuse me." I veered off. My pulse spiked in my temples.

Isabel stood in the back of the room, conversing with none other than Captain Lobo. She was clearly uncomfortable, and waved me over as soon as she saw me. I swallowed a groan as I waded through the chairs toward them. Fortunately, I was spared the need to speak to the horrible man.

Don Bernal made his entrance, guided by the young Maya boy he'd hired to walk him around town. We all clapped. I felt relieved to have an excuse not to talk, because my temper was hot enough that I was having trouble breathing.

"My friends, thank you for coming." He touched a hand to his breastplate. "I'm honored to have my dear friend and great supporter, Doña Isabel Ramirez, share with you a snippet of my final account, from the fall of Tenochtitlán. If you would do me the privilege of taking a seat, we shall begin."

The party clapped again as Isabel made her way to the front, a touch of color on her pale cheeks. Chairs scraped the floor as everyone took their seats. I sat near the window, next to Lobo, who reeked of tobacco and sweat. Don Bernal's new maid filled everyone's wineglasses before she stepped out.

"Thank you kindly," said Isabel as she picked up the manuscript. "It has been my honor and pleasure to help Don Bernal write down his accounts of the conquest of Mexico. This is truly a historical gem, and there is no doubt in my mind that it shall live on for generations. The people of this land, all of us, born and brought, are forever indebted to him for taking the time to chronicle his incredible experiences and achievements."

I had a moment where I thought I might burst into a fit of hysterical laughter.

I simply couldn't believe that I, the girl who'd had to lie, cheat, and crawl underground to rewrite a beautiful work of Mayan art, was sitting at this dainty little Spanish party, next to a thief and a murderer, about to listen to *another* murderer's account of one of the worst moments in living memory. *And* it was my one and only friend who would be reciting it. A friend who apparently had no inkling as to how sick this situation was.

My precarious situation did not escape me, though, so I bit my tongue, breathed through my mouth, and listened.

Isabel smiled. "Right. Let me set the scene. We, as in us Castilians and our thousands of Indigenous allies, have besieged the city of Tenochtitlán, and nearly three months have passed. Our soldiers have made a fleet of pirogues and have been fighting the Mexicans on the water. The fight's nearing the end. Here's where the writing begins."

She cleared her throat. "Fifty canoes set out. They were richly decorated, and we recognized them as belonging to the lord of Mexico, who was Cuauhtémoc, after Moctezuma's passing. The canoes were full of his property, gold, and jewels, and all his women. We quickly stopped destroying the houses and followed their flight through the water. We were warned not to molest Cuauhtémoc, only capture him."

Isabel took a sip of wine. "It pleased our Lord God that we should overtake his fleet. The Lord Cuauhtémoc knew then, he was defeated. But Hernán Cortés embraced him most respectfully, for he'd fought a brave fight, and defended his city as was his duty, and we couldn't fault him."

The room was silent; no one dared even to shift.

"It rained and thundered that night, the thirteenth of August, 1521, and it was curious. When morning came, we all became as deaf as if all the bells in a belfry had been ringing and suddenly stopped. I suppose because for the ninety-three days of our siege, there had been nothing but shouting at all hours of the day and night, and the unceasing sound of drums and trumpets, and cannons, and kettledrums."

Next to me, Lobo blanched and shuddered. His stinking breath came in great puffs, and I had to lean closer to the window to keep myself from retching. Isabel closed her eyes for a moment and took a deep, righteous breath. "But in the silence, we knew, we had triumphed. In the silence, we knew, God had led us to our new home."

"Bravo!" someone shouted, and everyone broke out into applause, except me. All hilarity had left me. I strained to think of a reason to get away.

Don Bernal rose and bowed, again and again, until the noise died.

"Surely there's more, Bernal!"

"Yes, yes, read us some more, Doña Isabel!"

I rolled my eyes. From across the room, Isabel gave me a querying look, and I responded with a taut smile and a shake of the head. I wasn't about to stand up and explain exactly how and why this dinner party was the most grotesque event I'd ever attended.

"Oh, if you're certain," said Don Bernal, and the room cheered. "Oh, very well. Dear Isabel, would you indulge me for a paragraph or two more?"

"Of course, Don Bernal." She found her mark on the page and hesitated only slightly before carrying on with a wavering note. "We finally entered the city, and I solemnly swear, all the houses and stockades were full of heads and corpses, many whose skin had been ravaged by the pox. Indeed, the stench was so bad that no one could endure it. The surviving men, women, and children were so thin and sallow, it was pitiful to see them. We—"

At the front, Doña Clara let out a moan, teetered to the side, and fell on her enslaved girl's lap. "She's fainted!" The room rose in unison, and I took the opportunity to slip away.

I took deep gulps of air as I emerged from the house. My feet were shaky, and I grasped my stick tightly as I walked in the direction of the small church by the hills, until I found myself sitting by one of the many graves. The image of the piled, diseased corpses swam behind my retinas, the sound of cheering rang in my ears.

No wonder Mother had never wanted to talk about it. No wonder she was plagued by nightmares, by bouts of terrible sadness. No wonder she had wanted every Spaniard to die. I thought of Cook as well, of whom she might've lost, whether she would've told me if she could've. One by one, I thought of all the deceased I knew, and all those I didn't. I closed my eyes and prayed for their peace.

I begged for their forgiveness too. I had to. I had to. For I could see that this immense crime, this cataclysm that had caused their suffering and loss, that had filled their lives with so much more bitter injustice . . . this was my legacy too. It would've been easier to pretend that it wasn't. I even had a right to claim to be a victim of the conquest, and in many ways, I was. But while my hand hadn't wielded a sword or lit a cannon, and in truth I wasn't responsible for the choices those men had made, I was living in a world that continued to be fueled by the colossal wound they'd inflicted. I had benefited from it, too, through my father. So I had to acknowledge this living, breathing hurt, and fight it. I had to fight with all my strength to try to heal it in any small way I could.

I would probably have to fight for the rest of my life.

This, I swore to do.

CHAPTER 20

Santiago de los Caballeros, Guatemala
Spring 1555

Much later, when I finally opened my eyes, I stared at the little house in the distance, hoping to catch a glimpse of Juan.

I didn't know if I wanted to shake him or kiss him, but every sinew in my body strained and pulled at me in desperation, to see him, to speak to him, especially right now, when I felt so alone in this world I could hardly breathe.

I'd stood and taken a step forward. I'd made up my mind to knock on his door when he emerged. I froze as he paused on the threshold to dust off his white trousers and adjust the red sash around his waist and then strolled away, toward the copse of trees to his right, my left. I took a moment to look around. There was an older woman laying carnations by a large stone cross closer to the church, but she was engrossed in prayer. I hobbled across the grassy field at a normal pace until I was under the shade. Then I broke into a staggered run in what I imagined was his direction, but I couldn't see him.

Surely he must've heard me, my ragged breath, my awkward footing, the swish of my skirts, but perhaps he thought I was someone else.

I called out softly, "Juan!" and kept walking as fast as I could. I wound around the pines until I felt that sensation on the back of my neck, and the hairs on my arms stood on end. I slowed down and walked past the thick, knobbly trunk of an ancient oak. There was a crunch of a leaf being stepped on. I whirled around and he was there, a mere arm's length away. My heart, already pumping, sped up to a frenzy.

"Catalina? What's wrong?" He stepped forward.

I shook my head, and it seemed to float away from me as I stared into his black eyes, full of concern and care. Perhaps he'd not forsaken me yet.

My bottom lip quivered, and my eyes filled with tears.

"What, what is it?" He leaned his head down toward mine, and I inhaled his scent, fresh, like citrus and cinnamon, like home.

I burst out crying and he wound his arms around me.

Everything poured out of me, every wound, hurt, and sorrow; in fits and starts, and with much stuttering, I spoke of Beatriz's betrayal, of Father's lies and punishments, of hearing Mother's voice and dreaming of her memories of her last moments on earth. I told him about the horror of waking up and being unable to speak, write, walk. My voice muffled into his chest. My tears and a fair bit of snot soaked his shirt, but he just listened, and held me, and stroked my back. His arms tightened as I told him about Nico's desertion, and the awful party I'd just been to, the superior looks on Isabel's and Don Bernal's faces that I had to bear with a smile. He let out a half growl and I broke away, still ranting.

"And all this while, I've had to wait, and wait, and wait. For Father, for Cristóbal, for you, for *men* to help me, to provide for me, to allow me a m-modicum of freedom, to fulfill your wretched promises! All I want, damn it, is for you to give me the old *Popol Vuh* and for us to finish writing the new copy!" I shouted.

Our eyes met, and I hiccuped when I saw that his were as tear-struck as mine.

He seemed at a loss. "I—I have summoned Nija'ib' as you requested. He'll be here within days and—" He shook his head, ran a hand through his hair, and took a tentative step back toward me. "Catalina—please, forgive me."

Fresh tears fell down my face.

"When I heard about your elopement, I—my whole world . . . sh-shattered." His voice fell to a whisper. "You were the one good thing that had happened to me since I could remember, and once again, *they* had taken it. I was enraged, and hurt, and so . . . *ashamed*. I—I thought maybe you'd finally seen me for what I was . . . a mockery, a pauper."

I shook my head. "No! I told you, Father was shipping me off to Spain!"

"I see it now. I couldn't before. I couldn't even see the nightmare you must've lived through, before and after that guard attacked you." He ran a hand over my cheek.

"I could've lost you," he breathed. "That is . . . if I haven't already, idiot that I am."

I didn't know what to say. My head and body, my heart and spirit, were in turmoil. I wanted to tell him he hadn't lost me, throw myself at him, promise ourselves to each other again, and let him press my back to that tree to kiss me senseless. But . . . he hadn't addressed the glaring problem I'd just raised. He nodded, as though he knew why I hesitated.

"You want your mother's manuscript back."

I blinked. "Yes, I do."

He looked torn for a moment, then said, "All right, let's go get it."

We made our way back to his little hut, side by side. The backs of our hands kept bumping into each other until he finally took mine in his, making my heart leap. The mottled pink light filtering through the trees faded, and the forest air misted and cooled. The leaves glistened with evening dew. Birds returning to their nests for the night called out to each other in greeting, livening our ears with their racket.

Outside his door, a pair of striking motmots flew over our heads in a flash of turquoise, and we smiled shyly at each other, for they were a symbol of destiny, and family. I began to feel a glow of anticipation, a thrill for what I hoped would happen next.

He let me into his home, a clean, square room with only a tiny oval opening for a window, a straw pallet covered by a woven blanket, and a large open trunk with barely anything inside, just some neatly folded clothes at the bottom. My heart twisted for him, because I knew it pained him to have so little. He, a king, and a good man too. He shut the door behind me and walked us to the trunk. I breathed in the scent of copal and dry grain as my eyes adjusted to the dim light. Like my drawer with the false bottom, Juan's trunk had a false top on the lid.

With his one free hand, he fiddled with the sides of it, tricking it open.

"Safe and dry for you, my lady." The corner of his lips curled up.

I scoffed a laugh and we locked eyes, then I gulped and fell into stillness. For several moments there was only silence, while our entwined fingers tingled and pulsed, beckoning us to close the distance between us. I began to move as though entranced, unable to tear my gaze away from his, unable to breathe until our lips were a feather's width apart, and I could sense the heat of his body and breathe the citrus on his breath. I felt both faint and more alive than ever before. A buzzing vibration spread from the tip of my tongue to the low, deep parts of me I was meant to keep in tight control because they could ruin me, my family, and my status.

Well, I had no real family now, and I no longer cared for status. The only person who mattered to me, the only person I loved, was standing in front of me, breathing hard, his black eyes reflecting the longing, the hunger, the need that was consuming me also.

I swung onto my tiptoes and kissed him, hard.

I wasn't hungry; I was ravenous.

My walking stick fell to the floor with a clank and rolled away. He made a sound, part growl, part whimper, and clasped his arms around my waist, and we stumbled, holding each other, kissing each other, onto the pallet. There, amid the crunch of straw and the waning light, we grasped, and bit, and claimed each other at last.

◆ ◆ ◆

Much later, he lit a candle, then came back to lie down next to me. I traced a line with my finger down his nose and jaw and around his Adam's apple. He was beautiful, and I told him so. His lips formed a sly smile.

"I know," he said. I smacked his arm.

He turned on his side toward me. "I missed you."

I turned, too, nuzzling my head under his chin and pressing my bare chest to his. We held each other in silence for a long, delicious time.

Then my gaze fell on the *Popol Vuh*.

"Why did you want it? Why did you insist on keeping it?" I asked. "For revenge?"

He shook his head. "Well . . . not really. You yourself said it, the book contains a list of all the generations of kings. That last part is still legible and it proves our lineage, our birthright. El Grande has been trying to gain an audience with the emperor. We think if we show that section to him, along with a few other documents we have, he'd give us back, if not complete dominion, then at least governance of our lands and people. In his name, of course."

My mouth opened in disbelief.

"Well, that was the plan at least. I shall have to tell him I've chosen otherwise."

I blinked, astounded, both at the realization that he'd chosen me over the possibility of gaining his lands back, but also at his credulity. How he thought there was any way the Spaniards would give him an inkling of power back was beyond me. Deep in my bones, I knew this was a completely pointless exercise, but I couldn't bring myself to say it. Not when he was suddenly looking at me with eyes so full of hope.

"That is, unless you wish to lend it to us, again." He could not keep the pleading note in his voice hidden. I cleared my throat and focused on one of the thousands of questions flitting through my mind.

"Wait, I mean, when you say 'gain an audience,' you mean you're to go to Spain?"

He shook his head. "I myself cannot. My post here has grown too important, and I will not leave you again. Grande will go, but I shall travel with him as far as Veracruz."

"How will the Spaniards understand the documents you're showing them? Surely they wouldn't just trust your word for it."

"I've made some Dominican friends. One of the monks, who speaks K'iche' and has learned to read our symbols, has agreed to travel with Grande."

"But how would you pay for their passage?" I looked around his little hut. If Juan was this poor, El Grande must've been even more so.

Juan shifted and ran a hand through his hair. "What's this, the Inquisition?"

"I have a right to know, for what you're asking for. Terrible things happen at sea. Grande might never return."

As though to distract me, he leaned over me and kissed me again. I pushed him back.

"How will you pay?" I repeated, brow raised.

He shifted to his back. "Let's just say, Nija'ib' has taken care of it."

I sat up. "That's what he's been doing? As the Ocelot? Collecting passage money?"

Juan rolled his eyes. "You women love his little heroics, don't you? Even Spanish ladies fan themselves whenever they speak of him."

"You're ridiculous." I wanted to add that I didn't think Cristóbal would notice, that I didn't think he cared whether women admired him, but that would've placed him in terrible danger. Even someone like Juan might not have understood. Better he felt jealous than afraid.

I thought hard and he kept quiet, allowing me time to consider, but I could feel his body constricting with anticipation. He wanted this, badly, although he was prepared to give it up for me. I glanced at him, at his eyes full of hope, even after everything he'd been through, after everything had been stolen from him. I couldn't take this away too. He needed to have hope. *We* needed to have hope, in each other, in the misty, fleeting notion of justice. Even if nothing came from it and we were denied, history would know we fought, we tried.

"All right. El Grande may take the *Popol Vuh* on two conditions."

Juan sucked in a breath.

"We finish the rewrite, and I keep the new copy. And Grande may only take the part of the manuscript listing the old kings."

"Those are three conditions," he said, but he smiled.

I leaned down and kissed him. This time, neither of us pushed the other away.

It was past eleven o'clock when I sneaked back into Isabel's house.

In a daze of happiness, I tiptoed up the tiled steps, running my fingers along the smooth banister, thinking of the warmth of Juan's skin on mine. I thought nothing could ever wipe the smile off my face, but I was wrong.

When I carefully opened the door to my room, Isabel was there, sitting on the edge of my bed. I froze and stared. The fire roared, but instead of glowing pink, her skin shone gray. Her lips were drawn into a thin, straight line, reminding me of the rods used to beat dissenting children.

"I've been looking everywhere for you." Her voice barely rose above a whisper.

"What, out in the streets? By yourself?"

She nodded slowly. "I was sick with worry—where have you been?"

"You won't believe it." I shook my head and grabbed my forehead. Before leaving Juan's, I'd already thought of what to say in case something like this happened. "I went for a walk and lost my bearings. You know my memory is still bad at times. Ended up by the river before I realized where I was."

Isabel snorted. "Well, you're right. I don't believe it."

"It's the truth. I don't know what else to say. I'm sorry I troubled you—you shouldn't go out by yourself, it's so dangerous!"

"I should say the same to you." There was a long pause. "Catalina, you've been acting strange lately."

"How?" I unlaced my gown and sleeves.

"Like tonight! Leaving Don Bernal's party? He was very upset, you know."

"I'll go tomorrow and apologize."

"And what about your father? When are you going to visit him?"

She waited, but I didn't respond.

"He's requested a formal visit from you! How can you not go after he helped with your annulment? He's going through a terrible time right now. He's being investigated."

"What?"

"The neighbors have accused him of nepotism, for giving land away to his sons-in-law, as if none of the previous presidents had done the same and worse. His health's in decline again. It would cheer him to see you."

I clenched my teeth and grew more annoyed with each passing breath.

"You know, if I didn't know any better, I'd say you'd found yourself a lover," she whispered.

My lips parted. I let out a laugh. "Isabel, that's preposterous."

"Is it? I'm no fool; I know the signs. Sneaking into the house, a vague look on your face, coming home late. It's as clear as ink on parchment."

"Is this about me?" I snapped. "Or should you take this up with your husband when he returns from Chiapas?"

She stood, face flushed and body trembling. "I keep hearing people whispering that you're heading in the same direction as your mother.

The good name you earned when you saved Bishop Marroquín is long forgotten. I'm trying to warn you."

I tossed my partlet and petticoat on a chair. My head had started thumping. I was tired and losing command over my speech. "I don't need warning, and I don't cuh-care for approval of stupid gossips like Doña Clara and Don Bernal. It's no crime to have poor memory and get lost. I've done no wrong."

"Suit yourself." She stormed off and slammed the door behind her.

CHAPTER 21

Santiago de los Caballeros, Guatemala
Spring 1555

I ran into Juan the very next morning, outside the busy palace gates. The sight of him sent a beating shock through me, and I could see he was struck in the same way. But we had to bow; we had to feign distance, coldness. The guards watched us. Isabel wasn't far off; she'd gone to buy dahlias from some of the vendors in the packed, noisy square, and I'd agreed to wait for her there.

Men hammered and shouted as they erected a platform with a stake at its center. Others piled firewood around it. The jacarandas with their purple blossoms swayed with the wind as Spaniards ran around and cried out the same news to one another. Over and over, they repeated, *Joanna the Mad is dead. Bless her poor soul to Heaven.*

"Lord Cacique." I looked quickly behind me. Isabel was no longer visible in the rushing crowd.

"My lady," he returned. "Are you here to see your father?"

I shook my head.

"Hmm. Perhaps you ought to. I hear he's very unwell."

"Is he?" A chill ran through me. I vacillated for the space of a blink before I remembered. I'd told myself I'd never set foot through those gates again, and I intended to keep my word.

"I'll see him another time," I said. "I have pressing matters elsewhere."

"I see." Juan leaned closer, a gleam of desire in his eyes. "I'd be happy to accompany you, madam. For your safety, of course. It is very busy today."

I flashed him a look of warning and lowered my voice. "Isabel suspects something. We must behave."

His face darkened. He whispered, "For how long? Even a day longer I cannot bear."

"Please," I whispered, then raised my voice. "It is warm today, is it not?"

He nodded. "Very warm indeed." He lowered his voice again. "I had word this morning that your cousin was spotted nearby."

"Good. Find a way to let Noble River or me know the plan, and I'll be there."

"So you'll risk yourself for him, but not for me."

I clicked my tongue and caught sight of Isabel beckoning me over.

"Have a pleasant day," I said, and we bowed goodbye.

I walked into the square and quickly realized it was a terrible idea. I'd left my stick behind, as I'd felt much steadier that morning. But now, too many people were shuffling around, bumping into each other, into me. I couldn't believe the death of our long-suffering, imprisoned-by-her-son, would-be empress could cause such chaos until a woman wailed, "The last of Isabella and Ferdinand's children is gone," and I began to understand.

It was the end of an era. Very sad indeed, but all I wanted to do was to get to Isabel and leave. I didn't like the look of that stake or the people around it. I caught the eye of a desperate-looking vagrant and shoved my purse deep into my bodice. I didn't have much, and Nicolao's generosity had been waning of late.

There was a greater commotion. The crowd pressed toward the center and carried me with them. I couldn't see Isabel anymore, and abandoned my quest to find her, but it was impossible to get away.

"They're bringing somebody!" a girl next to me shouted, and pointed to the right. The crowd hissed and heckled as a wagon carrying two bloodied Maya men plowed its way toward the platform. The younger man turned to face our way, and for one horrifying moment, I thought it was Cristóbal. I swayed into a doña next to me, who almost spat in my face before she shoved me back to my feet. When I took a second look, I realized it wasn't him. Yet, I was not relieved, because I did know him. I knew that boy.

Cristóbal's right-hand man. Jun Kaaj's son, Pablo.

Bishop Marroquín and Captain Lobo stepped up to the platform. The conquistador read, "These men have been convicted of theft and banditry. They're believed to be accomplices of the infamous Ocelot." There was a roar of shock and excitement. The bishop placed two wooden, painted masks onto the top of the pile of firewood. A horned devil and a feathered warrior. "Indeed, these ruffians were found with a stolen bounty of ten ducats and several jewels of great value. As such, they've been sentenced to death by burning."

The crowd muttered in surprise. Theft and banditry were usually punished with flogging, or hanging if the culprit was particularly notorious. Death by burning was reserved for traitors and heretics. This was much too much.

My breath came in fast. I looked at Lobo's scarred face and saw fervor there, relish. He looked up at the palace and could hardly conceal a grin. The bastard. This was his answer to Father's leniency. The Maya men's violent deaths would be a slap to his face.

The wagon jolted against the platform, and a pair of guards kicked Pablo and the warrior onto it. Pablo fell and failed to stand again. The guards raised him, shoved his back to the stake, and tied his neck, torso, wrists, and legs to the pole. There was no escape.

I made another attempt to get away, but we were too tightly packed.

The bishop, serious and solemn, whispered something in Pablo's ear. The boy whimpered in response. An executioner, masked with a black cloth, carried a burning log as thick as my thigh. The older Maya fainted. Pablo raised his head to look at the clear blue sky and let out two short but powerful howls, clear and chilling. A signal. The coyote crying for his pack.

The bishop stumbled back in shock. At the same moment, several arrows whizzed through the air from opposite directions, and struck the men's hearts. Pablo's neck and the side of his head were also pierced. He died on impact.

"We're under attack!" shouted Lobo. His tangled beard and doublet were drenched in blood. Another arrow whizzed through the air and struck him in the gut. With a grunt, he fell from the platform. The crowd shrieked and fled. Guards ran in the direction of the arrows, though no more were let loose. In my frozen state, I was knocked to the ground, but someone grabbed my arm and pulled me back up. Isabel.

"Come!" She urged us home through the maddened crowd. Women and children screamed and cowered. A group of men started a fistfight. Swords were brandished. A donkey brayed and nearly ran us over with its driverless cart.

Noble River and two other servants were waiting for us with frightened looks on their faces. They bolted the door as soon as we were through. For a moment, Isabel and I just leaned on our knees and panted.

"It's all right," I said to them. "We're all right. We just need water." Isabel's maid rushed away to bring us some.

"What happened, madam?" Noble River asked. "I was outside when people started running through the streets, shouting."

Isabel told them the story.

I watched Noble River's face, and the russet faces of the other servants, as they became blank masks. Perhaps if we'd been alone, I would've caught a glimpse of their grief, and their horror, although I imagined it would've been worn like old, faded leather.

"It was a mercy, what those archers did," I said, for it was true. The prisoners had been spared a long-drawn-out, anguished death. The worst type of death. I'd have taken the arrows, a clean-cut end, any day. Some of the servants looked down.

Isabel frowned at me. "They caused a stampede!"

"No, they didn't; that idiot Lobo did, shouting that we were under attack."

"And they shot him! For shame! They ought not have interfered," she responded.

"I'm glad they did," I hissed. Noble River flashed me a look, and I backtracked. "I'd hate for my hair to stink like scorched meat for a week. It's impossible to wash out the stench."

Isabel massaged her temples and groaned. "I'm going to rest my eyes and pray. My head is pounding."

Noble River and I walked up the stairs into my chamber.

"It's a fine line you're treading on," he muttered the second the door shut. "She might be your friend, but she's still a Spaniard, and the wife of a powerful judge."

"I know . . ." I watched as he dusted the windowsill. "I forgot myself."

"See that you mind yourself better. I've heard you two arguing a lot. It won't do."

"I will. I'm sorry." There was the creak of wood outside the room. Someone was walking past. I waited until it was quiet for some time before I said, "Perhaps it's time we left. You've been away from your wife and children for too long."

Noble River nodded. "I miss them so. But we cannot leave for another day at least."

"Why's that?"

"Because I've had word from your cousin. He requests your presence in the forest. Tonight."

"All right, sister," said Noble River. "She looked at me all kinds of funny, but the lady Isabel finally drank the cacao. That's the last batch of essence, so you best be sure to finish that blessed book tonight."

"We shall, brother. Thank you."

It was close to midnight when I left, dressed in my usual hood, dagger attached to my hip. I'd left my cane behind in case someone saw me and recognized it. I felt surprisingly stable, however, and this pleased me to no end.

I followed Noble River's instructions for how to get to the stela from Isabel's house. There were many people out tonight, even at this late hour, mostly drunk and rambling. The day's events had stirred up the town, and I narrowly avoided being trampled by a set of guards in search of the archers from this morning. I reached the stone bridge at the edge of town and crossed it. To my right was the forest. I took a deep breath and stepped forth.

Every sinew in my body flickered alive. My ears prickled at every sound, and I couldn't shake the feeling that something was watching me. I thought I heard footsteps on the bridge, and I hid behind a tree for several breaths before I carried on. Owls hooted and bats clicked overhead. I'd not brought a torch, and wouldn't have dared light it anyway. The only thing I could see was the murmuring river to my right, occasionally flashing in starlight. I stayed a few feet behind the tree line and followed it up for about half an hour until I spotted the field of maize and the old granary.

I crossed myself, said a quick prayer, and plunged into the living void. The only guide I had was the scent of burning copal. After what seemed like an age, I noticed a glow from a small fire. I approached it with great care, trying to stay silent, but it was no use. Even before I reached it, Cristóbal was there, with his back to the great mound between the two sacred ceiba trees, bow and arrow drawn and aimed in my direction.

"It's me," I whispered. He lowered the weapon and placed it across his lap without a word. He just stared at the fire with dead eyes.

I sat next to him and laid my hands over his, at a loss for words. All I knew was Juan would be with us at any moment, and I would lose my chance, possibly forever.

"Today, with Pablo—"

Cristóbal burst into tears. He leaned forward as great sobs racked his body.

"It's all my fault, God forgive me. It's all my fault." His voice was strangled, as if he were swallowing a terrible scream.

"No, no it's not, how can you say that?"

He looked at me, face twisted and mad with grief. "I got him into this filthy business. If it weren't for me, he'd be alive."

I shook my head, but I felt an argument would be useless, so I wrapped my arm around him and leaned my head against his. "I'm so sorry."

I rubbed his back and he cried some more, muttering some unintelligible words. I only caught the one thing he repeated twice, "My arrow, my arrow." Tears fell down my face.

It wasn't until Juan stepped into the light that Cristóbal wiped his eyes and stood, a murderous look on his face. "I told you we should've never gone after those jewels."

Juan's knees were bent, ready to pounce. His eyes were focused solely on Cristóbal. One palm was up in a gesture of peace, but the other held a long, glistening obsidian knife.

"Well?" yelled Cristóbal. "Admit it! You got greedy, and now Pablo and K'otuja are dead."

"We didn't have enough—"

"You had plenty, plenty for the passage for both Grande and that oily monk, and plenty for them to live in Spain for months and then return. Why did you order another raid?"

"They knew the risks. They should've been more careful," whispered Juan.

Cristóbal leapt over the fire and hissed, "Don't you blame them, you bastard!"

I ran and stepped between them.

"Please." My mind raced. "It's bad enough, what's happened. We can't turn on each other. We have work to do. Pablo would've wanted us to finish."

Cristóbal sneered at me. He didn't say it, but I knew his thoughts. What did I know of what Pablo would've wanted? What did I know at all?

"Let's finish, then," he said. "So I never have to see *his* ugly face again."

Juan scoffed and I glared at him to keep his mouth shut. He seemed to struggle for a moment, and his jaw set and twitched, but mercifully, he stayed silent.

We walked back to the fire. Cristóbal sat and tossed me a clanking sack, which contained both manuscripts, ink, fresh pages of amate, the wineskin, and two panaches. Everything was scrambled together with bits of pottery from a broken jar. I swallowed my displeasure at the irreverent treatment of these sacred objects, and pulled them out as carefully as I could.

"I shall write," said Juan. He took the ink, quill, and paper and laid them out near the fire. He returned for the headdresses, and picked out the one with the bright-red feathers.

"Red for fire." He tied it around my forehead and sealed it with a kiss.

I glanced at Cristóbal, who was stabbing the soil with his arrow-head, and I took the other headdress to him.

"Come now, cousin. Tonight we dance in his honor. The Horned Devil shall not die in vain." I pulled him up and tied the blue panache around his head. Both men were silent, so I took it upon myself to begin the prayer.

I raised my arms and whispered, "Heart of Sky, Heart of Earth, your children praise you. Mother-Father, Maker and Begetter, we ask for your blessing. We, the children of the Kaweq, the Nija'ib', and the Ajaw-K'iche'. We pray you take away our falsehood and our stain, and give us the strength and courage to preserve your teachings forever."

"Amen," said Juan and Cristóbal in unison. To my surprise, they had no more to add.

Cristóbal drank the *balché' ki'* and handed it to me.

I took my first-ever breath. It was perfumed with the honeyed breath of the gods, and the scent of maize from Grandmother of Day and Light, who had molded my every limb and hair and that of my brothers.

We looked around for our creators in the semidarkness and felt their magnificence in the outline of the trees and the sparkling stars. We knelt and prayed, offering thanks for our lives.

"Kaweq, Nija'ib', Ajaw-K'iche'," they named us in reverberating voices. "Meet your wives and multiply."

We could hardly see our beautiful wives, or our beautiful children. The world stood in eternal twilight, shade, and mist. Such wonders in this world, and we could only guess at their true splendor. Yet deep inside, we knew a new day would come. The gods had given us Sight, and though we grew weary of this endless dusk, we never ceased to be grateful.

"Go to the mountains," the gods said, taking pity. "We shall favor you some more."

We walked across grasslands and plains, marshes and rivers, jungles and valleys, until we found the mother mountain. There, we received great blessings, amid blackening storms and white hail, amid indescribable, bitter cold.

First to appear, in a rumble of steam and ash, was Hacauitz, lord of the Fire Mountain. His body was sculpted from a mix of black, porous stone and crystals. "I am bound to you, Ajaw-K'iche'." His voice spat bright-orange sparks. "Through me, your house will prosper." I dropped to my knees and kissed my god's feet, trembling with awe.

Next, a delicate woman appeared. Her lustrous skin glowed like quartz, and her eyes were pupil-less and as black as the pit of night. Every movement of hers was exquisite, a dance, a joy. "I am Auilix, the lady of the moon, bound to Nija'ib'," she said. "Through me, your house will rise."

Lord Nija'ib' took the hem of her starlit skirt and pressed it to his lips.

Then there was a flash and the roar of spitting fire. A tree split in half and went up in flames. The side of the mountain lit up, and Tohil stepped forward, magnificent, brightest of all. "House Kaweq, greatest of all three Houses, meet your master. I bring you my fire and my rage, to keep you warm and steadfast."

Lord Kaweq prostrated himself. He dared not touch Tohil, but sang him praise nonetheless.

It was only then we saw that others had followed us, Rab'inals and Kaqchikels, and Mexican people who spoke strange words. We could not see them before without fire, but now we did.

They observed our flames with jealousy and said, "Give us some, or we shall steal it!"

Tohil asked them, "Is it truly your . . . *hearts'* desire . . . to embrace my flame?" The others replied that it was, all except the trickster Kaqchikels, who simply stole a branch away.

"Very well, for your hearts, who wish it so, you shall have my flame." The others were joyful; they failed to realize they'd been tricked.

Time passed by, and our grandchildren had children of their own. We built our gods grand pyramids to rest in. All the while we knew, we sensed, the time of the first dawn drew close.

One morning, there was a great cry in all of nature. Pumas roared; parrots, eagles, and vultures cawed and screeched, spread their wings, and took to the sky. All the countless people in the world followed their eastward journey and there, in the distance, a faint span of orange began to swim amid the dusky blue.

"Look!" we shouted, and began to sing together, all the people, the Rab'inals, Kaqchikels, Mexicans, us K'iche', and many more.

"It is as our Sight predicted. Hunahpu and Xbalanque have defeated the eternal night, the underworld!" said Nija'ib'.

The twins lit up the world, bathed it in warm, golden-yellow light. Every color on this earth sparkled fresh, like a budding leaf in spring, a crisp winter morning. Tears poured down our faces at the sight of this wonder, this miracle. We were born again. Our families grew and multiplied. We became a great nation, and we kept our prayer, our praise. We offered blood and lymph to all our gods, the blood of birds and deer. We burned resin, marigolds, and stevia in gratitude. Yet it was not enough.

"Our gods are too good! Our offerings are pitiful," said Lord Kaweq.

"So, let's bleed ourselves," I said. "Like this." I took my dagger, slashed my palm, and poured my blood into the fire.

"It's still not enough," said Lord Nija'ib'. "They ought to have more, but what?"

Finally, the gods gave us the answer. "You must win great victories. You must abduct other tribes."

We armed ourselves with lances and shields. War came, inevitable as the first dawn. Tohil ensured we were victorious. He revealed his trick, the secret bargain he'd struck with the other peoples. They'd asked for his fire, and in return he'd gotten their hearts.

"Finally, the gods have the perfect offering," I said as I extracted a beating heart from my enemy's chest. "Heart's blood, pure blood."

"It *is* good, but we are old. Our time draws near," said Lord Nija'ib'.

"We must leave instructions to our sons and daughters," said Lord Kaweq. "We must leave a book, with our counsel, our knowledge, our Sight. So they may never walk in darkness, so they may never be lost."

And so we summoned the *Book of Council*, our greatest gift and treasure.

"Here, my children, take this and keep it safe. Defend it with your lives," I said.

The words of Lord Ajaw-K'iche', my oldest ancestor, rang in my ears as the forest slowly came into focus. The smell of copal and sweat singed my nostrils, and my palm throbbed where I'd sliced it, but I felt little pain, for I was still partly between this world and the other, swaying.

I heard a rustle by the tree line and spotted four delicate, pale fingers, which quickly disappeared into the shadows.

Intruder! The spirit of Lord Ajaw-K'iche' shouted and spurred me on.

I gave chase, though I couldn't feel my feet on the ground. I flew through the trees. The darkness was nothing to me; the light of the otherworld still shone from within my eyes. I easily gained on the hooded figure, a woman, by the pitch of her screams.

"Quiet!" I shouted, but she kept screaming and running, so I threw my dagger.

It wheeled through the air twice before it pierced the base of her hood with a thud. She fell forward, her arms outstretched in the same way she'd run. I lingered above her, transfixed by the gurgling, gagging sounds spilling from her throat.

Heavy footsteps approached from behind. Juan stared at us, panting. The noises faded. His face was ashen, and it was the last thing I saw before the otherworld left me fully and darkness crept back under my lids.

"Are they dead?" he asked.

I couldn't answer. The darkness had brought a chill, and my entire body shivered.

"Nija'ib'!" hissed Juan. "Cristóbal! A torch!"

Neither of us spoke as Cristóbal stumbled toward us, eyes glazed over and confused. Juan took the torch from him, leaned down, and pulled the hood back from the woman's face.

A strange cry swelled in my chest and knotted around my throat.

It was Isabel. Her eyes stared into nothingness.

Only the bejeweled hilt of my dagger stuck out of her nape. The blade had gone in deep and was entrenched. It pinned her hood to her body. Juan struggled to dig it out. My stomach turned and I hurled its liquid contents by the side of a tree, holding on to the trunk to stop myself from falling to my knees. Either Juan or Cristóbal placed a hand on my back and said something, but my heart was pounding in my ears, and I couldn't hear. Her face was burned into my retinas, her lifeless eyes, and the knife, the knife, *my* knife!

"Catalina, stop it!" Juan shook me by the shoulders. "Stop screaming."

They'd covered her face again and hidden the dagger out of sight.

"What's happening?" I cried. My breath came hard and fast, and my chest felt like a block of ice, blue and painful. "What have I done?"

"Listen to me, listen!" said Juan. "You need to go back now. Go back."

"To her house? *Her* house?"

"Yes, to her house. You need to go back and pretend nothing's happened."

I shook my head. "I can't."

"You must," said Cristóbal. He stood next to Juan and held the torch so low their faces were distorted. They looked like apparitions, demons from hell. Fear clawed at my thundering heart and I stepped away.

"We'll take care of this," said Juan. "Go now, and don't let anyone see you."

CHAPTER 22

Santiago de los Caballeros, Guatemala
Spring 1555

I couldn't sleep a lick the rest of the night. I lay in bed, straight like a cadaver, every fiber in my body tensed so tight I wondered if I'd turned to stone. The only parts of me that felt vaguely alive were my thudding palm and the piercing stab in my temple, but I welcomed the pain.

Sometime after the ten o'clock bell rang, Noble River arrived with a silver tray. He took one look at me and nearly dropped it.

"What happened?"

I shook my head. "I—I couldn't sleep, thinking about those men killed yesterday."

Noble River's face softened. My gut twisted from lying to him.

He said, "Here, eat some papaya, it'll make you feel better."

I took the tiniest bite and steeled myself to ask, "Has, has the lady Isabel gotten up yet?"

"Yes, servants say she must've gone out early. She's not back yet. I think they're relieved. They all overslept, though none will dare admit it."

I nodded. "I wish to apologize for my outburst yesterday. Do let me know when she returns?"

"Of course." Noble River touched his hand to my forehead. "You need to eat more. I'll go make you some eggs, with fried tortillas and bean soup, how about that?"

"Thank you," I said, only to please him. I had no desire to eat.

I spent the rest of the day on the patio, trying to steady my hands enough to sew, trying not to imagine how they must've looked in spirit, covered in blood. No, I had to stop thinking like that. I attempted to sew again. My palm ached, but it was a shallow wound. I didn't even need a bandage for it. I ignored it, ignored everything, and concentrated solely on a singular purpose, to get away with murder.

By supper, the servants began to whisper.

"Has your mistress sent word?" I asked the housekeeper. Every duplicitous syllable stuck to the dry roof of my mouth. She shook her head.

"This is unusual, is it not? Send someone to Don Bernal and my father. Send a message to the convent. See if she's there, tending to the sick as she does sometimes. We shall wait a little longer, so we can eat together."

I returned to my room and waited. Pushed away the terrible images fighting for my attention by staring out the window at the mess left behind from the stampede yesterday. There were bits of cloth and broken jars, and an upturned wooden cart missing a wheel. Several people passed by—a pair of Dominican monks in their black-and-white habits, a young Spaniard who plucked at his lute, and a Maya boy with a colorful woven scarf around his head, pushing a wheelbarrow loaded with tomatoes.

Finally, the servants returned, a laundry maid and a kitchen boy.

I took a deep breath, arranged my features into a mask of mild concern, and walked downstairs, calmly, one step at a time, holding the rail for support. "Well? Where is she?"

"Ma'am, we checked everywhere you told us and more. We went to the cathedral and Doña Clara's house, too, but no one's seen her today."

"But—how can that be?"

They had no answer, of course.

"She spoke to no one this morning? She left no note?"

"We're not sure, ma'am."

I gathered the rest of the household and asked the same questions. Except for the housekeeper who answered, the rest of them stood in line, shoulder to shoulder, stupefied. It was as Noble River had said: none would admit to having slept through this morning.

"This won't do." I paced around the room and wrung my hands. "I fear something terrible has happened. I shall go to the palace and raise the alarm myself."

I rode to the palace on horseback as the sun set. The distant volcanoes were cloaked in a blush of pink and orange. The stable boy helped me down.

"Haven't seen you in a long time, señorita. Heard you'd become one of those incurables, if you don't mind me saying, but you look fine to me."

I smiled in spite of the heaviness in my bones and the nerves that rattled my spine. "Yes, I'm better now, thank you. Who is in charge?"

"There's a new judge in charge, the one brought to investigate your father's practices of nepotism. But he's gone out." The stable boy looked around to check we were alone and beckoned me closer. "And I hear Captain Lobo ain't so good after that arrow pierced his belly. I'm bettin' he'll be worm food by the end of the week."

"Poor worms," I whispered. "But listen, child. Who can I speak to? It's urgent!"

"I guess your father, señorita. He's up in his chambers."

I sighed and thanked him, then rushed through the archway. There were more guards than usual, and they did a double take as I walked past, but they seemed to remember me. I stumbled up the stairs, wishing I'd brought my wooden crutch.

I took a deep breath to compose my face and reined in my thoughts. I was innocent, I told myself. I was simply a concerned friend. I had no knowledge of what had happened. I was desperate.

I closed my eyes and knocked on Father's door. Maloso barked from within.

"Who's there?" Father barked as well.

"Your daughter," I said, grateful for my clear voice.

There was a pause, and then a shuffle. He opened the door slightly, then attempted to push the scuttling, whining dog back inside with his cane. Despite the warm evening, an overpowering heat slapped my face. The stuffy, sickly-sweet stench from the room filled my nostrils. He managed to shove Maloso away and looked down at me.

We stared at each other for a long while. He'd aged, and not well. He'd still not regained all the weight he'd lost during his illness. His skin was tinged yellow, and his beard was long and messy. He looked so frail that for a moment, the child inside me who longed so badly to be held almost reached out and touched him.

But the time for that had long passed. He'd shut his heart to me. He'd not written or visited after I'd nearly died. So I curtsied and said, "Sir, pray forgive this disturbance."

He blinked. "They told me you couldn't speak, or walk, for that matter."

"The Lord Jesus saw to my recovery, and I am almost back to my old self."

"Yes, I see that, bold and proud as ever." For a moment, I thought I saw a spark of pride in his eye. Then he said, "Not even being jilted by your asinine husband seems to have taught you some humility. Back, boy!" Maloso nearly knocked him to the ground as he pushed through the door toward me.

"Down, down." I rubbed his gigantic head, which he thrust into my belly. I was grateful for the momentary respite, for the chance to gather myself again.

"Well? This is clearly no formal visit, like I requested. What do you want?" He drew his thick black velvet robe tight around his midriff.

"Isabel left this morning. No one knows where; she left no note. She spoke to no one, and she's nowhere to be found. I'm worried sick, and I don't know what to do."

"Have you looked in our idiot governor's house?"

"Yes, I sent servants to Don Bernal's to check. I sent them everywhere."

"The nunnery? The almshouse?"

"Yes, Father! She was expected home for supper hours ago!"

He rubbed his unkempt beard, which pulled his sagging cheeks down with it. "I'll put together a search party and go out looking."

"You? Can't you send the captain of the guards or someone else? You don't look—"

"Yes, I look like I'm dying, but aren't we all? The captain's busy mopping up Lobo's mess and searching for those mystery archers, who could very well be involved in this, if you ask me. So, send up a servant to help me change. Get my steward to prepare the guards and send word to Bernal. I'm sure that prissy swashbuckler would love the chance to play the hero."

"Are you sure you're strong enough?" I whispered. He stood, but from the way he was panting, he might as well have been running a race.

"Do as I've asked and stop wasting time. When you're done, head back to Isabel's house and send word if she returns."

I've done it. I've fooled him, and I didn't even stumble on my words, I thought as I walked away and down the stairs, but each step seemed to unravel the thin tapestry of lies I'd patched together in the last day, the last five years in fact, and my veneer began to crumble as the truth seeped out. Isabel's blood was on my hands.

It dripped and gurgled out the back of her throat, and pooled around my feet.

I found Father's steward and a maid near the fountain. The steward rushed away to do Father's bidding. I knew I should leave, go back to

Isabel's, but instead, I stood there, shaking. I felt as though any movement would set me screaming.

A flash of white caught my eye, and I looked down at the fountain. A rush of gratitude so immense surged through me that tears sprung to my eyes. Two orchids. He knew I was in the palace. He was there too. I hurried to his office and didn't give a second thought to the crowds around me who may or may not have been watching.

Juan opened the door. "I'm glad you came."

The room was dark; only one candle flickered on the windowsill. I reached out and kissed him, pulled him toward the desk, and tore at the cloth belt around his trousers with frantic fingers. He grabbed my hands.

"What's this, Ab'aj Pol?"

"This is me wanting you, Q'anti," I said, and kissed him again.

His grip loosened.

"Let's forget everything for a moment." I reached out to his belt again.

He pulled away, gentle as a breeze, but it still hurt. The tears returned in a flood, and I doubled over and almost fell off the desk, except he caught me and sat me down beside him, pulling my head to his chest. Then I began to wail.

"I'm sorry, I'm sorry," I said, over and over.

"I know, I know, my love." He rubbed my back and kissed my head.

I cried harder. "I'm a terrible person. I don't deserve love."

"Yes, you do."

"No, I'm awful. I'm an awful, evil person. A coward, a liar, a—a killer! What have I not done? What sins have I not committed? Who have I not hurt?"

"Enough now. Enough of this." Juan stood up and faced me. The light of the candle wavered in his dark pupils, rendering him more jaguar than man. "We've been at war. Did you think the conquest was over? It'll never be over, not until every bit of our heritage is destroyed, and that'll never happen as long as there's people like you and me, willing to fight, to kill for it. You did what you had to do. Do you think she would've kept our secret?"

I grabbed my head, which was splitting in pain along the scar. At first, a part of me wasn't sure, but then I thought yes, she would've told. She'd seen me praying in K'iche' and cutting my hand for a blood sacrifice, just like my mother. I couldn't have done a more barbaric, unchristian thing in a Spaniard woman's eyes. She would've run to my father like she'd done countless times, or to Don Bernal, and I would've been shown no mercy.

Still, the guilt ate at me. "Thanks to me, we'll never know. Thanks to me, she's dead."

"Thanks to you, the *Popol Vuh* is safe."

I looked down. "I don't know how I can live with myself. I can't face going back to her house again. The walls feel like they'll crush me. I can't breathe there."

"It's only for a little while longer, a few weeks at most. Then we can leave."

"We?"

He took my hands. "Yes, we. You and me. I've had a little house built near Santa Cruz, close to Chichicastenango. If you'll still have me, it's yours."

I gaped at him, at a loss for words.

He ran his fingers through my hair. "Well, say something."

"I love you," I choked out. He huffed a laugh and trailed a thumb over my cheek.

"There it is," he said, "at last."

The search went on. Judge Ramirez arrived midmorning on the fourth day, dusty and stinking from riding nonstop since the news had reached him in Chiapas.

He staggered toward me in the hall with a wild, desperate look in his eyes, and reached out with a filthy hand. "Any news? Has she returned?"

I shook my head, and my lip quivered. "My father's doing the best he can. Others have joined his search."

He rubbed his hands on his face. "It's because of me. She's finally left me. I've been no good to her. No good at all."

The pain in his voice tugged at my heartstrings. "She didn't take anything with her, though, and she would've needed money, clothes."

"No, no, I'm sure she's left me. I must—I must speak to your father at once."

"Surely you need to wash, to eat something?" I said, but he twisted on his heel and walked back out the door.

Not too long after, Don Bernal paid me a visit as I sat out on the patio. An unopened book lay flat on my knee. Don Bernal's Maya boy guided him near me and bowed away.

"Dear girl, there you are. I wondered if Ramirez was home?" His beard was unkempt, and it looked like he'd slept in the same clothes for several nights.

"He's gone to see my father, Don Bernal. He's probably joined the afternoon search."

"Ah, I see. I wish I could be of more use, but, well." His grating voice quivered.

"You've been a great help, sir, sending those messages out to nearby towns."

"Always so kind." He took the seat next to me and we were silent for a moment. Doves fluttered and cooed in the far corner. He cleared his throat. "To be truthful, I also came here to advise you, child, about your stay in this household."

"Oh?" I looked at him.

"Yes, well. I—I don't know if dear Isabel will ever return." His voice cracked. "Everyone believes those archers are involved, or the Ocelot. God, I pray she does not suffer."

"Me too," I whispered. Tears fell down both our cheeks.

"But, my girl, now that Ramirez is back, it might be . . . prudent, for you to, you know."

"Ah, I should leave before tongues start wagging."

He shuffled in discomfort. "Ramirez is well known for . . . you see, I wouldn't wish for your reputation to suffer." *Any worse,* I thought I heard the words spoken, in his mind.

"Nor I," I responded, though I couldn't have cared less. I was relieved to have such a perfect excuse thrown at my feet. Another day in that house would've ended me.

"I know it'll be hard to have to return to your father," he said, "but it's for the best."

Thus, I was spurred to action. I asked Noble River to help me pack. The next few hours blurred like the colorful satin and cotton skirts waving in the air before being folded, one after another, in a neat pile.

I'd closed the trunk when the sound of hooves and barking reached me from the open windows. Someone banged loudly on the door. Heavy footsteps resounded on the wooden floor and the tiled stairs. My door was thrown open. Noble River and I jolted and turned to look at the imposing hooded figure framed by the door. My pulse spiked and my mouth dried out.

"Leave us," said my father. As he stepped forward, he appeared to deflate. He panted and, with the back of his hand, rubbed down the sweat and dirt on his face. His eyes had sunk to his cheekbones, and his face was pale yellow. He held on to my chair for support.

"Sir, shall I bring you some wine or water—"

"Leave us!" he barked at Noble River, who shot me a wary look before walking out. He closed the door.

"Father, surely some water—"

"Out of all my children, alive and dead," he rasped as he took out something from the inside of his cloak, a long object wrapped in brown cloth, "I loved you best."

He unwrapped it and threw the object at my feet.

It was the dagger. My dagger.

Juan and Cristóbal had obviously tried to get rid of it. It was covered in soil, and the leather hilt had been burned off, but somehow, he'd found it and there was no mistaking it, not with those three perfect rubies gleaming as bright as the blood I'd shed.

"Whoever lit that fire, whether it be you or your accomplices, intended to conceal whatever crimes were done to her. It was a good job. Only your dagger remained."

I stared back at Father, too weary to pretend, too heartsick to lie. In fact, my bones felt less heavy, oddly enough. I was finally seen for what I was.

"What will you do?" I whispered.

Father shook his head. A tear fell down his cheek into his wiry beard as he pointed at the dagger. "Take it. But know that from this moment on, I renounce you, in the eyes of our Lord Jesus Christ."

I gasped. His words did not surprise me, but the blow to my gut and chest did. Why did I care still? My lower lip trembled. Was it his mercy? That he loved me enough to spare me? Or was it the finality of his tone? Because I knew my father, I knew that tone. He'd set his will against me, and I would never win it back. But . . . did I want it?

No, not really. I wanted my freedom, which was hanging by a thread, his thread. So I kept my mouth shut, one last time.

"I never wish to see you again," he whispered, as though to drive the point home. I nodded through my tears. He clutched at his heart before he turned back out the door.

I picked up the dagger, shoved it under my pillow, and listened to him descending the staircase. The door slammed, and I turned and watched through the window as he left the house. He didn't mount his horse again, but dragged his feet forward, kicking up plumes of sandy dust, which was unlike him. Maloso pressed his nose against his hand and tried to win a pat, but Father pushed him off.

Halfway along the street, he stopped and groaned, then fell to his knees.

Without a second thought, I ran. I yelled for help and sprinted out the corridor and into the street. My heart hammered, and the dry air burned my throat. Down the street, a pair of Maya men closed in to try to help him, but the dog growled, and they were frightened back.

"Come, come, Maloso!" I screamed, and the dog ran to me.

Father turned to the sound of my voice and raised an arm.

At first, I thought he was beckoning me closer, and I stepped forward. But then he moaned, "Begone," and I saw his palm was up. He was warding me off, true to his word to the very last. I halted and his arm fell by his side.

The men shouted for a doctor, a surgeon, a priest. A Spaniard ran off to get help, and others crowded around, watching the scene. A boy led the horse away.

I clutched at Maloso's collar and waited. All the while a sense of frantic pressure built in my body, an earthquake of emotions. Guilt, panic, frustration, helplessness. I didn't know what to do, so I just stared and trembled, stared and trembled.

"Who is it?" the people gathered around me asked.

"It's—it's," I stuttered, and my hands shook.

One of the men leaned into my father's chest, and I saw his ragged face.

My knees failed me. An arm wrapped around my shoulders. Another hand gently took hold of Maloso's collar. I didn't need to turn to know Juan and Cristóbal had arrived by my side.

"His heart's stopped," one of the Maya men said, and his voice cracked. "Don Alonso, oh, my sons. The lord president is dead."

Maloso let out a howl, and I began to sob.

CHAPTER 23

Sololá, Guatemala
Autumn 1555

Cristóbal and I walked arm in arm along the shore, and I leaned on him for support. Gentle clinking sounds rang from within Cristóbal's sack. The cool water of the lake lapped our bare feet and ankles, and the hot sun bore down on our shoulders. My hem was soaked, as were his cotton trousers. I could see my old house, now Carmen's house, high up the hills in the not-too-far distance ahead. Noble River had written to say Carmen was with child. I wished her and Nico good luck.

Cristóbal pointed to a flat, jutting rock ahead, under a canopy of palm leaves. He helped me climb and we sat. From his sack, he took out tiny jars of colorful pigments and the two *Popol Vuh*s. We were copying as many of the drawings as possible from the original, trying to replicate them as closely as we could. It was difficult work, requiring our utmost concentration. I was always exhausted by the end of the day, my mind fuzzy and slow and sore, but each time we did it, it felt as though tiny pieces of our old selves were also colored back into our blackened, fractured souls.

Maybe this is what I should do—find old Maya books and copy them. Make sure they lived. The thought made my heart glow.

Somewhere behind us, among the tall trees, there was a clanking of several hammers and the murmur of men's voices. A sharp, indecipherable note from Juan's voice reached my ear.

"Someone's in trouble," said Cristóbal.

"For once it's not me." I pretended to flick a drop of sweat from my forehead.

He gave me a pointed look. "And yet you're marrying the man."

I shrugged. "The offers weren't exactly pouring in once they found my father's will." He'd left everything to his Spanish relatives, although I was not surprised.

"Catalina, it's better to be alone than trapped in an unhappy union. You know that, right? I know Godfather made it hard for you to believe, perhaps." He took my hand. "But you have other options. You can always live with me."

"Oh, cousin! No, I'm sorry. I'm awful." I kissed his hand. "It's this . . . poison . . . inside me. This endless guilt. Sometimes I just don't know how to sound happy anymore."

"But you are happy? With him?"

"Yes! Yes, I am. I swear. It's hard to say aloud how, how *good* he is, but he really is." I looked into Cristóbal's eyes, to show I was sincere.

He shook his head. "Must be buried deep inside."

I laughed and leaned my head on his shoulder. He'd been so very kind to us, even though his feelings for Juan were complicated. He'd let us stay in his hideout by the lake. But we would be leaving soon, to Chichicastenango, to live in the home Juan had built for us.

I worried about Cristóbal, how he would feel, all on his own. After a while, I dared to ask him. Even though I was afraid of opening up his wounds again, I wanted him to know how much I cared. "What about you? Is there . . . love? In your life?"

He pushed my arm. "Fiend! What of you?"

"Well, of course *I* love you! But I meant—you know." I looked around to ensure we wouldn't be overheard and lowered my voice. "Someone else, someone like, like P-Pablo."

His eyes filled with tears.

"I'm sorry," I said quickly.

He raised his palm. "No. It's good of you to ask, to see. I—didn't know if you did."

"You're my oldest friend." A beautiful jay with striking blue plumage landed above us and let out a series of chattering calls.

"*I* didn't see," he said. "With you and Juan. I should've. It would've saved us all much heartache. It would've saved you so much pain." His eyes flitted from my legs to the side of my head, where my great scar still shone under a thick layer of hair. "I am so sorry for being the cause of it. I thought I was doing what was right for you."

My body and mind were better. *I* was better, although I didn't think I'd ever be the same again. It didn't help to dwell on that too much, so I said, "It's in the past now."

Cristóbal shook his head. "You're too good. I still bear a grudge against him, for Pablo's death. But truth be told, I miss his company."

I shifted so I could sit with my back to the lake. I waved at the jungle, toward the place where the hammering continued unabated. Some men sang in unison. The scent of grilled poultry and smoke reached my nostrils, and my mouth watered.

"What he's doing now, helping build your school, it's his way of making amends."

Cristóbal rubbed his chin. "I suppose he's a king, after all. Begging forgiveness is against his nature."

I took his hand and squeezed it. "Lucky for us, you're a forgiving person, like me."

He squeezed it back and smiled. "Indeed, cousin. I am."

I closed my eyes as a warm breeze filtered through my loose hair. I caught another fragrance, of yucca and earth, and thought of Mother. Was that her touch in the wind? Her kiss upon my forehead? I'd not heard her voice again, but from the way some of the pages fluttered, I knew she was here, and that she was proud, and at peace.

I smiled to myself.

I'd kept my vow, and I'd continue keeping it as long as I lived.

EPILOGUE

Santa Cruz del Quiché, Guatemala
Spring 1557

I followed the glow emanating from Juan's torch, and descended the old hidden steps beneath the ruins of the Kaweq palace on my rear, as I'd done many years ago.

I slithered slowly, like a snail, not from fear, but because my legs still gave me trouble sometimes, and I was too heavy with child to manage a faster pace. I hoped for a little girl, my very own Daughter of Fire, although a Son of the Jaguar would've made me happy too.

I pictured her, toddling in our garden, climbing her father's back, picking oranges from our trees, sitting in our small living room by the fire, sipping cacao, and listening to our myths and songs. Then I winced as I thought of how we'd have to keep our voices low, we'd have to teach her at night, we'd have to warn her, *These songs are our little secret.*

But another defiant voice, mine or maybe hers, said, *Only for a little while.*

"Careful, careful," Juan's voice echoed. "Nearly there."

He helped me up from the floor, and I kissed him to let him know I was fine. The damp air and closed space still sent a barb of unease through my large belly. I moved out of the way and allowed Cristóbal and El Grande to enter. They discussed reports of a savage bishop terrorizing the Maya in Yucatán. Juan lit a fire. The flames rose, and we sat for a moment on the carved stones arranged in a circle around it.

"So, brother, you leave tomorrow for Spain. Are you prepared?" Juan's excitement was palpable. After many years of service, he had valid reasons to hope for some concessions from the Crown. The Dominicans attested to his good name. He had a solid case in hand. I was still unsure, but as he said, for our children, we had to try. We could never stop.

El Grande nodded. "I have all the documents required, thanks to your lady wife."

"Take as good care of my old manuscript as I'm taking care of the new one," I said, "lest you wish for my mother's spirit to haunt your dreams."

"That wouldn't be new to me, nor unwelcome," he said.

I gave him a sad smile.

"We'd best get on with the blessing," said Cristóbal. "Grande, kneel by the fire."

All three of us—Cristóbal, Juan, and I—walked to the carved wall. By the foot of one of the larger sculptures, there was a trunk full of beautiful panaches and other K'iche' treasures, some of the haul recovered by Cristóbal during his days as the Ocelot.

It was hard to believe that this cousin of mine, with his kind brown eyes and easy smile, had once been a fearsome brigand. His school continued to flourish. He'd even had to hire a handsome Tz'utujil fisherman to help teach some of the classes. The man had built himself a hut next to Cristóbal's, to help him get to work on time, of course.

I rummaged through the trunk and picked out my favorite headdress, the green macaw. Cristóbal donned the blue and Juan the red. Juan tied it wrong, on an angle. I reached out to fix it, but Cristóbal got there before me. Juan grunted his thanks, and Cristóbal thumped him on the shoulder.

We turned, took a pinch of copal from the vase in front of us, and threw it in the fire. The scent of smoky resin enveloped us, as though the gods themselves were breathing into the cave, awaiting our worship.

"Heart of Sky, Heart of Earth," we chanted in unison. "We, the K'iche', speak to you, praise you. We ask for your favor."

I closed my eyes, and let the spirits take me.

AUTHOR'S NOTE

By implementing the New Laws almost single-handedly, Don Alonso López de Cerrato achieved one of the most extraordinary feats of administration in the New World. Yet, he has been largely forgotten by history. The president was reportedly buried in the monastery of Santo Domingo in what is now known as Antigua, Guatemala, previously Santiago de los Caballeros. His gravestone has since been moved, and its location is unknown.

Don Juan Cortés's boat was attacked by French pirates on the way to Spain. His documents, which likely included a number of unknown pre-Columbian codices, were lost. Despite this, Don Cortés managed to reach Spain and was granted audiences before highborn officials. Unfortunately, even with Dominican support, the Franciscans successfully argued against the restoration of the rights and privileges of the K'iche' nobility. They claimed that additional power would foster further revolt by the Indigenous people.

Don Juan de Rojas continued in his post as minister of native affairs, although records show he ceased to sign official documents in November 1558. His impoverished children continued to advocate for the rights of the K'iche' nobility.

In 1562, Bishop Diego de Landa ordered that a large number of Maya codices and thousands of cult images be burned in Yucatán, as part of his campaign against idolatry. These manuscripts would've contained knowledge of Maya religion, history, and civilization. Only four codices are known to have survived the conquest and subsequent Inquisition, as well as the only known version of the *Popol Vuh*, written by the friar Francisco Ximénez.

Between 1701 and 1703, Ximénez somehow managed to get a look at the "original" *Popol Vuh* during his tenure as parish priest in Chichicastenango. He made his own copy and added a Spanish translation. His work remained in the possession of the Dominicans until Guatemalan independence. The original manuscript may have included a few illustrations and even an occasional Maya symbol, but it is thought to have been written phonetically, in Latin script. Friar Ximénez's version, however, contains only columns of alphabetic prose.

Out of respect for the authors, this novel has retained the original spelling for proper names used in the *Popol Vuh* (e.g., Tohil, Auilix, Hacauitz), whereas present-day orthography has been used for K'iche' words and terms with obvious etymologies.

The identities of those authors and the whereabouts of the purely K'iche' version of the *Popol Vuh*, last seen by Ximénez over three hundred years ago, remain a mystery to this day.

ACKNOWLEDGMENTS

I would first like to thank the beautiful people of Guatemala, especially the K'iche' people. With the utmost respect and reverence, thank you, *gracias, maltiox che la*. I don't know why the search for my roots brought me to you and the *Popol Vuh*, but I am infinitely grateful and humbled. If you are, too, reader, please consider sponsoring a Girl Pioneer for the MAIA Impact School, an organization led by Indigenous women to empower other Indigenous women to continue their education, reach economic autonomy, and plan their families on their terms. Visit www.maiaimpact.org for more information.

Also, if you ever get the chance, visit Guatemala and don't skip the Museo Popol Vuh in Guatemala City. They have a world-class display.

I also want to thank Professor Allen J. Christenson, from the bottom of my heart, for your herculean efforts in capturing the soul of the *Popol Vuh* and translating it to English, as well as for taking the time to read this manuscript. Your care and patience in providing so many wonderful and detailed notes and answering all my follow-up emails is greatly appreciated. My spiritual thanks as well to Professors Dennis Tedlock and William L. Sherman. If any readers are interested in more factual details about this time period and some of its characters, I would recommend Sherman's little-known but very important *Forced Native Labor in Sixteenth-Century Central America*. It's a hoot (not).

To my first readers, Katherine and Constance, thank you for your care, your feedback, and your support with this baby and the last one too. Constance, thank you as well for writing the #PitMad tweet that landed me an agent. I'm forever indebted to you, you brilliant creature. I can't wait to see Iphigenia out in the world where she belongs!

To my brilliant agent, Johanna Castillo, and her team at Writers House (Erin and Victoria), thank you for reading, editing, cheering me on, and knocking on all the doors until we got our yes. To Alexandra Torrealba, my editor at Amazon Crossing, thank *you* for that yes. Having you all in my corner has made a world of difference. *Mil, mil gracias.*

Thank you to my writing community, for all of you who have read and taken the time to make this book better, including the fantastic editors Elaine Colchie, Jon Reyes, and Lauren Grange. Thank you for your vision, wisdom, and eagle eyes. Thank you to authors Tina Chan, Xiran Jay Zhao, and Jordan Kopy. Tina and Xiran, you are both superstars, and I am in awe of you. If anyone has been living under a rock and hasn't read Xiran's *Iron Widow* yet, please do yourself a favor. And to Jordan Kopy, thanks for all your guidance and support over the years, and for pushing me to get a move on in writing this novel. *Theodora Hendrix* is the cutest and spookiest—anyone with kids, check out the series.

To all of you who have encouraged me, friends and family. *Mama y Papa—gracias por todo su apoyo y su amor siempre, los amo con todo mi corazón.* Thanks especially to my mother, for believing wholeheartedly in the supernatural powers of the psychic who read the soles of her feet (yes, her feet) and convinced her years ago that my books would be a success. I really, *really* hope this lady is for real.

Thanks also to my mother-in-law, Connie, and in heaven, a big thanks to the lovely Aunty Jan, for also cheering me on and mentoring me when I was just getting started.

And to Craig . . . my patient, kind, loving, and devoted husband, who is probably cringing while he reads this. Thank you for being the most wonderful example to our son. Thank you for supporting my impractical dreams of becoming an author. Thank you for working full time so I could write one day a week, and for all the solo parenting hours you've put in when I needed to get edits done. Thank you for reading my first-ever novel ten years ago and encouraging me to continue, even though the thought of writing anything gives you unbearable anxiety. Thank you for being you. I love you.

And finally, to you, reader, thank you for undertaking this journey with me and those who came before me, those ancestors whose voices I hope always to hear.

ABOUT THE AUTHOR

Photo © Michael Oosthuizen

Sofia Robleda is a Mexican writer. She spent her childhood and adolescence in Mexico, Saudi Arabia, and Singapore. She completed her undergraduatrees in psychology at the University of Queensland, Australia. She currently lives in the UK with her husband and son and splits her time between writing, raising her son, and working as a clinical psychologist supporting people with brain injuries and neurological conditions. For more information visit https://sofiarobleda.com.